THE BAJA PROJECT

By
Jim Hughes

ISBN: 1-4196-5709-7
ISBN-13: 9781419657092

Visit www.booksurge.com to order additional copies.

ACKNOWLEDGEMENTS

Both my son Jim and my editor, Bill Greenleaf, said, "Show it, don't tell it." Hopefully I've succeeded. An experienced seafarer, Wesley Penney, gave me some advice on ships, and an experienced pilot, Fred Bellows, on planes. Many family and friends were supportive, especially my wife and photographer, Eleanor, and my sons Jim and Brett. Although the historical and geographical facts in this story are for the most part accurate, it is a work of fiction.

PROLOGUE
EARLY IN THE 21ST CENTURY

The sun was setting and the air heavy and still. The bearded Iranian looked over his shoulder to see if he was indeed alone as the door creaked open for him to enter the missile launch site. He saw no one else. He did not see the satellite hovering two hundred miles above, which noted his entrance.

One thousand miles north, in the caverns beneath Cheyenne Mountain, a red light began to blink on the computer screen in front of Colonel Charles Longley. He was slumped in his chair from fatigue, but, alerted by the blinking light, he snapped alert and bent forward to watch the screen closely. He picked up a phone at his side and pressed a button. The call was answered after the first ring.

"Yes?"

"He's entered the site," said the colonel slowly and deliberately.

Silence for a few seconds. Then he was asked, "Are you sure it's him?"

He answered, "No question. It's him."

A few more seconds passed.

"Okay, Colonel, execute the plan."

"Yes, ma'am," he said crisply.

He disconnected with one finger and pressed a second line with another.

The satellite surveillance had begun two months earlier, conducted under the direction of the Iran Group within America's National Counterterrorism Center. It was the culmination of three years of intelligence-gathering that had begun with Iran's announcement that it had achieved uranium enrichment and would continue those activities. The surveillance did not occur, however, in the Middle East. Rather, it focused on the Baja Peninsula, that 1,000-mile-long, stiletto-like projection extending south from California. The peninsula was part of Mexico. At least, it had been, prior to recent events . . .

CHAPTER 1

SIXTEEN MONTHS EARLIER, IN NOVEMBER
TEHRAN, IRAN

The Ayatollah rolled over with sleep still in his eyes as the soft alarm music wakened him. He squinted at the clock by his bed. *Seven o'clock. Time to rise*, he thought. He turned to look at the young virgin lying next to him. At least she had been a virgin. She looked so young and pure, with her dark hair cascading about her bare shoulders. And she was so small, lying curled into a ball. He justified his debauchery by viewing it as his preview of heaven, where six dozen virgins awaited the dead martyr. He viewed himself as a living martyr. Others carried bombs around their waists; he paid for the bombs. And he was still shy of seventy-two maidens.

He had been born in 1935, just as Persia became Iran, and he was beginning to think he was too old to spend his nights in a young man's pursuits while leading his country during the day. Just yesterday, he had spent most of the day in meetings with his economic advisors.

They had pressed him: "Your Excellency, we must do something about these sanctions from the West. We are buying more gasoline than selling. Our resources, although bountiful, are not unlimited. As in the Azadegan oil fields, we need foreign assistance, which is barred by the sanctions. And our refineries require foreign partners. Someday we must also begin to grow beyond oil."

He had replied to their pleas in a soft, resigned voice. "Yes, I have read your reports. I pray daily for a solution. Allah surely will provide one. You must have faith." Remembering those words as he woke, he was glad that he had already devised a solution. *A daring one*, he smiled wryly. *Now to another day of worldly affairs.*

"Time for you to leave, my dear," he said, patting the girl gently on the bare rump he had so enjoyed last night. He watched her slip from under the sheets and pull a robe around her small body with trembling hands before scampering away. Her footsteps were muffled on the carpet until she reached the bath area. He heard her descending the back stairs, where she would be met and taken back to her family.

The Ayatollah smiled again. She had not been asleep. *Just lying frozen, hoping I was finished with her.* She was just fifteen years old.

He looked about his simple room, containing only a bed, a hard reading chair, and a small table. Opulence was not one of his sins, with the exception of the beautiful Kashan carpet which had muffled the girl's footsteps. He tossed off the sheets and knelt on the carpet, bending low and facing Mecca to pray for guidance and forgiveness.

Ayatollah Ali Jalil was the Supreme Leader of the Islamic Republic of Iran. He shared governing authority with an elected president, Tariq Talabani, and with the leaders of the nation's Muslim council. In reality, the Ayatollah was in control. President Talabani tried to straddle the line between the country's young moderates and the religious conservatives, but his core allegiance was to the Ayatollah. The Ayatollah ran Iran with the support of his close confidante and cousin, General Mahmoud Mussahrah.

General Mussahrah frowned on the Ayatollah's sexual escapades. He often told him so, but the elder cleric would usually respond by clasping his hands and bowing his head, saying, "I try to do as Allah directs, cousin. But I am weak. I am human, with human frailties. Please pray for me to gain more strength." Those were the Ayatollah's words this morning, as the two talked while walking to the meeting which had caused the Ayatollah to hasten the young girl away.

At least they're girls, the general thought to himself with disgust, as he and his cousin prepared for the meeting.

The Ayatollah and General Mussahrah were not without world experience. The Ayatollah had been educated at Oxford before returning to Iran while the Shah was still in power. Mahmoud had attended Princeton and, thanks to the propensity of the United States to share its military knowledge with others, the U.S. Army War College in Pennsylvania. There he had learned some of the skills which had helped him fend off and defeat attempted incursions from neighboring Iraq and Afghanistan. Both the Ayatollah and Mussahrah were fluent English speakers. The Persian dialect Farsi was their native tongue.

This morning, the Ayatollah and Mahmoud were meeting in Tehran with representatives from Hamas, al-Qaeda, and the Palestine Liberation Organization. It was a conference of terrorists being held in Tehran to decide on funding for the ongoing terrorist activities against Israel.

They sat around a large marble table in a private dining room in the basement of the popular Alborz restaurant. Coffee, bottled water, and snacks had been set out on the table. The air was dense with cigarette smoke. There were only five of them in the room. No aids. No assistants. General Mahmoud ran the meeting standing in front of a chart, on which he listed how Israel had been hurt over the past year. Each terrorist incident had a line next to it for a cost figure to be inserted. They were creating a blood budget: the cost of the Israeli blood which had already been shed, and what it would cost to wreak more havoc.

The general spoke to the group: "Suicide bombers are cheap, less than a thousand dollars a bomb, if we ignore what we pay the surviving families. Even the Hezbollah missiles are not costly. We need to send more bombs and more missiles. Tell us what you need."

These terrorists seldom met together, but their common hatred of Israel brought them into one room to deal with money. Their martyrs and rockets and car bombs cost money. Iran had always provided great sums. During the meeting, the talk turned to how Israel's presence and power had been guaranteed when it was placed in their midst by the United Nations.

The PLO representative, Abu Mazen, spoke bitterly while exhaling smoke with every word. "The Jews are so close. That is the problem. Yes, they occupy our land, but the real problem is that they are next door – in our backyard! If Israel were in southern France, or Ireland, or in the vast reaches of Russia, we would not mind so much. But here...." He rose and thumped the location of Israel on the wall map with his knuckles. "Right here! It's impossible. Insulting! Such closeness gives the Jews their power over us. We must destroy them."

The Ayatollah in his seat turned his head slowly to look directly at each of the three visitors. "Yes, here also. We could abide Saddam next door, since he was so predictable, and incompetent. But now we face the Americans next door in Iraq and in Afghanistan. It is the closeness – the proximity of our enemies – which is so worrisome. But do not worry. We will destroy Israel. It is only a matter of time, and money."

.   .   .

General Mussahrah stepped aside a few paces as the men vented. He remained silent, stroking his short black beard and looking pensively at the broad mural on the side wall. The fresco depicted the spread of the ancient Persian empire before the Christian era, from Egypt on the west running over three thousand miles into central Asia. It depicted great warriors, large cities, and prophets with gold-leaf scrolls reading to the people. His goal was to regain the prestige and power of that ancient empire. He knew the goal was almost within reach. He wondered how much of their plans he should disclose to this group.

Very little, he thought to himself. *Tell them very little.* Then he spoke in a quiet voice:

"Yes, we will destroy Israel. And we have a few surprises for them and for the Americans. Do not despair. Allah is with us. We will prevail."

The others nodded and murmured in agreement, but the thoughts were transitory and mere asides from the main business of the day, which was to raise money. They continued to plan their attacks and assign costs. The next year would be a busy one – and bloody for the Israelis.

.   .   .

A few months later, the Ayatollah remembered the comments from the Alborz restaurant while attending a conference for emerging and underdeveloped nations in

Mexico City. The conference was run under the auspices of the United Nations. It attracted representatives from almost one hundred countries which were starting to develop their resources and attempting to gain entry into the more developed world court. As the Ayatollah heard pleas for financial support from the poorer nations, his mind went back to the meeting with the revolutionaries in Tehran, who had also been holding out their hands for money.

President Chavez of Mexico chaired the conference. He welcomed the delegates with a photo mosaic tour of his country, while standing before them in front of a wall-sized map of Mexico. During his talk, the attendees sat restlessly in the large university auditorium. They spoke quietly among themselves as the president spoke.

The Ayatollah was thinking to himself: *How much will I have to give to buy favor here? What's going to be the cost of world recognition? And respect?* He thought the opening remarks by Chavez were dull. He knew very little about Mexico, other than that it shared a long common border with the United States. He wasn't interested in learning more about what he viewed as a second-rate outpost of America with little Muslim presence.

He did, however, take notice of the long peninsula which ran down the left side of the map, almost like an extension of the American state of California. On the map the United States was colored green, but this strip of land was colored pink, as if part of Mexico. President Chavez said nothing about it during his presentation.

Afterward, the Ayatollah leaned over to the representative from Brazil sitting next to him and asked, "What is that long piece of land on the left?"

"That is the Baja Peninsula."

"Is it part of Mexico?"

"Yes, but I think an unimportant part," answered the Brazilian. "It is mostly a desert, with some mountains, and it is largely unpopulated."

The Ayatollah remembered the earlier conversation about the threat caused by the closeness of Israel in the Middle East.

I wonder, he thought, *is there perhaps a way to make the Baja Peninsula more important? To make it fit into our plans?*

• • •

When the Ayatollah returned to Iran after the Mexican conference, his cousin Mahmoud was waiting to hear how much of their money had been spent. As they sat in the comfortable anteroom to the Ayatollah's chambers, the general looked at the older cleric and wondered, *how many young Mexican girls?*

He was jolted back to reality when his cousin spoke excitedly about his fantasy concerning the strip of land called the Baja.

"A foothold in the West," explained the grey-bearded Ayatollah. "Our own Israel in America's backyard. It is what we have talked about, what we need for our plan to succeed."

"So, what are you saying, cousin?" responded Mahmoud. "Ally ourselves with Mexico? Why in Allah's name would they even consider it? Mexico is a Christian country, under the thumb of the Americans. Even our money could not accomplish that."

"Maybe not, but maybe there is a way," said the Ayatollah, gazing into the distance, as if in deep thought. "I think

I will at least have some people look into this Baja. It seems strange, just sitting there. A part of Mexico, but not really, and so close to America. Let me investigate."

"Fine," said Mahmoud, with a shrug of indifference. "Investigate. And Allah be with you."

CHAPTER 2

SIX MONTHS LATER – APRIL 15
THE BAJA PENINSULA

Corporal Martinez was the first to see the body as he did his morning beach walk. Actually, the gulls had seen it first. He saw them screeching and hovering, and then diving, around an object at the water's edge. As he approached, he had to wave them away with his arms. Standing over the body, he saw that the birds had already gotten to the eyes.

He lit a cigarette as he stood staring down at the dead man. Although the face was damaged, it was definitely the fisherman Plarez. Just yesterday, Plarez's wife had reported him missing. Martinez turned and headed toward the village in search of a tarpaulin and assistance to recover the corpse. As he walked away, he heard the gulls returning to the body, screeching at him in anger for his interruption. There was nothing he could do about them. *But,* he thought, *there's something wrong about the body. Something doesn't look right.* The scene lingered in his mind as he walked. Suddenly he snapped his fingers and nodded as he realized what it had been.

The fingers. Something was wrong with the fingers. One arm had been stretched out in the sand, and the other folded over the dead man's chest. The fingers of the hand on the chest were not lying flat like normal. Some were sticking up in the air, as if they had been bent back and broken. *The birds couldn't do that,* he thought. *Only a man could do that.* He had seen a similar condition once before.

While in the army, a comrade had been captured and tor-tured by the rebels. His fingers had been broken. That was what Plarez' fingers looked like.

It made no sense to Martinez.

CHAPTER 3

MAY 2

MESA VERDE, COLORADO

A loud *crack* startled Professor William Abbey as he sifted through the ashes of the ancient Pueblo cook site. On his hands and knees, he scrambled to the cave entrance and looked down. The forty-foot ladder he had just climbed to reach the cave lay broken on the adobe roof below. It had bowed as he climbed up, but he didn't see why it had broken now, with no one on it. A chill ran up his spine, as he wondered if someone else had been climbing up. He tried to look closer, at the roofs below and the surrounding areas. *No one in sight … Don't hear anything … Guess I'm just imagining things.*

Thirty-two years old, Abbey had been teaching at the University of New Mexico in Albuquerque for six years. His lanky six-foot frame now bent low as he knelt at the cave entrance. This Saturday afternoon, he was mixing business and pleasure, exploring the cliff dwellings of the Pueblo Indians in Mesa Verde National Park. He had been there most of the afternoon. His academic task was to find samples of the maize that the Pueblos had eaten over 700 years ago. By carefully sifting through likely cooking sites, he had located a half dozen of the small kernels. They were now hard and petrified, like small pebbles. He put each into a small plastic bag with a scrap of paper noting where he had found it, and stuffed it into his jeans pocket. As an academic, he was permitted to remove artifacts for purposes of research. He was also pursuing his hobby of photographing ancient Indian wall drawings, or petroglyphs. He hadn't seen any in this cave yet, but there had been a few in other areas.

He was now in a bit of a pickle, having lost track of time and remained in this remote cliff cave up to the park's closing time. Now his only means of climbing down from the cave was gone. He thought some of the staff must still be around. He called out for help.

"Hello! Anyone? I'm stuck. I need help!" He waited a few seconds and repeated his shouts, but no one responded. He looked out over the valley, with its brownish-red adobe huts stacked like stepping stones along the cliff walls. No one was visible. *Everyone's left,* he thought to himself. He shivered for a second and took a deep breath. He realized he was alone.

• • •

Under a trap door in the roof below the cave opening, the Iranian Abdul Kazam crouched in a stairway while Abbey shouted for help. Kazam knew no one would respond; the staff would not return tonight. He had called them all away to an accident in another area of the park, where they were attending to an old man who had been badly injured in a fall from one of the roofs. The fall had also been the work of the Iranian. A firm shove in the back when the tourist leaned over to wave to his wife had been sufficient.

Earlier, Kazam had followed Abbey to Mesa Verde and watched him leave his car. Looking through the car's passenger window, he had seen a cell phone on the console between the seats and an open laptop beside it. *These careless Americans,* he had thought, *leaving such things in plain sight.*

Kazam now moved quickly down the stairs and hurried toward the parking lot, moving in the shadows next to the adobe walls. Tonight he would carefully examine the phone and laptop. Professor Abbey, unaware of what was going on, was being vetted for a new assignment. The dark-skinned Iranian chuckled to himself at his cleverness. *In the morning, he won't even know what I've done.*

Reaching the car, he rifled the driver-side window with a thin rod and popped the lock. He then reached in and removed the phone and computer. He would later review and download their memories. His movements at the car were awkward because they were all done with his right hand. The left sleeve of his shirt was neatly folded and pinned above the missing elbow of his left arm. He had no left hand.

• • •

As an amateur rock climber, Abbey was concerned, but not panicked. Lying on his stomach, he leaned out over the edge of the cave entrance and looked carefully down the rocky wall below the cave. The setting sun highlighted a few small depressions and rock shelves, but nothing that would give him a good way down. That didn't surprise him, since the purpose of the ladder entrance was to make the cave inaccessible without one. He knew the staff would be back in the morning, but that was twelve hours away, and he had no food or heat. A little water and a power bar remained, but the mesa and the cliff cave would be cold during the night. He couldn't even call home, although he wasn't sure whether anyone really expected him back tonight. *Why didn't I bring the cell phone? Doesn't do much good in the car.*

As dusk approached, Abbey crawled back into the cave to explore it more closely. There was nothing helpful – not even any wall drawings to help pass the time. As he crawled further, he realized that the cave was deep enough to retain some of the day's heat. That was good, because his short-sleeved shirt wasn't going to help much against the nighttime desert chill. Crawling back to the entrance, he sat with his feet hanging over the edge and ate his small snack as the sun continued to drop. The shadows of the cliffs he faced lengthened and marched toward him until they touched his perch. Slowly, they merged together into dusk, then darkness. He slid backward on his stomach, tapping the ground and air behind him with his sneakers to find his way. His feet finally came up against a wall, where he curled up to try to sleep.

The ground was hard and the rocky pillow cut into his scalp after a few seconds, even when he tried to cushion it with his hands. He could see nothing. No light reached this far into the cave. It took what seemed like hours, but he finally fell asleep.

He slept fitfully, hearing the desert nighttime sounds and sensing small, scurrying creatures. He dreamed, as he had before.

Mommy, I want to go out and play!
No, dear. Not today. You must stay in today.
But, Mommy, I'll be good.
I know dear, I know.
But for today, you have to stay.
Tomorrow will be another day.

They were always in rhyme. Not the same dream, but always involving his mother, and always in rhyme. He had loved her very much growing up.

She had been his rock. His first seizure had occurred as an adolescent on the bus ride home after school. He had passed out in his seat with convulsions. Epilepsy, the doctor later diagnosed: "A seizure disorder, but easily controlled with medicine." The doctors could only guess that an earlier head injury had planted the seed for the seizure. A daily regime of anti-convulsant capsules was initiated. In high school, his mother had ensured that he took the pills every night. He never told her of the two seizures he had in college when he skipped the medication.

Tonight, he had no pills with him. He had left them in the car.

Twice he was awakened by little feet scurrying over his face. Each time, he brushed his face and short hair frantically to shed whatever was on him, but he couldn't see anything in the darkness. He curled into a ball, with his knees up and arms clasped, but still shivered much of the night. Wide awake by daylight, he waited impatiently for the park to open. *Where are those rangers?*

Finally, when his watch said 8:30, he began to yell again. "Help! Someone help me . . ."

After fifteen minutes, he heard sounds and voices below. "Are you okay, mister?" someone shouted. The trap door swung up and over and a uniformed ranger climbed onto the roof below, staring up at the cave entrance with his hands hooding his eyes. "Hold on, we'll be right there," he yelled to Abbey.

The professor waited impatiently until a new ladder was pushed up through the trap door to his perch. "Don't you come up," he ordered. "I'm coming down."

When he reached the roof below, two ashen-faced rangers were waiting. "Sir, I don't know how this happened," apologized one young ranger, almost in tears. "I'm so sorry. I don't think your car was in the parking lot when we left last night, but it's there now. We all left in a hurry last night because a man had fallen off a roof and hurt himself. And now this."

"Well, I doubt if my car drove out and back this morning on its own," Abbey replied sarcastically. "It was in the parking lot."

"Can we get an ambulance, or a doctor? We'll drive you."

"No. I'm okay now, but you really need to be more careful. That ladder was a disaster waiting to happen. I can drive myself. I'm fine." *What? I'm consoling them?*

When they inspected the broken ladder, it appeared the base had slipped into the stairway under the trap door and then snapped off. "But how'd the trap door then close?" asked Abbey. "Makes no sense," The rangers just shrugged their shoulders. "Maybe the falling latter pushed it shut," one said. None of them could figure out how it had happened.

"Maybe," Abbey responded. He was just glad to be on the ground. He gave them his name and address and drove away, looking for breakfast. Once in his car, he quickly swallowed the pills he had missed the night before. Without water, he worked his cheeks and jaw muscles to get enough saliva to swallow them. He assumed he had not had a seizure during the night, but there was no way of knowing for sure.

He was famished; his stomach achingly empty. Once he reached the nearest diner, he tried to use his cell phone to call his girlfriend, and then his computer, but both batteries were dead. He knew they had been charged yesterday. Maybe the chill of the night had drained them. An omelet, sausage, and plenty of coffee filled his stomach. He then started the long drive back to Albuquerque. He stopped to nap a few times and was home by five o'clock that evening.

Karen was waiting for him.

"Where have you been?" she scolded as he walked inside through the garage door. "I expected you last night, or you should have at least called!"

"Sorry, sorry. Actually, I had quite an experience last night. I got stranded in a cave in Mesa Verde. Couldn't get out . . ."

"What do you mean, stranded? Why couldn't you leave?"

"Well, the main problem was a forty-foot cliff between me and the ground. I chose not to jump."

The conversation went downhill after that. Abbey grew discouraged, feeling that she blamed him for the broken ladder.

Eventually, she relented and agreed that it wasn't his fault that he had been trapped in the cave. Then she looked at him and shook her head in resignation. "You're smart, Bill. You're handsome. Your blue eyes and crooked smile bring me to my knees. But you want to play at life, not work at it. You want to climb mountains and explore caves. That's not what I want. I love you, but not what you do. We've talked about this too often." She got up from the couch and started toward the bedroom. "I've thought about it a lot. I should leave. I'll get my things. We each have to do our own thing."

Abbey stayed seated with his head down. Nothing seemed to be going right. But, he thought, *she's right. We're not having fun together. We're just arguing all the time.*

CHAPTER 4

MAY 3
ALBUQUERQUE, N.M.

The next morning, Professor Abbey went to work. He was deep in thought about his personal life as he climbed the stairs to his office on the third floor of the library. He had come to the University of New Mexico because of its location and courses. The University occupied an open, six-hundred-acre campus in the center of Albuquerque. Its department for Latin American Studies was probably the most noted in the country, in part simply because it was one of few such departments, and in part because of the Hispanic heritage of America's southwest.

He knew the department was also strong in its own right. Its courses included languages of today and those of the original indigenous natives. A number of literature and archeological programs were offered, and also studies of the Incas, the Mayas, and the Anasazis. Additionally, the program offered studies about the current political situations throughout Mexico and Central and South America. Most academic sources rated the department high in Latin American affairs and Southwest Hispanic studies. William Abbey was one of the department's four professors.

Since his college days in southern California, Abbey had followed his interest in the southern deserts and their early residents. As an undergraduate, he had majored in archeology, with an emphasis on the Southwest and Mexico, loving to spend his spare time trekking and hiking in the vast deserts of the Southwest. He had earned his doctorate with a thesis involving the history of the Baja Peninsula and how that region had become a part of Mexico in the nineteenth century, rather than a southern extension of the state of California. Although he had a good mind, Abbey didn't consider himself an academic. From his parents he had developed a strong sense of what was right and what was wrong. He tried not to cross that line and didn't like people who did. These and other thoughts all ran through his mind as he reached his office on the third floor and greeted his assistant.

"Good morning, Marge."

"Good morning, Professor. How was your weekend?"

"Oh, it had its ups and downs. I collected some interesting maize samples from Mesa Verde to add to our collection. I found them near an old campfire site. And I camped out in one of the caves – somewhat unexpectedly, it turned out. I'll tell you all about it later. He stood pensively for a second, then added, "Also looks as if Karen will be leaving and heading back to San Francisco. She'll be coming in later to pick up the article you're helping her on – and to settle up with you. Guess the Southwest just isn't right for her." He was subdued and spoke quietly, rather than with his usual enthusiastic voice.

"I'm sorry to hear that, Professor. I'm sure it'll work out."

"Yeah, it'll be fine. Guess it has to be. Let's see what's going on this week," he murmured as he walked into his office, shuffling and skimming the mail which he lifted off his assistant's desk. Some was in English, some in Spanish. Although he was the only Anglo in the department, Professor Abbey was fluent in Spanish.

He sat down at his desk and looked out his one small window over the arid desert landscape. He was still distracted by what had occurred at the Pueblo cave dwelling Saturday night and the events of the night before. Although Karen had finally shown some sympathy about his harrowing experience, she had clearly prepared to discuss ending their relationship, a conversation that was going to take place no matter what. His thoughts turned to how they had met.

They had been a couple for almost two years. He had met her when she interviewed him for an article she was writing about the living conditions of the remaining Apache and Pueblo Indians. Karen was a freelance writer, but her real source of income came from a modest family trust fund. She traveled quite a bit, and since they met, she had spent more and more of her time in Albuquerque. She stayed with him when in town. Last night, she had seized upon what had happened at Mesa Verde as an example of their different life interests. She said his unstructured and unplanned cave exploration represented the way he led his life. He could still remember her words: "You take off for a weekend with no planning, no cell phone, no consideration whatsoever of others. You're only interested in yourself." He wasn't ready to be tied down. Her departure was not really a surprise to him, since they had talked and argued about their future a number of times. She had finally had the strength to call it off.

He turned his thoughts to his future. The chairman of his department had recently left the school for another position. Abbey wanted the chairmanship, but he wasn't sure he wanted to work for it. He was exploring the Southwest but writing very little, and he was beginning to wonder whether academia was really for him. He would have to decide soon, because he was close to the time when he would be evaluated for tenure. Without having published much, and certainly without any important patron, he was pessimistic about his chances. Students flocked to his lectures about the origins of the Southwest and the original Indian inhabitants of America's southern neighbors, but teaching skills were not what earned tenure. Professors had to be sufficiently recognized in their field to attract professional attention and the resulting grants. That had not happened for Professor Abbey.

Unknown to him, this was all about to change.

As was his routine on Mondays, he opened the calendar on his desk to get ready for the week ahead. The previous week had been end-term exams, and he knew he had a lot of reading and grading ahead of him. He noticed an appointment on his calendar which Marge had booked. Abbey was scheduled to meet the next day with a John Duprey from Denver. It was unusual for him to have an appointment with someone he didn't know.

"Marge, who's this John Duprey?"

"I don't really know. He called and said he was an attorney from Denver with a very interesting research project involving Mexico. He was quite insistent about meeting with you as soon as possible. He laid it on pretty thick about having been told you were the best authority in the Southwest on Mexican history. I hope it's okay that I scheduled him."

"Sure, it's fine. It'll give me a break from reading the exams. Guess I didn't know how widespread my reputation had become," he added with a self-deprecating chuckle.

• • •

The next morning, Marge showed John Duprey into Abbey's small office. Duprey was overdressed for the university, wearing a conservative tan suit and a muted tie on a blue shirt. He looked like a lawyer.

"Professor Abbey, thanks for seeing me," Duprey said, offering his hand.

As Abbey stood, he looked down a few inches at the shorter man, who immediately struck him as officious and filled with self-importance. Extending his arm over the desk to shake hands, Abbey said, "Glad to. Do we know each other from somewhere?"

"No, no. Not at all. I'm on an assignment for a client to start a research project. Your name has come highly recommended because the work involves Mexico."

Abbey sat down behind his desk, while Duprey took one of the other chairs. "Well, I'd be glad to help. I have some doctoral students who write papers about and do research into various Mexican matters."

"Professor, we're looking for you to conduct this work. Personally. Hands on."

"I don't usually do that. I have a fairly heavy teaching load, and I'm just starting a research project on the origins of what we today know as corn – previously known as maize. I'm trying to determine how natural genetic modifications of maize over the centuries compare to today's artificial modifications being engineered by man. Probably sounds a bit dull, but it's taking a lot of my time. And I'm pretty much occupied full time on the payroll here."

Ignoring Abbey's statement, the lawyer went full speed ahead. "Professor, my client is a bit stubborn. She's also very wealthy. She thinks you are the one she needs. It could be very profitable."

"I'm flattered," Abbey responded, "but I'm on the teaching staff here. I can't just take on outside projects without approval from the administration, and even then, only if they have an academic purpose." He was starting to become a bit impatient with Duprey's persistence. *A little pushy, isn't he?*

"Professor, please give me a moment to explain further. We have a way to do this which we think will be acceptable to you and the university. We assume your department isn't highly funded. We're prepared to help change that. We're prepared to make a substantial donation to fund an academic chair, which I hope you would hold. We would do it at a level commensurate with chairs at the most prestigious universities. In return, all we need is for you to devote about six months of your time to our project. I'm sure the university will find that the work has an academic purpose."

Abbey took pause, remembering his disquiet about his future. What Duprey said was beginning to sound intriguing. He didn't know what to say, or whether even to believe what was going on.

"What research do you want?" he asked.

The lawyer leaned on the desk in front of him and shifted his eyes side to side, as if to see if anyone else was listening. He lowered his voice, almost to a whisper.

"This is all very confidential, Professor. Let's just say it involves the Baja Peninsula and its history."

"That's my field of expertise! I wrote my doctoral thesis on the Baja."

"We know, Professor. We've read your thesis."

"Well, you have my attention," said Abbey. "I'm not sure what to say. But I can't just take six months off."

"Professor, I understand your reaction. I've sprung this on you out of the blue. I've put everything in writing in this packet." He took a manila folder from his briefcase and handed it to Abbey. The folder was labeled *Professor William Abbey Research Project*. Inside were about a dozen typed pages. "Maybe you could look these over and we can talk again tomorrow morning. In the meantime, if you have any questions, call me on my cell phone. Here's my card. I'll be staying in the area for a couple of days."

Putting the folder on his desk, Abbey raised one last question.

"What exactly about the Baja are you interested in?"

Duprey leaned forward to answer, his voice again dropping to a whisper.

"I must repeat, this is confidential. I hope you'll respect that." He hesitated for a moment, then added, "Let's just say we're intrigued by the question raised in your thesis about a missing deed . . . a missing deed to the Baja." The lawyer watched Abbey's face closely to see his reaction.

"Yes. I did raise that question," Abbey said, almost offhandedly. "I remember I found some interesting documents, but that was a while ago. I'd have to get my research papers out and look at them. Let me look over your proposal and give you a call."

• • •

Once Duprey left, Abbey looked at the pile of exams on his desk and then flicked his eyes to the folder. After a moment, he picked up the folder and opened it. The papers in it didn't give much additional information. There was a long, complicated confidentiality agreement, and a proposed chair in Latin American Studies to be funded by a one-time gift to the university of five million dollars. Abbey was stunned when he read the number. *Five million dollars!* he thought excitedly. The university had a number of fully endowed chairs, but he wasn't sure whether any of them were funded at that level. Although not stated, the clear inference was that he, William Abbey, would be the first holder of the chair.

All of a sudden, he had thoughts of financial independence, travel, and academic work that he had never before even dreamed possible. He forgot his doubts and pessimism about his future. It didn't take long to decide that he was interested. He almost picked up the phone to call Karen and tell her of the new assignment, but then realized it wouldn't make any difference to her. He didn't want to look like he was begging her to stay. It was over between them. Instead, he decided to find out a bit more about Duprey. He turned to his laptop and went online.

Abbey found the lawyer in his computer search. Duprey was the head of a small law firm in Denver. Two other lawyers were in the firm: Jonathan Polk, who did wills, and Wendy Outlander, a divorce lawyer. It was unclear what Duprey did, but his credentials were from the East, Syracuse undergraduate and Cornell Law. He looked reputable.

• • •

Duprey walked to his car parked in front of the library. He got in and turned on the engine to start the air-conditioning. He was sweating. He thought Abbey looked like a good choice: young, impressionable, and probably not suspicious by nature. He pulled out his cell phone and called his office.

"The retainer check from the New York group cleared," his assistant told him. "And I just FedExed the biggest check I've ever seen to your hotel. What's going on?"

He ignored her question. "How's everything else?"

"Smooth, as usual. One will-signing today, and Wendy just landed another client."

"Great. I'll be back late tomorrow." He added, "Don't you worry about what's going on. You'll know soon enough."

Duprey was not sure of the identity of this new client he was representing in Albuquerque. A contact in New York had given him the assignment. Most of Duprey's questions about the matter had been rebuffed, but the $25,000 retainer had convinced him to take on the work. He was given the bare outline of what was required from Abbey, and he himself scripted much of what he was presenting to the professor. When he got back to his hotel, the FedEx was waiting at the desk with a check inside.

Abbey heard from Duprey the next morning.

"Professor, sorry to jump the gun, but I've been able to get an appointment with President Overton this afternoon. Don't want to push you, but it'd be great if we could see him on this project. *I know he's interested,* he added to himself. *He's seen the five million dollar figure. He's creaming in his pants.*

"Well, that's moving pretty fast, Mr. Duprey, but, yes, I'm interested. This afternoon? President Overton?" Abbey swallowed nervously.

"What time?"

"Two o'clock," answered the lawyer.

"How'd you get an appointment so quickly?" asked Abbey.

"Money talks, professor. Money talks. I told his assistant I wanted to discuss a large gift to the university. He was very available. Why don't I come by and pick you up just before two."

"Sure," Abbey said, trying not to display his excitement and nervousness. "I'll see you then."

•   •   •

President Overton sat in his office behind an impressive mahogany desk as Professor Abbey and John Duprey were ushered in.

He looks like a university president, thought Duprey. *Tall and thin, with a full shock of grey hair.*

They took seats facing his desk. Earlier in the day, Overton had gotten a message that Duprey wanted to meet with him to discuss a large gift to the university. He couldn't figure out why Abbey was there, but he greeted them both politely, even acting as if he remembered the young professor. After preliminaries, Duprey summarized his proposal.

"That would be a very generous chair endowment," responded Overton after he caught his breath. "One of our largest gifts." *The biggest by far*, he thought to himself.

Duprey added with a serious look, "Yes, sir, my client has a true fondness for the university and a great interest that this research goes forward quickly. She attended the school years ago."

"Who *is* your client?" asked Overton.

"That I can't disclose. She's a bit of a recluse. As the agreement says, the gift is conditioned on confidentiality. We want absolutely no publicity about the gift or the assignment. Naturally, you'll need to disclose the funding of the chair. But you must be circumspect."

"I think we can meet those conditions," responded President Overton. Looking at Abbey, a junior associate professor he barely knew, he asked, "But what exactly is

Professor Abbey going to do?" For a gift of this size, he didn't really care if Abbey had to stand on his head, but he would have to get approval from the Board of Regents and provide them some information. Many gifts had conditions, and although this was starting to sound a bit unusual, he saw nothing at all improper about having Professor Abbey conduct some research in return for five million dollars.

"We're in the planning stages for a grand new real estate development in Mexico, on the Baja Peninsula," Duprey explained. "We need Professor Abbey to work full time doing important historical research concerning the Baja to help us with land acquisition. It is in his field of expertise and directly related to his doctoral thesis. My client thinks this is a great way to combine her commercial and altruistic goals. She gets assistance for the proposed development *and* she benefits the school."

Overton tented his fingers in front of his face and nodded knowingly, even though he knew nothing about Abbey's thesis, and not much more about his field of expertise.

"It's the first step in this development," Duprey continued to explain. "We need the research to be done quickly – within six months. We need his full-time effort during that time. If you agree to the proposal, I have here a check in the amount of five million dollars. The agreement does say, however, that we may request it back if you breach our confidence."

"Does that mean we're to hold the check?" Overton said, with disappointment in his voice.

"No, no. It's yours to spend and fund the chair. We're confident there will be no problems."

Overton smiled broadly. "Well, I'm sure we can handle this. Professor Abbey, sound okay to you?"

Abbey nodded enthusiastically. "Definitely. I think it's a very workable project. I know a lot about the Baja. The research is right down my alley, and I think it's a terrific way to fund a chair."

Duprey handed the check to President Overton, who took it casually and placed it on his desk, as if it were a normal event. They stood and shook hands.

Duprey turned to Abbey. "Before I leave, you and I need to go over some details of the assignment."

"Let's go to my office," responded Abbey.

As they departed, President Overton extended his thanks. "Thank you very much on behalf of the university, Mr. Duprey. And thank your client. I'm sure we won't disappoint either of you. Do you have a preference as to what we name the chair?"

"Not at all," answered Duprey. "We'll leave those details up to you."

• • •

Duprey and Abbey walked the short distance to Abbey's small office. Abbey sat down behind his desk, which was strewn with the student essays he was in the middle of reading and grading. His office walls held pictures he had taken of places he had visited and explored: a view of Half Dome in Yosemite taken from Glacier Point, the back country of Alaska, and grizzly bears at Brooks Falls. There were pictures from the Baja, one of a long mountain range disappearing into the distance, and another of the sea breaking on a rocky shore with white, foaming spray reaching up the cliffs. These last pictures were from the days of his doctoral thesis, when he had trekked the Baja by foot and by vehicle for two months, interviewing Mexicans and occasional Americans about the land and its history. On one shelf sat samples from his collection of pottery from the indigenous people of the Americas. At home and in his office, he would look at these ancient eating and drinking vessels and think of the people who had used them in their daily lives. He would often wonder: *Why did all these people disappear?*

His real treasures, however, adorned the walls of his condominium: photographs of the petroglyph wall and cave drawings he had taken throughout the Southwest and Mexico. The simple, ancient drawings depicted hunting, farming, and warring scenes from centuries before. He used a 35mm Canon Elan with a filtered strobe light that he had devised to illuminate the drawings in dark caves without glare. He still used film for most of his pictures. The surprise and memories of the developed prints were more satisfying to him than the instant gratification of digital images. He often carried a digital camera body for spot-checking, but film was his preference.

As Duprey took a seat, Abbey leaned forward with his forearms on his desk. "So, what's really going on, Mr. Duprey? Where's all the money coming from, and why in the world are you making this proposal?"

Duprey began his story: "I can't identify my client, but I can tell you a fair amount. Remember back in the 1960s, when Walt Disney began planning for his huge Disney World complex in Florida? It took him years to assemble the thousands of acres he eventually purchased. It was swampy wasteland then. Orlando was just a bump in the road. He knew prices would escalate greatly if his plans became known. So he hired a number of separate brokers and agents to go into the field and start buying land. He didn't tell them the plans, and none of them knew that others were doing the same thing in adjacent areas. It was a stroke of genius. He kept his land costs much below what he would have paid if people had known what was happening. When people finally realized, he had assembled most of the land he needed."

"So is Disney now going to the Baja?" asked Abbey.

Duprey hesitated for a moment, staring at the professor and crooking a finger to his chin in contemplation. Then he pointed the finger gently at Abbey.

"I can tell you it's *not* Disney, but you're not far off. As I explained to President Overton, I have a client with great wealth who hopes to develop a first-class destination resort and retirement community in the Baja. It will cater mostly to Americans and will be an hour's plane ride from Los Angeles. It will be high-end. As you probably know, there are millions about to retire in America who are looking for a dream retirement home. In Mexico, we can build a luxurious community at very affordable prices. We see this as an enormous opportunity. But, as I think you know, purchasing real estate in Mexico is difficult for foreigners.

"In our research, we've decided that the northern portion of the Baja Peninsula holds much more potential than all of the current development in the south around Cabo San Lucas. We came across your doctoral thesis. You'll remember that you briefly mentioned the legend that a lost deed exists for a large portion of northern Baja; that title to that area might be in some doubt. But you gave very few details in your thesis, and your working papers are not publicly available. We looked into it and ran into a dead end.

"So we need your help. We need to find out if there really is a lost deed. If there is, we want to find the living descendants of the old owners. We then want to quickly and quietly purchase their interests. Since it was your research in the first place that uncovered this issue, you're the perfect person to continue the investigation. It will appear normal for you to pursue the matter as part of your academic research. Your activities should not raise questions. And, of course, everything is perfectly legal. You simply won't explain exactly why you're doing the work." His hands opened in a gesture that suggested the task would be easy.

Duprey continued, "You're on the ground floor of a very exciting development. The endowment has been paid and has no strings attached, other than the confidentiality requirement. To reward your success and as a form of bonus, if we are successful, you will be given a home of your choice in the new community. But time is important. As I told President Overton, we need results within six months."

"Okay. At least it now makes some sense," said Abbey. "And a home in Mexico is exciting. I've often thought I would like to spend more time there. So, essentially, I take a six-month leave of absence and find out more about the deed and the people connected to the deed."

"Exactly," responded Duprey, with a clipped firmness to his voice.

"It will require some travel and some expenses."

"Don't worry. Your expenses will be paid. What if I advance you ten thousand now toward expenses?" Duprey took a loose check from his briefcase, filled it out, and handed it across the desk. "If you need more, let me know."

The check, as with the one given to President Overton, was drawn on a bank in New York City but contained no printed customer identification. Abbey took it, saying, "Thank you very much."

"No, Professor, thank you. I will look forward to your reports. I would appreciate receiving some type of update every couple of weeks."

Duprey was ready to leave. He stood, reached over to shake Abbey's hand, and walked out, saying goodbye to Marge on his way by her desk.

• • •

Professor Abbey spent the next two days clearing his calendar of all teaching responsibilities and completing the grading of his students' exams. Not surprisingly, President Overton's office was fully supportive and assigned other professors to his classes. Marge couldn't figure out what was happening. "Are you leaving the school?" she asked.

"No, Marge, but I've taken on a special consulting assignment which will last about six months. I might be away for some travel, but I'm certainly not leaving the school."

A few days later, she received an internal university announcement that Professor Abbey was being granted tenure as a full professor, with an endowed chair in "Baja Studies."

Abbey himself was figuring out how he was going to proceed on the new project. Karen's departure was fading from his mind. He felt a new sense of purpose and excitement. This was exactly what he needed: an important new assignment and, finally, someone who recognized the value of his work.

I'm going to succeed, he thought. *I'll find the deed. I'll find the people. And I'll show them all that Bill Abbey is someone to be reckoned with.*

CHAPTER 5

MAY 4–5
WASHINGTON, D.C.

Colonel Charles Longley was beginning to think that things were not quite as expected in Iran as he reviewed the minutes of his group's last meeting. He was chairman of the Iran Group within the National Counterterrorism Center. The group included a senior representative from each armed service and each intelligence agency. Its mission was to monitor Iran's nuclear program to determine when and if the Iranian nuclear enrichment program reached a stage at which weapons were probable – when Iran achieved "bomb ready" status.

The sons of bitches are just too self confident, he thought to himself in his small Pentagon office. *Talabani sits with his shit-eating grin and makes speeches to the world that Iran is a peace lover – a threat to no one. I don't buy it.*

Longley reported directly to the secretary of defense and was the marine representative in the Iran Group. At fifty-five years old, he was a career marine and had served in both of America's military quagmires – Vietnam and Iraq. In Iraq, he had been the senior officer in the country responsible for the storage and possible deployment of tactical nuclear weapons. Although the subject was seldom discussed publicly, he knew that almost every conflict involving American troops had the nuclear option available. Naturally, that availability depended on a very complex chain of command and authorization protocol. Longley knew the protocol. He assumed his duties in Iraq were what had qualified him for his present assignment.

He knew the press had been reporting for years the expert consensus that Iran would not have nuclear weapon capability for another decade. But he also knew there really were no such experts. Each press report fed on and repeated the previous one. Few were based on fact. He suspected the reports were instead based upon a disinformation campaign being conducted in Iran. Colonel Longley's staff had correctly determined that no one really had any idea about what was going on in Iran. The same had been true in Iraq before Saddam's fall.

In Iran, the one possible exception was Israel. Because of the close ties between the United States and Israel and their commonality of interests, Israel was an informal member of the Iran Group. Its representative, Henre Morad, was an Israeli diplomat whom most knew to be more from the intelligence community than the diplomatic corps.

Always the gentleman, thought Longley, as his mind went over the last meeting. Morad attended many of the group's meetings, stepping out when top secret matters came before a meeting. Morad had contributed some helpful information at the last meeting. At the same meeting, John Muffin, the CIA representative, had disclosed that Iran had more nuclear capabilities than had been suspected. Muffin's report had been startling to Longley.

"We now believe that Iran has an adequate supply of uranium oxide yellowcake to produce weapons," Muffin had explained. "As you know, everything starts with yellowcake. No yellowcake is produced in Iran, so we always figured that they were limited by the very small quantities they could obtain off the record from ore-producing countries like Russia and Libya. Enrichment of the powder to create uranium-235 requires five tons of yellowcake to create the approximately one hundred pounds of enriched uranium needed for a single weapon. That's a lot of powder. Ten thousand pounds for just one bomb. Unfortunately, we've just received new information. We now think Iran quietly purchased twenty-five tons of the stuff from Niger. Niger's yellowcake shipments are closely monitored by the IAEA, but we've just come across some documents showing deliveries of over two hundred sealed barrels to Iran in 1999. The docs don't reveal what was in the barrels, but there's really nothing in Niger of interest to Iran other than yellowcake. It couldn't have been anything else."

"That was seven years ago!" Longley had exclaimed at the meeting. "Why the hell are we only hearing about it now?"

"We only recently received all shipping documents from Niger, rather than just those designated as yellowcake shipments," answered Muffin. "In these new documents, we found the suspicious shipments. It was a period of political instability in Niger. Looks like someone needed some money." The Israeli, Morad, had absented himself for that discussion but had made some unsettling comments when he returned.

Reading more of the minutes from that meeting, Longley recalled more of the conversation.

"Our sources suggest that Iran is much closer to successful uranium enrichment than suspected," Morad had said.

"What do your sources say?" Muffin asked.

"I have to be careful here because I have to protect our source at all costs." The Israeli had paused, obviously thinking how to word his disclosure. Then he had continued,

"There is a strong possibility that enrichment activities are taking place in Iran at a location in addition to Natanz. We all know about the Natanz facility, but materials which should be going to Natanz are being diverted elsewhere, to the south. And a small number of key scientists from the Natanz facility are no longer there. We don't know where they are. But they have left Natanz. Additionally, President Talabani has been strangely quiet since his nuclear pronouncements last year . . . almost as if he has been told not to stir the pot."

Muffin said, "The U.N. inspectors at Natanz have reported nothing unusual."

"That's the point," Morad replied. "Little is happening at Natanz. Things have been too quiet. And our source reports these other activities."

The colonel suspected that Israel had someone on the ground deeply embedded in Iran. He knew better than to ask that question in an open meeting. The United States had no one placed on the ground in Iran, but the electronic monitoring devices which surrounded Iran were sending some troubling signals. A number of short and mid-range missiles had been fired in Iran's southern deserts, and Longley knew Iran was buying materials on the international market which were more appropriate for weapons manufacture than peaceful purposes. Everyone knew that Iran was trying to build a bomb.

Longley was most troubled that he really had no idea how close Iran was to the possession of nuclear weapons. When he reported that position to the National Security Council, he was usually asked for supporting data. The point was, he didn't have any. The experts kept saying they had time, but he wasn't so sure. He decided to meet privately with Morad to see if he could obtain more information. The two met alone in Colonel Longley's office in the Pentagon. Longley the picture of a full-chested and uniformed marine colonel; Morad lithe and small, with his usual well-tailored suit and tie.

"Henre, I'm concerned," Longley began. "A sudden announcement of nuclear weapon capability by Iran would be catastrophic. What do you really know?"

"We know a bit more than I said on the record – and this meeting is not on the record. We, too, have grave concerns that something is about to happen. Luckily, we've been working on this for decades. We have a very good source in Iran. What I said at the meeting was accurate. What I didn't say is that Israel should receive some warning if any type of attack is imminent. For us, that is the difference between life and death, survival or annihilation. No measures can defend us against such a sudden attack. America has always had the luxury of great distances between it and its enemies. The one exception was Cuba, and you then acted quickly and decisively to make sure that no missiles would be near your border . . . but I digress. I am confident that Israel will receive advance warning of any attack."

"What kind of warning are you talking about?" asked Longley.

"We should have at least twenty-four hours' notice, based upon the resources we have in place."

"Do you know where the new facility is?"

"No."

"Well, then, what can you do, even with twenty-four hours of notice?"

"If we receive the warning, we can and will destroy much of Iran. We might not know their specific missile launch point, but the devastation we will cause will be so widespread that a surviving missile launch from any location would be unlikely."

"You'll use nuclear weapons?" asked the colonel in a shocked tone, springing to his feet and looking down at the still-seated Israeli.

"You know I cannot answer that," Morad responded, smiling wryly through clinched lips and shaking his head slowly. "The official policy of Israel is that we have none. Suffice it to say, we will not sit back and let Iran destroy us."

There wasn't much more to say. Colonel Longley thanked Morad for meeting with him and sharing the information. He gave him his personal phone number and asked the Israeli to please keep him posted of anything new. Morad said he would. Longley had always been impressed by the Israeli, who was a master of the diplomatic understatement, while Longley usually charged forward in the marine way. As he walked Morad back to the reception area, Logley realized they made an odd pair in the hallways of the Pentagon. Even their hair styles contrasted. Morad's thinning, grey, and cut long, alongside Longley's short but full marine cut.

After the meeting, Colonel Longley directed his staff to initiate even more intense satellite and electronic surveillance over Iran. He told them to focus on the southern coastal area. He wanted to know of any unusual truck movements into areas where they would not be expected. He wanted more intense infrared screening of southern Iran to determine patterns of heat emission and any changes in those patterns.

"I want both Lacrosse and Keyhole spy satellites deployed over Iran," he directed to his staff. He knew the Lacrosse had a resolution of under twelve inches, and by interfacing its digital pictures with a land-based computer, a traffic count could be generated for almost any road in the world. The Keyhole's strength was its infrared capability. Much of the earth's surface had been measured for heat baselines. A significant change from a baseline could be detected by the satellite. Longley had been advised that the large centrifuges for uranium enhancement involved very large machinery that generated a lot of heat. He issued appropriate orders to reposition the two spysats so that they would each pass over southern Iran twice a day. For the time being, he thought it was all he could do.

CHAPTER 6

MAY 6

IRAN

The Ayatollah received a short communiqué that Abbey had been hired. It came through the Iranian Information Office in Manhattan after John Duprey had dutifully reported the hiring to his New York contact. The cleric passed the information along to his cousin, whom he knew had been very busy running Iran's uranium enrichment program.

His cousin, General Mussahrah, had quietly acquired a large network of centrifuges to spin yellowcake's uranium hexafluoride gas into highly radioactive U-235. The yellowcake Iran had purchased from Niger contained only minute quantities of U-235. The centrifuge spinning was extracting and concentrating the necessary quantities of the radioactive poison, and the general's staff advised him that they would soon have one hundred pounds. That was what they needed for a single fission bomb of about fifteen kilotons, the size of America's Hiroshima weapon.

Mussahrah and the Ayatollah had agreed from the outset that they didn't have the time or resources to assemble a large number of bombs. They knew they couldn't win a head-to-head nuclear battle with the West. Instead, their plan was to attack with precision and finesse to achieve the destruction of Israel and the capitulation of America.

They talked privately in the Ayatollah's study after learning that Abbey had been hired.

"We will protect ourselves and initiate the final death spiral of Israel," said the Ayatollah. "And then, as they might say in the West, we will make them an offer they have to accept. Our position will be considered reasonable by many. We will be seen as heroes around the world."

The general nodded his agreement, adding, "It is as we have discussed. Once we are in a position to hurt the United States, they will capitulate to our demands. They do not like to be hurt. They are fearful of another September eleventh attack within their borders. As Allah would say, 'They have the way, but not the will.' We will soon have both. And our will cannot be questioned."

He continued, "Everything depends on secrecy until we have the weapons in place. Our news agency is doing as I have ordered and disseminated such disinformation that our enemies have no idea what we are planning. When they discover something, we simply change our story. We'll cooperate with investigations as long as they mean nothing. Look at Natanz. Their investigations have found very little there because they are looking in the wrong place." He puffed out his chest in his beribboned uniform, which he always wore. "They have met their match, and we will win," he added proudly.

"Let us not forget our President Talabani," added the Ayatollah. "He can meet and speak with them almost as one of them. I think they believe him because he can speak so well, even in English when he chooses. They believe we are all ignorant desert rats, and they are so pleased to find a Muslim they can talk to."

"Yes, cousin," responded the general, "Talabani has been helpful. But we must keep him at a little distance. Remember, he resisted my contacts with Saddam before the

American invasion. I managed to get those centrifuges out of Iraq and to Jask just in time. Talabani wanted no part of Iraq – or Saddam. I didn't either, but I thought I could pretend otherwise and play the man for a fool."

"Saddam actually believed me when I promised to help him escape to join us. Him, a Sunni, help us? I wonder if he ever realized that I initiated the tip which led to his capture. He would have been more hindrance than help. Now the Jask enrichment facility is up and running smoothly and almost invisible to prying eyes. I believe I have orchestrated things perfectly," he concluded with a smug look. Then, seeing a frown come to the Ayatollah's face, he added quickly, "With your help, of course, my Excellency."

"Yes," added the Ayatollah. "Your efforts have been successful. And now, maybe I have solved the last hurdle. Maybe my *fantasy*, as you put it, will provide us with a launch site in the West. Because, as you know, we must have one. We cannot otherwise deliver the bombs to their doorstep over such a long distance. For Israel, no problem, but for America, we must be closer. So, my general, although I have my weaknesses, remember that I, too, am pursuing the everlasting strength of Islam and the inevitable victory of Allah over the heathens."

"I did not mean to suggest otherwise," answered Mahmoud, spreading his hands in acknowledgment. "With Allah's strength, we work together. I will concentrate my efforts on Jask and hope to soon have three weapons."

The two Iranians had discussed the political picture in the United States, with a new female president and a country tired of the Afghanistan and Iraqi incursions. If a nuclear threat was to be made, this was the time to do it. In particular, they wanted to spring their nuclear surprise during the first term of the new American president. She had never been tested, and, as a woman, they felt she would surely fail. They were glad to hear that this Professor Abbey would now be doing some of their work for them. For, unbeknownst to Abbey, he was looking for their missile launch site in the Baja Peninsula.

First, though, the Iranians had to set the stage so the Americans would believe them when they eventually claimed they could fire a targeted missile over a thousand miles. Almost all of the Iranian missiles fired by Hezbollah in the past from Lebanon had been unguided projectiles like the Katyushas rockets, traveling under fifty miles. Iran was a big country, extending over one thousand miles north to south. So General Mussahrah scheduled a test shoot of the new Shahab-4 medium-range missile at a defined target one thousand miles from the launch site, all within Iran's own borders. He wanted to satisfy himself that the guidance system worked. Furthermore, with appropriate planned leaks of the test shoot, he wanted the West to know that Iran had the capability. No threats or wide publicity; simply making a point. The firing occurred that summer. General Mussahrah reported to the Ayatollah that he was sure it had been noted by American intelligence sources.

CHAPTER 7

MAY 7
WASHINGTON, D.C.

Madeline Cartright was a career project manager from the Department of the Treasury who had been transferred to Homeland Security when it was organized. This morning, she settled her large frame heavily into her chair, beginning her day with a cup of tea as she reviewed the emails and reports which had come in overnight. One document in the pile was a hard copy of the foreign funds report. She winced at its size. *So much paperwork,* she thought with a sigh. She saw that the input clerk had written a note on the front page in black magic marker: *Note pages 7 and 8 – circled checks.* She turned to the designated pages, and her curiosity was piqued. First, a five million dollar payment to the University of New Mexico was circled on page seven. Then, at the top of page eight, a ten thousand dollar payment from the same account to a Professor William Abbey was also highlighted.

Madeline knew that the regulations only called for scrutiny of payments in excess of five million dollars, but the clerk had been perceptive enough to combine these two checks and treat them as one, even though they were dated a few days apart. She agreed with that decision, and, when combined, they exceeded the threshold. *Not by a great amount,* she thought, but her training was to deal in decimal points and details.

Although she had seen large donations from foreigners to American universities in the report before, she dug further and researched the two checks. The New York bank on which they were drawn was a reputable small, boutique bank used by the wealthy. She was able to trace the source of the funds by reviewing inter-bank transfer records. She found that these particular funds had gone through a number of convoluted transfers before reaching New York. The money had been wired to New York from a small bank in Macau. Prior to that, a number of letters of credit had issued from Dubai shipping companies connected with an originating Dubai bank, making the money look like payment for goods shipped into Dubai. But the path of the funds was too convoluted. Cartright had seen money laundering before. Someone was trying to conceal the source of this money, which was clearly in the Middle East.

Madeline warmed her tea before reviewing her other incoming mail. Then she returned to the funds report.

She assumed Abbey was connected with the school. She went online to the university website to see what she could find out about him. Sure enough, there he was in the department of Latin American Studies. *Probably a radical liberal wanting to welcome the unemployed and downtrodden from the south with open arms*, she mused. *And open wallets.* But his curriculum vitae was not all that far out. No revolutionary articles published, and, after looking at a classified government site, she could find no record of demonstration arrests. Everything she found painted him as a middle-of-the-road type of guy. There was even a picture. She saw a thirtyish, clean-cut man with short dark hair and a slightly crooked smile. *Handsome guy,* she thought with a smile.

She decided to contact the university.

• • •

President Overton was dreaming about how the huge endowment could be used when the call came in. He had confirmed that the check had cleared. Certainly the chair would be established, and Professor Abbey had already been named its first holder. But it took less than five million dollars to endow a chair. *A new addition to the library, or a new administration building?* he wondered. He knew this was probably his last academic post. He was sixty-four years old and had earned his academic stripes in a number of second-tier Western universities. President of the university for three years, he knew he didn't have many years left to place his imprimatur on the school. This was his chance.

"Mr. President, a Mrs. Cartwright from the Office of Homeland Security is on the line."

"For me?"

"Yes, sir. She asked for the president."

"All right. Put her through." He heard the line open. "This is President Overton."

"President Overton, I am Deputy Counsel Madeline Cartwright from the Office of Homeland Security. Thank you for taking my call."

"Glad to. Must be important. What can I do for you?"

"No, no, probably not that important. This is a routine inquiry concerning a recent large payment to the university involving foreign funds. These transactions pop up in our computers from time to time. When they do, we look into them."

His heart in his throat, Overton asked in as casual a tone as he could, "What payment are you interested in?"

She answered slowly, thinking that he wasn't being all that forthcoming. "Well, sir, a pretty big payment. Millions of dollars. Actually, five million dollars, paid by a check dated May 3, drawn on the Wall Street Bank in New York."

"Oh, yes, certainly I know of that gift." He remembered the confidentiality requirement and hesitated. "But, as you say, it was drawn on a New York bank, not a foreign one. Actually, from a very wealthy alumnus who wishes to remain anonymous. I can assure you, he's as American as you and I. No foreign funds at all." *A few stretches of the truth shouldn't hurt,* he thought to himself.

"Well, maybe my information is wrong, Mr. President. I'll check further. One other question. Did that alumnus make any other gifts or payments at about the same time, even smaller ones, to anyone at the university?"

"Oh, no. We were most satisfied with the gift as it was. There was nothing more."

"Okay," she said slowly. *If that's the way you want to leave it.* "Well, thank you, President Overton. As I said, this is just a routine inquiry. I'll check further on my information."

"Very well. Glad to be of help."

Not much help, Cartright thought as she hung up. *Why didn't he disclose the other $10,000 to this Professor Abbey?* Since Abbey was a professor at the school, she felt Overton should know of the payment. She put together a short report and sent it along to the Investigations Division for them to pursue if they wanted. *Probably nothing*, she thought. She copied her report to the passport office, aware that it would cause the name William Abbey to go onto the TSA Watch List for at least ninety days in connection with any international travel. She also knew it would tentatively label him a money launderer.

• • •

After hanging up, President Overton nervously drummed his fingers on his desk while considering his options. He didn't really care where the money had come from, and he certainly wasn't going to give it back. He decided to go forward with his plans as if nothing had happened. After all, the check had cleared. He resumed his planning to spend the gift. Faculty and administrative offices were spread around the campus. *An Overton Faculty and Administration Building would be a nice remembrance*, he mused. He could endow the chair for about a million dollars. That would leave four million for construction seed money. He could raise any necessary additional funds. *And then they'll remember me,* he thought with pride. *Then they'll remember President Overton.*

CHAPTER 8

MAY 4–7

ALBUQUERQUE

Duprey's question about the "missing deed" had jogged Abbey's memory. As soon as the lawyer left, the professor retrieved his doctoral thesis and research notes from the library's archives and began to review them to recall the details about the missing deed. Looking over the papers, it all started coming back to him.

His thesis had focused on the ceding of the Baja Peninsula to Mexico by the United States in 1848. The United States and Mexico had fought over much of America's Southwest in the mid-nineteenth century. The Baja Peninsula even today carried the full name *Baja California, Mexico,* on many maps, where it looked like a southern extension of the state of California. He had studied the geography of the region and had seen that the Sonoran Desert of southern California ran a thousand miles to the southern tip of the Baja, where Cabo San Lucas was guarded by its famous portal cliff. Overlooking that desert, a single mountain range ran from California along the middle ridge of the peninsula, north to south. In the nineteenth century, many had thought that the Baja was more naturally a part of the United States than Mexico. His research showed why it had not happened that way.

In the mid-1840s, America had sought to take possession and partial control of Mexican territory, including what was now the state of California and parts of the Baja.

The result was the Mexican-American War of 1846–1848. The hostilities were ended by the Treaty of Hidalgo in 1848, where the United States ceded to Mexico its claims to the Baja. Mexico, in return, gave up its claims to California and portions of New Mexico and Arizona. Soon thereafter, in 1850, California became the thirty-first state.

In his doctoral research, Abbey had come across some unique language in at least one version of the Treaty of Hidalgo. While at the National Archives in Washington as a student, he had reviewed the original treaty document. It was inscribed on three pages of parchment paper which were sewn together in the top left corner. He had to sign a withdrawal card to remove it to a table for review. Since it wasn't stored in the area of highly valuable documents, his university credentials had been sufficient to give him access. The treaty was in English, with signatures and wax seals of American and Mexican officials. He found the text to be the standard formal language of international treaties, with more uses of *whereas* and *now therefores* than he thought necessary. He read it carefully and saw nothing unusual.

Then, when he was about to close the folder and return it to storage, a loose page fluttered out of the folder and dropped to the floor. He still remembered how, when he had picked it up to return it to the folder, the rough texture of the paper on his fingers had caught his attention. It wasn't smooth like modern paper. Instead, it had felt crinkled and rough, like old parchment paper. So he sat back down to look at the page.

The paper was the same type of parchment paper as the three-page treaty. At the top of the loose page was written in large letters, *ADDENDUM*. Some loose threads stuck through the paper in the top left corner. Looking back to the treaty, he realized that this page had originally been attached to the treaty document. At some time it had apparently ripped off and thereafter remained unattached and loose in the file. The addendum contained seven numbered paragraphs. Looking again at the treaty, he had seen that there were seven footnotes in the text written with small numerals. He had overlooked the numbers before.

Abbey had then gone back to the addendum and read the seven paragraphs. The first six were fairly innocuous references to metes and bounds and land descriptions. The last, number seven, was a bit different, and caught his attention. It referred to the last footnote, just before the signatures in the treaty. His doctoral notes, which he had been reviewing, refreshed his memory of the wording of footnote 7. He remembered he had written the words down verbatim, since photocopying such an ancient document would have been difficult. He now read what he had copied six years before:

7. As for the Baja Peninsula Territory, nothing herein shall have any effect whatsoever upon private property rights to tracts within the Territory which have been perfected by actual cultivation and livestock grazing for a period of at least twenty contiguous years.

None of the history he had ever seen made any reference to such a clause. It had confused him as a student. Even today, six years later, he was still uncertain of its meaning.

For his thesis, Abbey had next traveled to Mexico and continued his work in the Mexican national archives in Mexico City. There, he had read the diplomatic records and correspondence from officers in the field about the war and eventual negotiations with the Americans. It was coming back to him as he continued to read his notes, and he remembered what he had found in Mexico.

Late one morning, he had been sitting at a table in a dark basement reading the original treaty in Spanish, including an addendum page which was attached. In the body of the treaty, he had seen the footnote numerals 1 through 6, but there had been no footnote 7 on the signature page. Turning to the addendum, he found the same omission. The exclusionary footnote 7 language he had uncovered in Washington, D.C., was missing in Mexico City.

He had spent the rest of the day pouring over the diplomatic records, but he was unable to discover any reason behind the inclusion of those words in the English version or their absence in the Spanish text. His first inclination had been to ignore the issue and put it down to some type of 150-year-old scrivener's error. After all, most of the Baja had remained untouched over the years. No one appeared to have ever asserted any claims under the provision. Then, as he continued to review the old files in Mexico City, he had found the letters. They were in English. As with footnote **7, he had copied the letters into his notes and now looked at them again.

March 6, 1850

Señor President,

I and my family have raised cattle on our land grant here in Baja Norte for over 20 years. I have been informed that this gives us some rights. Instead I am being assaulted by your policia and demanded to make tax payments, grant passage, and many other things. They laugh at my claim that I have property rights. They say I

*am a foreigner with no rights. I protest. I wish to be left
alone in my Baja Norte.*

> *Yours respectfully,*
> *Jonathan Van Huessen,*
> *of Bahia de los Angeles*

Next, another letter from Mr. Van Huessen, dated six
months later:

*Again I write, having had no response to my earlier
letters. I am not Mexican nor a part of Mexico. I insist
on recognition.*

Finally, in a note written in the shaky and trembling
hand of an old man:

October 1854,
*I write again after these years of your insulting si-
lence. My rights will not die with me, if that is your hope.
I have today deeded all of my right, title, and interest to
Baja Norte to the new American who has come to settle
here and establish a new country, William Walker. Here-
after you shall deal with him.*

Abbey had known of the "new American," William
Walker. Walker had brought a group of desperados to the
Baja in 1854 and purported to invade the peninsula and
establish a new nation called the Republic of Sonora. He
named himself the president of the new Republic. One
of the reasons for the incursion was to provide a base for
slavery, as the institution was eroding in the United States.

Another was simply the extra-territorial movement of the times, under which Americans thought they had a right to the lands to their south.

After some months of skirmishes with the Mexican authorities, and marching north along most of the peninsula, Walker and his band were chased across the border back to the United States. His new state in the Baja was very short-lived. Abbey knew that Walker continued his colonization efforts in the following years in Central America, until he was executed by a Honduras firing squad in 1860. Apparently, Walker had met this Mr. Van Huessen in Walker's march up the Baja Peninsula in 1854, and Walker had purchased some land from Van Huessen.

While conducting his doctoral research, Abbey had developed a good working relationship with the chief Mexican archivist, Juan Montego. So, after he discovered the unusual documents, he talked to Montego about the conflicting treaty language and the letters from Van Huessen. In his notes he had summarized his conversation with the archivist. As he now reviewed the notes, he remembered the conversation.

"Señor Abbey, what can I say? Naturally, our version of the treaty in our language must be correct. No doubt someone in the United States added some words in English after the translation. Possibly there were political motivations to appease some malcontents. We have over one hundred and fifty years of settled law on this. There is certainly no basis for those words you say appear in some English translation of the treaty."

Abbey nodded to himself as he also recalled what else Montego had said: "As for Señor Van Huessen, I am not familiar with these letters, although his was certainly an important family in the history of the Baja. Indeed, I believe his descendants continue to live in the Baja today, in the same area of Bahia de los Angeles on the east coast of Baja Norte, which is stated in the letters. We also know of the Mr. Walker mentioned in that last letter. An unfortunate occurrence in our history. Too often, people from your country have tried to subjugate us. But that is all behind us now. That is all I can add. I wish you well in your education and in this thesis you are writing."

Abbey had then dropped the issue because he was under pressure to complete his paper in time for the upcoming doctoral dissertation defenses. His thesis focused on the border conflicts between Mexico and the burgeoning America in the mid-nineteenth century and how they were eventually resolved. He did refer to his discovery in a footnote in his thesis, stating that no further information had been uncovered. He put in a cryptic heading to the footnote: *A Missing Deed?* But the footnote and thesis disclosed very few of the facts he had discovered. Most of the information was only in his working papers, which were stored in the university library private records section. Someone Googling *Baja* would find reference to the footnote and Abbey's thesis, but very little more about the missing footnote 7 was in the public record. Abbey had intended to go back to the subject at a later time. He had thought it would be a good subject for a future research paper. Since he didn't want to alert others to the matter until he had a chance to pursue it, he had disclosed very little. But he had never gotten around to revisiting the subject. *Another detail of academia that I let drop*, he thought to himself.

Now, however, he had been hired to further review those issues.

He decided to start by trying to find out the identity of Jonathan Van Huessen of the 1850s. Online research turned up nothing beyond a line of fancy men's shirts. The records of the early pioneers trekking west contained no such name, and he couldn't find the name in any of the indexes to available history books. After two days of fruitless efforts, he finally went back online and entered *Van Huessen* into the white pages, narrowing the search to Mexico. There were over a dozen possibilities, some in the Baja, but only one in the area of Bahia de los Angeles. He placed a call to the number.

A man answered, "Si?"

"Good morning," Abbey replied in Spanish. "I am looking for a Señor Van Huessen. Is he there?"

The man's voice responded gruffly, "What do you want?"

"Just to talk to him briefly."

"Why?"

"I'm conducting some research on the Baja and its original settlers."

"He's not around."

"Can you help me reach him?"

"No," was the curt reply as the phone was hung up.

It seemed he had found at least a trace of Mr. Van Huessen, but not a particularly cooperative one. He would have to go to the Baja and meet this man and maybe others. At the same time, he knew that he was going to have to get more information about the infamous William Walker and his descendents. That was a perfect assignment for one of his graduate students, an approach that President Overton had agreed to. He contacted his student John Modesta and gave him the assignment.

"Develop information on William Walker and his incursion into the Baja," Abbey explained. "See if any of Walker's living descendants exist today. If so, they might be able to add some type of family historical perspective. There's a lot written about Walker. Focus only on his invasion of the Baja. If you come up with names of living heirs, just hold them. I'll contact them myself."

"Sure, Professor. What's the project?"

Abbey had thought of an answer to that question.

"I'm planning an article comparing Americans invading Mexico in the nineteenth century to the Mexicans coming here illegally in the twentieth. Obviously very different, but an interesting juxtaposition. The opinions of Walker's descendants might be something I can use in the piece. So do your best to come up with some names for me. Probably start with the Mormon Genealogical Library in Salt Lake City. I've used it before. You can do a lot online. If necessary, I'll go to the library. As I said, though, I want to make the contact with these people. Just try to get the names."

• • •

By Friday, he was ready to go. After making some inquiries, Abbey found that the only operating airport in the Baja close to Bahia de los Angeles was in the village of San Felipe. That was itself a long drive from his destination. So, instead of flying, Abbey decided to drive from Albuquerque. That would give him the best flexibility if he had to travel to a number of locations. He drove a black, five-year-old Toyota Highlander. The car had 95,000 miles on it and looked a bit beat up, but it ran fine. He had made many trips across the Southwest in the car.

Then he remembered that his passport had expired. It had been a few years since his travels had taken him out of the United States, other than to Mexico. New laws passed after September 11, 2001, would probably make a passport necessary to enter and return from Mexico. He asked his assistant Marge if she could see about a quick renewal so he could leave within a couple of days. Time was important. In the meantime, he continued to read the available resources about the history of the Baja.

His efforts refreshed his recollection that, during the 1700s and 1800s, the Baja was colonized first by the Franciscans and then the Dominicans from Spain. The monks started in the south and moved north along the coast, setting up missions which eventually stretched all the way to San Francisco. They took control of certain lands and made land grants to natives who converted to Christianity. Then Mexico gained its independence from Spain in 1822, and Mexico made more land grants. During the next thirty years, there was confusion surrounding land titles in California and the Baja as the western-expanding America began to make its own claims in the area. Abbey was surprised to learn that even John Sutter of Sutter's Mill in Sacramento, where gold was first discovered in the California gold rush, originally based his ownership of the mill on a fifty-thousand-acre grant from Mexico. After the Treaty of Hidalgo in 1848, Sutter had simply changed the flag over his flower mill from Mexican to American. Most of the conflicting claims were in the northern half of the Baja above the 27th parallel, an area which eventually became the Mexican state of Baja California Norte.

Abbey would drive to Baja Norte. The passport, however, was creating problems.

Marge reported back: "I faxed a form for an emergency renewal which is supposed to work in twenty-four hours. I stated you had a sudden academic assignment in Mexico. But the response said no renewal is possible without an interview."

"An interview? That's crazy. Let me call. Let's see the fax response. Yeah, there's a phone number there."

He called the passport office and got through to an indifferent operator, who simply said that his name was on a hold list which prevented issuance without a face-to-face meeting. A routine matter, said the operator, but one to which no exceptions were made. If he was on some sort of hold list, he might have trouble at the border, he thought. Los Angeles was not that much out of the way, so he decided to drive via L.A. He made the appointment with the passport office for Monday.

• • •

Abbey's passport application had bumped into the electronic barrier just put in place by Madeline Cartwright. His appointment at the passport office triggered a computer alert to her. When she received it, she saw that the alert also went to the National Counterterrorism Center (NCTC), which had been set up after September 11, 2001, as a cross-agency "czar" to oversee all intelligence efforts in the United States. Since she had initiated the first report, she now filled out and sent another to the Los Angeles passport office. She put a *code 03* into the report, knowing that it signaled suspected money laundering. The funds she had noted a few days before had now electronically branded Professor Abbey a trafficker in funds. Cartright smiled to herself as she did the paperwork. She remembered her phone call with the university president and how he had not been very forthcoming. She thought to herself, *Maybe something after all. Why does this Abbey suddenly want to travel, and in such a hurry? What's going on out there?*

CHAPTER 9

MAY 10–11

LOS ANGELES

Abbey knew that Albuquerque to Los Angeles was a long, one-day drive west starting on Route 40. He made his appointment at the passport office for late Monday morning so he could leave a day early and camp overnight at Joshua Tree National Park. The park was slightly south of Route 40, not far from Palm Springs. He knew it wouldn't be much of a detour. There was a rock outcropping in Joshua Tree which he had recently read about in his favorite climbing blog from an outdoor shop in Mohab. According to the blog, fifty feet off the ground was a ledge and shallow cave which held some old Indian wall drawings. He hoped to climb to the ledge and photograph the art. He would then drive to L.A. early the next morning for his meeting. He gave Marge a loose outline of his schedule and promised to check in from time to time from Mexico.

"I'm not sure about my schedule other than I'll end up in Bahia de los Angeles within a few days. If attorney Duprey calls, let him know where I am and that I'll contact him as soon as I come up with any useful information." He packed street clothes and hiking gear and loaded the Toyota with a small tent, ground tarp, and light sleeping bag. For food, he took dehydrated meals, some fruit, and a six-gallon container of water. Remembering that Joshua Tree often prohibited campfires, he also picked up a salami, a small block of cheddar cheese, and a loaf of bread for a cold meal that night. He left Sunday morning.

• • •

Abbey didn't know that his departure was noted by the one-armed man who had been at Mesa Verde. A call was placed to Denver. John Duprey took the call in his office.

"Sir, this is Abdul Kazam. I'm associated with the group who hired you for the Baja research."

"Yes, how can I help you, Mr. Kazam?" answered Duprey.

"We've read your report about Professor Abbey with interest, Mr. Duprey. We had a few questions for the professor, so I just tried to call him. I've been told by his assistant that he's away on a trip. I wondered whether this trip is on our project. Has he started the work yet?"

"I'm sure he's started, Mr. Kazam. I'm not sure about the trip, but I can find out. But I was told I'd be the only contact with the professor. Why are you calling him?" he asked in an irritated tone.

"You're probably right," Kazam answered quickly. "Maybe you could let me know about the trip."

"Sure, I can do that," Duprey answered with a quizzical tone. "But why were you trying to reach him?"

"Oh . . . uh . . . to get information on his car," the Iranian stammered. "To make sure he's covered by our insurance."

"I'll find about his car, too. Give me a number, and I'll get back to you." Duprey took the number and hung up, thinking the phone call had been a bit strange. He then called Marge.

"Hello, this is Charles Duprey from Denver. I met with Professor Abbey a couple of weeks ago about a research project. Is he available?"

"Yes, Mr. Duprey, this is Marge, his assistant. I think we met while you were here."

"Yes, sure, I remember."

"The professor actually just left on a trip involving your project. He's driving to L.A. first, and then south to Mexico. He said he would be checking in with you."

"Yes, I knew he'd be going to Mexico. I guess I'm a little surprised he's not flying."

"Well, he said his eventual destination is Bahia de los Angeles, on Baja's east coast, and that airport connections are pretty bad down there."

"Bahia de los Angeles, did you say?"

"Yes."

"What's he driving?"

"His black SUV. A Toyota."

"Okay, that's great," responded Duprey. "Please call me when you hear from him, or ask him to call me himself."

"Certainly. I'll take care of it, Mr. Duprey."

• • •

Later that day, Duprey called Kazam back.

"Just wanted to let you know, Mr. Kazam, you're right. Professor Abbey is away on our project. He's driving to Mexico for his research, to a place called Bahia de los Angeles."

"Did you say Bahia de los Angeles?" Kazam answered slowly.

"Yes, that's the place," said the lawyer.

"That's good, very good indeed, that he's started," Kazam commented, again speaking slowly, as if he were deep in thought. After a slight pause, Kazam added, "Just be ready to help him down there, if necessary."

"Help him? What do you mean?" rejoined Duprey.

"Maybe his questions will not be welcome, Mr. Duprey. Some secrets are not easily uncovered. Just be ready to help the professor if he has trouble in this Bahia de los Angeles. That's all I mean. Just be ready."

"Sure," answered the lawyer. "I'll make some arrangements. Oh, by the way, to answer your question, he's driving a black Toyota."

After hanging up, he sat thinking a few moments. Then he picked up the phone and placed another call to a contact in Mexico.

• • •

Abbey loved the small size and unblemished landscape of Joshua Tree National Park. It was a desert, named for its large concentration of the cactus-like trees which appeared to be beckoning a traveler forward, as the prophet Joshua had done in biblical times. Abbey knew the history of the area. The Mormon pioneers crossing the desert in the 1800s had named the trees. Amazing rock outcroppings also dotted the landscape, which were often covered with rock climbers inching upwards. Otherwise, it was sand and scrub vegetation of ocotillos and cholla cactus. Some saw it only as an arid desert. Abbey viewed it as a beautiful sea of sand, with rocky peaks and fork-shaped masts rising above a calm, brown surface.

The blog from Mohab had given precise directions to the rock outcropping known as the Canyons. From the eastern entrance to the park, he was to drive 3.4 miles, where he would find a trailhead and a dirt footpath heading north. Then he would park his car and hike two miles on the path until he saw the unique rock outcropping on the west side of the path. He was to look for six rocky peaks separated in places by narrow gaps no wider than twelve inches, about one hundred yards wide and fifty yards high.

As he entered Joshua Tree, he purchased a permit for an overnight stay to leave in his windshield. *Only fifteen dollars. Better than a hundred-dollar motel room.* Driving through the park, he was awed, as he had been before, by the scattered rock outcroppings growing skyward from the sand. He reached the trailhead and took his overnight pack and climbing gear from the back seat. While locking the car, Abbey saw his face reflected in the side window and realized he still had his glasses on. He took them off and left them inside. He often didn't wear them.

After a short hike, he reached the designated location and looked up the narrow slit between the rocks at the northwest corner where the directions said the cave was located. He couldn't see any ledge or cave entrance, but this was the site described. He pulled on his climbing shoes and organized his line and pitons. Fifty feet wasn't that far. *Should take less than an hour.* He hung his camera from his belt in a padded bag.

The climb started out quite easy. He found a number of footholds and handholds, and even some old pitons which previous climbers had not withdrawn from crevices. After ten minutes, he was thirty feet off the ground, beginning to break a sweat, but still not breathing hard. Things then began to get a bit more difficult. An overhang prevented him from going up, so he started edging to his right into the narrow gap between the rocks. It was only about twelve inches wide and appeared to get narrower inside. He couldn't look down or see his feet, so he felt with his toes for depressions in the rock. With his left foot securely planted, and holding on above with his fingertips, he gingerly moved his right foot sideways and up and down to find a perch. After he had moved sideways into the narrow crevice for about ten feet, the overhead projection merged into the cliff and disappeared. He could climb again, although only by lifting and scraping his knees sideways. *Only another ten feet*, he thought, as sweat dripped into his eyes.

Sure enough, after a few more minutes, he was on top of the overhanging ledge which had earlier blocked his ascent. The ledge was two feet deep and extended to his left around to the face of the rocks. Once on the ledge, he saw a shallow cave, the perfect location to hide from one's enemies or scout for an attack.

The sun was low in the west, but he could see well enough to notice traces of old campfires. Lying on his stomach, he stuck his head into the shallow, cave-like depression. Sure enough, he spotted simple stick drawings of animals and what looked like hunters. They were scratched into the rock walls, with some of the indentations still colored brownish-red with ancient dried blood. He quickly set up his camera on his miniature tripod and shot a full roll of pictures. Then he sat on the ledge, drank some water, and gazed over the desert landscape with its Joshua trees and rocky projections. It was beautiful. But it was dusk. Not having any fast film, he switched his lens to a digital body and took some scenic shots. Then he quickly descended by rappelling down from the narrow ledge. He ate his simple cold dinner and spent the night at the base of the Canyons with a Joshua tree in the distance, beckoning him westward.

In the morning, he hiked back to his car and drove west on Route 10.

• • •

Abbey approached L.A. in mid-morning. He disliked the tall buildings and street canyons of big cities. That was one of the reasons he had settled in Albuquerque, which was a large, sprawling metropolis, but without the towering steel and glass towers of many cities. After having slept under the open skies the night before, Abbey felt unsettled as he approached the city. Sometimes reentering civilization made him nervous, with all the sounds and sights and movements of people running about their tasks, like ants moving frantically to gather, frolic, or eat. He had only spent one night in the desert, so the re-entry feeling was brief, with just a mild feeling of disquiet.

Reaching the federal office tower in downtown Los Angeles by 11:00, he parked under the building, and took the elevator up to the fifth floor. The doorway was labeled United States Immigration Service. He looked around as he entered the room. Inside was a reception area with eight straight rows of chairs: hard plastic seats and backs on shiny metal legs, with no arm rests. Not a welcoming or comfortable room; just a holding area. There were a dozen people seated in the chairs, mostly Hispanic, Abbey observed. He checked in at the desk, where the receptionist stamped his parking ticket and asked for his license plate number. That seemed strange to him. *Why does she want my plate number?*

A Mrs. Juarez soon came out to meet him and took him to a small office. He wondered why he was reached so quickly, while all the others sat waiting. Her office had a desk with computer screen on it and a chair facing it. She gestured for him to sit while she sat behind the desk. Abbey was annoyed that such a big deal was being made of his passport renewal.

"What in the world's going on?" he asked. "I simply want to renew my passport. I've never heard of such complications over a passport."

"Professor Abbey, I apologize for the inconvenience. Our computers tagged your name for reasons even I don't understand. There's a computer-generated profile for persons who could be terrorists. Emergency renewal requests often trigger the profile. When it is triggered, we have to have a face-to-face meeting. In part, it's to make sure you're a real person – you're who you claim to be. Regular renewals take four to six weeks, and many of these things are looked into routinely during that period. Sometimes a request for speedy action suggests that something is not as it seems. Obviously you are who you claim to be, and you're a responsible citizen. All I need is for you to fill out this form concerning your planned trip. I'll be able to have your passport by this afternoon." She handed him a four-page form which looked like a tax return.

Juarez turned briefly to her computer, which had dinged an incoming message. She looked at the screen, nodded to herself, and turned back to Abbey.

"No problem at all, Professor. You can fill out the form outside and leave it with the receptionist. Come back after three o'clock for your passport. But remember, we close at four o'clock."

As he walked out of the office, he saw her turn back to the computer and start typing.

• • •

In Washington, Madeline Cartright read the message as it came in from Mrs. Juarez:

> *Our mobile currency sniffer machine detected no unusual amount of currency in his car. He does not appear to be taking American currency into Mexico. I will, however, code his passport 03 as a suspected money launderer.*

• • •

Abbey found the form to be a pain in the neck, but he filled it out. It called for his travel schedule and itinerary and names of contacts at his destination. He put in the rough schedule and itinerary in the Baja, but he didn't really know who his contacts might be. Not wanting to involve Marge too much, he named President Overton, since Overton knew generally what he was doing. After leaving the form with the receptionist, he went out for lunch. He returned at three o'clock to pick up the passport. He spent the night with some old friends in Venice Beach, and in the morning, he headed south.

Abbey crossed the border in Tijuana without difficulty. The Mexican border agent quickly scanned his passport and wrote down the car and plate number. He continued south along the Baja coast on Mexican Route 1 for about two hundred miles, until he reached the town of Rosario. This stretch of coast was the developed area of the peninsula, with many small villages and a few American tourist destinations. The area held little interest to him.

At Rosario, the highway turned east and inland. Before making the turn and heading inland, he decided to spend the night in a small motel on the Pacific coast which had beautiful views of the sea breaking on the rocky shore below. He had spent a night there six years before when he was in the Baja for his thesis. It was called the "Pacifica." He found a small café within walking distance, where he ate quesadillas and chicken enchiladas smothered with a wonderful mole sauce. His waiter was friendly.

"And what brings you to Rosario, señor?"

"Just stopping on the way to the east coast. I'm going to do some fishing. I'll head on in the morning." No sense getting into a complicated discussion with the waiter.

"You're smart to stop for the night, señor. We still have some banditos along the highway at night. But seldom do they bother anyone in the daylight. Good luck with your fishing. Make sure you buy petrol in the morning, since you will not find any inland. "

In the morning, Abbey did fill his gas tank, and he then drove east and down the center of the peninsula for about a hundred miles, until Mexican Route 12 branched off toward the gulf coast. Route 12 was two-laned, unpaved, and pot-holed. He was barely able to drive forty miles an hour, but he was approaching the gulf coast by evening. There had been almost no signs of people or development between Rosario and the east gulf coast, but he enjoyed the drive. This was his type of country, he thought. The dry desert with cactus and dwarf pines leading up to the more vegetated foothills and, eventually, the mountainous spine running north and south. The sky was deep blue, with very few clouds. Professor Abbey was in his element. He was content and happy.

CHAPTER 10

MAY 10

IRAN

The Ayatollah and his cousin General Mussahrah had received reports about Professor Abbey and were following developments with great interest.

"This Bahia de los Angeles is where we sent Kazam, isn't it?" the Ayatollah asked his cousin.

"Yes, it's the same place," replied Mussahrah. "The same town where he killed that stupid fisherman. I'm concerned about this professor going back to the same place, but I think we have to let him proceed."

"Maybe a message of warning to the lawyer," the Ayatollah thought out loud. "Let him know that there could be trouble in Mexico. Tell him to be ready to help the professor, if necessary."

"It's been done," replied the general. "Kazam says he has given the warning. But we have to keep Kazam in the background. He has his strengths, and I want to save him for what he's good at." He pictured Abdul Kazam in his mind as he spoke.

Kazam's specialty was torture. He had lost his left arm at the elbow to a piece of jagged shrapnel in the war with Iraq. *That's probably why he's so good at hurting others,* thought the general. Even without his left forearm and hand, he was fast-footed and dexterous, a bear of a man. Broad, strong shoulders and lightning-fast reflexes compensated for the missing arm. Milky brown eyes stared out from a swarthy, mustached face. The general had befriended Kazam after the wartime injury and seen that he was nursed back to health. He knew the man would do anything for him. Earlier in the year, General Mussahrah had sent Kazam to the Baja to find Van Huessen after the name had surfaced from Abbey's thesis.

Kazam had provided a full report about his trip. He had flown through Paris to Los Angeles on papers identifying him as a Middle Eastern businessman. In Los Angeles, he had purchased the medical supplies he needed and a pistol, with little difficulty. He had then driven to the Baja Peninsula and the area of Bahia de los Angeles.

He reported that he had found an old man named Van Huessen in a ranch in the foothills. The two had argued, and he had been ordered off the property. Rather than further accost the man, Kazam went to talk to a niece named Maria who had been mentioned by Van Huessen. After observing her and her husband, he had decided to start with the husband.

Kazam's report had detailed, almost gleefully and boastfully, the events which followed. Mussahrah remembered the words as Kazam reported almost verbatim what had happened on the fishing boat he had chartered. Once they were well offshore, he had confronted the Mexican.

"Captain Plarez, it is really information, rather than fish, that I am after."

"What do you mean?" the captain had queried, with fishing line in his mouth as he tied the leaders.

"I mean, I am not who I said I was. I have no interest in fishing. Instead, I want information . . . information about your family, and your uncle in particular."

From the stern of the boat, Captain Plarez had looked steadily at the dark Iranian, still holding the fishing line in his teeth and hands. He then dropped the line from his right hand and quickly reached for the knife on his belt.

"I kicked him in the balls and told him we would save the knife till later," Kazam had reported.

But no useful information had been obtained, and the fisherman had died during the interrogation. Kazam threw the body overboard and left the boat to drift at sea. Once he learned what had happened, Mussahrah had ordered the agent to suspend activities and return immediately to the United States. Mussahrah had been explicit in telling Kazam to stay away from the niece.

The Iranians couldn't care less about the death of an unimportant fisherman, but their plans called for absolute secrecy. They could not risk another bungle. That was why they had decided to hire Professor Abbey. First, they had sent Kazam to Albuquerque to check out the professor, giving him clear instructions:

"Find out if anything in his background makes him unsuitable to be our front man. Are there any skeletons in his closet? Don't let him know what you're doing. Utmost secrecy is necessary. And we don't have much time."

Mussahrah smiled as he remembered the report on Abbey based upon the Mesa Verde encounter. *A brilliant idea,* he thought. After spending the night going through Abbey's electronic files, Kazam had reported back that Abbey was uninteresting. "Plain vanilla," were his words. "No skeletons." So they had given Duprey the green light to hire Abbey. With Abbey, they added legitimacy to their search. They thought that no one would question a college professor, and he had no possible foreign connections.

After all, it was his doctoral thesis that had given them the lead about a missing deed in the first place. Thinking now, Mussahrah realized that they should probably have used this professor in the first place, rather than sending Kazam. The payment to the university wasn't large in the overall scheme of things.

CHAPTER 11

MAY 12–13

BAHIA DE LOS ANGELES

Abbey had read about the area before he left Albuquerque. Bahia de los Angeles was a small village nestled next to a bay of the same name. It was a simple fishing village, with easy access across its bay to the gulf which separated the Baja Peninsula from mainland Mexico. Some maps he looked at labeled it the Gulf of California, and some the Sea of Cortez. The village was three hundred miles south of the American border, and its bay was guarded by a ring of mountainous islands, the largest being Isle Angel de la Guardia – the "Guardian Angel." He learned that, in the 1940s, the area had been a popular fishing destination for actors like John Wayne and his friends from Los Angeles, California. John Steinbeck was supposed to have written some of his work in Bahia de los Angeles. Although a small airstrip sat on a plateau above the town, the literature explained that there were no scheduled flights and no ground support whatsoever. It was simply a dirt runway. It looked as if time had passed the area by.

This was where Mr. Van Huessen's telephone number had been listed, so this was where Abbey came to find the uncooperative man. It was close to dark when he approached the coast and the road started to descend from the foothills to the water. He imagined there would be very few guest facilities in the village, so he pulled over to camp.

His dinner was freeze-dried beef stew heated over a small campfire. *No rules against fires here*, he thought. Later, sitting before the red coals after dinner, he thought about how lucky he was to have had this assignment drop into his lap. But he was a little nervous about Van Huessen. The man had been rude and uncooperative on the phone. *How am I going to get him to help?* Abbey knew he didn't do well with conflict. *What will I find in the village?* he wondered as he fell asleep.

In the morning, he rose and had a snack before heading down the dirt road to the coast. He saw a number of small buildings scattered next to the water. As he drove toward the village, the bay and surrounding islands spread before him. He could understand why it was called the Bay of Angels, the angels being the islands grouped around the entrance to the bay. The biggest angel of all was the Isle Angel de la Guardia – the Guardian Angel – which guarded the southern entrance to the bay with two towering peaks. The literature said that the island was usually called Guardian Island. At both sunrise and sunset, its two mountains looked like the wings of an angel taking flight as the mountain shadows moved across the water. In the morning, they moved to the west side of the island, and then flew away to the east at sunset. Abbey viewed that idyllic morning scene as he drove down from the hills.

The village appeared to be a typical slow-paced rural Mexican community. A small adobe structure with a veranda looked like a general store, and the dirt streets were lined with ramshackle structures, with few people in sight. The ever-present dogs lay in the sun. One building looked a bit more substantial than the others. The sign over its door read *Comisaria*. Abbey decided that would be a good place to start. He parked in front, got out of his car, and took a deep breath. *Here goes*, he thought.

Walking through the front door, he paused for a moment to let his eyes adjust to the darkness. A police officer was leaning back in his chair behind a big wooden desk. Smoke filled the air from a cigarette in his hand.

"Buenos dias, señor," Abbey said.

"And what can I do for you, sir?" the officer responded in a clear, gruff voice.

Abbey switched to English. "Hopefully you can help," he answered. "I am a professor from the United States trying to write a paper about some of the history of the Baja Peninsula. Part of my work involves the old families of the Baja." He had decided on this approach the night before. It wasn't far from the truth. "I've been trying to find a Mr. Van Huessen who I think lives in this area."

The Mexican sat upright quickly and snubbed out his cigarette in the metal ashtray on his desk. He was suddenly alert and stared intensely at Abbey through the smoke and dim light. "Mr. Van Huessen, you say?"

"Yes. Can you help me find him?" Abbey was beginning to feel nervous. He seemed to have touched a sore spot.

"Maybe . . . maybe," the officer responded. "But what is it you want of him? Maybe I should see your papers to see if you are who you claim. Your passport, please."

"Sure," said Abbey, digging out the booklet from his pocket and handing it to the man. He detected hostility from the officer and felt intimidated.

"Just issued the day before yesterday," the officer observed. "Isn't that strange. I hear that many false passports are now being produced."

Abbey bit his tongue and didn't say that those false passports were usually going from Mexico to the United States, rather than the reverse. This policeman didn't seem to be in a mood for quips.

"You're looking for Mr. Van Huessen, are you," muttered the officer as he continued to look down at the booklet. He lifted his eyes to Abbey with pursed lips, thinking for a moment. "Well, Señor Abbey, I will have to report these papers and your request to my superiors before I can do anything. I will keep your passport while you are in our little town."

"I really don't want to leave my passport," said Abbey. "What is the problem?"

"You have no choice, señor. You are in Mexico. Hopefully there is no problem. Come back in the morning, and I might have an answer for you. In the meantime, without a passport, you may not lawfully travel outside this town."

Abbey decided that an argument would only worsen the situation. He had to stay for a while, anyway. He had clearly started at the wrong place. He would try the general store and see if someone else might be more helpful. "I'm sorry you feel the need to treat me this way, since this is a simple visit and a simple request for some assistance." He turned and headed for the door. "As you require, I will return in the morning."

• • •

The officer was Corporal Juan Martinez, a junior policeman in a very small outpost. What he didn't say to Abbey, but what he was thinking, was that Abbey was the second person in a month to arrive looking for Van Huessen. Martinez had only learned of the first visitor after he had come and gone, and he knew very little of what had happened during the first visit. Mr. Van Huessen was a local recluse, not prone to dealing with the police. About a month ago, however, Van Huessen had come into the station and reported to Corporal Martinez that a foreigner had come to his ranch. Van Huessen said the visitor had asked a number of questions about Van Huessen's background and ancestors. When Van Huessen had tried to send the stranger away, they had argued.

Van Huessen had reported those events, but not much more, when he came to the station to complain that he had been bothered. He said that the stranger was dark-complexioned and possibly a government official. "And he only had one arm. No question about that. Only his right arm." Martinez had made some inquiries and determined that no one from the Mexican government had made the visit.

Then, two days after Van Huessen's complaint, Martinez had found the body of the fisherman Jaime Plarez on the beach. Plarez was married to Van Huessen's niece. His fishing boat was later recovered drifting in the gulf. After having observed the condition of the man's fingers, Martinez had inspected the body carefully. Plarez could have been the victim of a fishing accident, but the policeman thought the condition of the body suggested otherwise. The fingers were broken and jutting at different angels, and some of the fingernails were missing. What looked like cigarette burns covered the face. Martinez made the appropriate reports, but a poor village and an unimportant fisherman didn't receive much attention from the authorities. The official response was that fingers were often broken by machinery or nets in fishing accidents, and that the facial disfiguration could have been caused by feeding fish or parasites. The body was buried with no autopsy or further investigation.

All of this was going through Martinez's mind while this gringo college professor was talking about looking for Mr. Van Huessen. The officer could not ignore the suspicious coincidence that a second visitor was now looking for the old man. He was going to have to do something.

· · ·

Abbey drove the short distance to the general store, got out of his car, and walked in to try again.

"Buenas dias, señora," he addressed the old, Mexican lady behind the counter. She was very short, barely taller than the top of the counter.

"Buenas dias, señor."

"I'm looking for Señor Van Huessen," Abbey continued in Spanish. "I think he lives nearby. Can you help me with directions?"

"Yes, I know him. He shops here. He lives on his ranch in the mountains." She pointed up the road on which he had driven into town. "About four kilometers up is a small road to the left. That goes to his ranch."

She pointed up the road again with her left hand and circled her ear rapidly with her right finger, switching to broken English. "Crazy, señor. A bit, how you say, crazy. Be careful, señor."

"Muchas gracias, señora," Abbey said as he nodded his thanks and left the store, feeling even more worried than before. As he drove north out of town, he saw a small, hand-lettered sign with an arrow pointing in the other direction, labeled *Van Huessen Turtle Museum.* He decided he had to try the ranch first. *But what did she mean, be careful?*

He headed into the mountains to find Mr. Van Huessen.

CHAPTER 12

MAY 13

BAHIA DE LOS ANGELES

Abbey knew he had picked the correct dirt road when he saw the signs:

PRIVATE PROPERTY KEEP OUT!
YOU WILL BE SHOT IF YOU GO FURTHER!
I MEAN IT!

The signs were crudely hand-lettered in both Spanish and English. He didn't know what to do. He assumed the signs were more bark than bite, but he wasn't sure he wanted to test his assumption. He stopped his car and got out to survey the area. Ahead of him was a long, winding dirt road rising to a small canyon between two rocky cliffs. He decided that it would be best to announce himself.

"Hello, Mr. Van Huessen?" he yelled. "Are you there? Mr. Van Huessen, I'd like to talk to you!" With no response, he leaned in the window of the car and blew his horn, followed by the same shouts. Still, no one responded. He got back into his car and drove slowly toward the opening in the rocks. He continued to shout his greeting as he leaned out the window. After about two hundred yards, he saw more signs with the same messages.

Suddenly, two loud blasts rang through the air.

"Oh my God," cried Abbey as he slammed on his brakes. He looked towards the opening and saw a man holding a shotgun pointing in the air. He stopped and started to slowly open his door to try to get out and speak. Two more blasts.

The solitary figure yelled, "Can't you read? This is private property. My private property. And I don't want you or anyone else here." Abbey put the car in reverse and started to slowly back up. The figure stood still and watched until he was back to the first set of signs. Then Abbey got out of the car and tried to yell his message of accommodation. The response was another blast. He decided he would have to go back to the village and regroup. *Maybe the museum?*

His armpits were drenched with sweat as he drove back down the mountain. His hands trembled on the steering wheel. First the uncomfortable confrontation with Constable Martinez, and now someone was shooting at him. This was not what he had expected. *Why is everyone so upset?*

He headed to the general store, where he had been pleasantly received in the morning. The reception now was different. The lady would barely speak to him. She kept saying, "No comprende. No comprende," with hands raised, even when he spoke in Spanish. She seemed scared of something. Evidently Officer Martinez had spoken to her. *Why all this hostility?*

He drove to the sign for the turtle museum and headed south, as its arrow directed. He would give it a try.

He soon found himself on another dirt road. After about a half mile, he saw a small, nondescript wooden structure near the beach with a faded sign over the front door announcing that it was the Turtle Museum de Bahia de los Angeles. A majestic title for the nondescript building. It was only about ten feet tall. The wide wooden planks were brown and weathered, with a low-pitched roof also made of wood. A hundred yards of beach and grass separated the building from the bay. He parked and walked slowly to the front door, looking carefully to his left and right. He knocked loudly on the door. He certainly wasn't going to enter unannounced.

"Hello . . . Are you open?"

No answer, so he repeated himself. At least there were no warning or trespass signs here.

Then a young woman walked around the corner of the building to his right. She was dark-complexioned, with long brown hair, but she didn't appear to be a native Mexican. Dressed casually in jeans and a short-sleeved top, she was wiping her hands on a large towel. She was an attractive woman.

"Si, señor, may I be of assistance?"

At least he wasn't being accosted or challenged. A bit flustered, Abbey broke into Spanish, thinking that would create a better impression. "Hopefully you can help me. I'm a college professor from New Mexico doing some research about the history of the Baja. I drove down yesterday, and I'm trying to find members of the Van Huessen family, which I understand was one of the first American families to settle in the Baja. Unfortunately, I'm not having much luck."

A faint smile crossed her lips as she answered, "Señor, I speak English, and I'm a Van Huessen. Maybe you're in luck." She pushed her long, dark hair out of her face, while looking at him with sparkling brown eyes. "My name is Maria Plarez. I run this turtle museum, which is really more of a hatchery, since we have very few visitors."

Abbey couldn't help but notice the quiet confidence and the lilting tone of her voice. He found it hard to take his eyes away from her.

"As far as the Van Huessens go," she continued, "I'm the niece of John Van Huessen, who lives on his old family ranch in the mountains." She pointed north, where Abbey had come from.

"Well, I think I met him this morning," Abbey said with hesitation, "and he was carrying a shotgun. And shooting. At me," pointing his hands at his chest. "Could that have been your uncle?"

She chuckled, showing a pleasant smile full of straight, white teeth. "Oh, yes, that's him. He doesn't like outsiders. Pretty much likes to be left alone in his mountains. He probably wasn't really shooting at you, just trying to scare you off. He's been very good to me over the years. But I don't think you'll get any cooperation from him. If you want to learn about turtles, however, you've come to the right place."

Since she was at least a Van Huessen, and he had nothing much better to do, he took her up on the offer to learn a bit about the local turtles. She took him to the tanks in the rear of the building where she had been working with young, injured turtles and gave him a lively and informative explanation of the species.

"I have mostly green turtles and leatherbacks," she explained, holding two tiny turtles in her palms to show him the differences between them. "Push the shells with your fingers. The softer, rubbery one is the leatherback. Otherwise, they look pretty much alike."

Abbey stroked and pushed on the shells and felt the difference. Maria explained that, as adults, the leatherback would grow much larger than the green and weigh as much as two thousand pounds, making it the largest reptile in the world. She seemed eager to have the opportunity to share her knowledge with someone.

After a few moments, they walked back inside the small museum building. It was quite simple, with displays and photographs of the local habitat. There were also photographs and information about the large island which loomed across the bay. She explained that the Guardian Angel Island was a national park and preserve. It remained in its natural state and was totally undeveloped. She used the island for many of her turtle experiments and observations. Both the greens and the leatherbacks nested on its beaches.

As Abbey explained his background and studies in archeology and indigenous societies, they found they had a number of common interests. Both loved the outdoors and had spent much of their time in the deserts and mountains of the same terrain – even if in different countries.

"As I grew up in the Baja and hiked the mountains," Maria said, "I found many signs that ancient people lived here long ago."

"Yes," Abbey responded. "I think they were mainly Indians and natives from what is now the American Southwest moving southward along the peninsula. The Mayas, Incas, and Aztecs appear to have stayed on the Mexican mainland and never crossed the gulf to the Baja. At least, no one has reported signs of them being here."

After about an hour, he steered the conversation back to his search for Mr. Van Huessen and members of the Van Huessen family.

"I'm here looking for signs of more recent people. Your family, actually. I've read that the Van Huessens were important settlers in this area back in the early 1800s and owned a lot of land in Baja Norte. I'm trying to find out what happened to them and their land. It's for a paper I'm writing on the history of the peninsula."

She nodded thoughtfully. "I've heard such stories about my ancestors. My uncle has told me that he is the last Van Huessen. There might be other distant family members on the peninsula, but he says his father passed on only to him the information about their history. As he says, 'The story dies with me.' But I don't know what he means." She said she had lived with her uncle for a number of years before she married. Even in those early years, he had been eccentric, but not to the extent of his current rage toward outsiders.

"He now seems to hate almost everyone. Even at my husband's funeral a month ago, he sat in a corner in the church and afterwards refused to talk to anyone but me."

"Oh, I'm so sorry," Abbey said with embarrassment. "I didn't know about your loss. I should probably leave."

"Well, you're here now." She shrugged. "What exactly is it you want from the Van Huessens?"

"What I'm really looking for," he finally said after an awkward silence, "are some of the old papers or deeds about the Van Huessen land ownership. I need some documents to rely on if I write something about the family history. And I would really like to hear your uncle's story."

"I know my uncle has some papers," she said brightly. "Over the years he described the old leather trunk in the library as his file box. He said the family jewels were stored in the trunk. I remember once, when I was young, I peeked in the trunk, looking for jewels. All I found were a bunch of old dusty papers." She laughed. "No jewels. I'd be glad to talk to my uncle for you. No promises. He might be willing to shed some light on the Van Huessen name, but as I said before, it's a long shot."

"That'd be great," exclaimed Abbey. *Maybe some progress.*

A couple of hours had gone by, and Abbey thought it best to return to town and see about lodging for the night. He asked her about available rooms in the village. The sun was starting to approach the mountain peaks to the west, and he knew it would be dark within an hour. He had that important meeting with Corporal Martinez in the morning to get back his passport. He also told her that he might have to leave the next day and was wondering when she might be able to talk to her uncle.

"I'll probably go see him tomorrow. He's asked me to come visit. As I mentioned, I recently lost my husband. At the funeral, Uncle John asked me to come see him. Said he wanted to talk to me about a few things. I've been putting it off. Now you've given me a good reason to go." She was quiet for a moment before continuing. "As for a room, there's really not much available. We have very few visitors."

He knew he should leave. He said some awkward condolences, gave her his card with his university phone numbers on it, and asked her to call him after her meeting with her uncle.

"Even if I'm not there, my assistant Marge would be able to take any information. I really appreciate your willingness to talk to your uncle."

"No problem, Professor. I don't have much else to do. No problem at all."

Outside, before he could get into his car, he heard another vehicle approaching rapidly over the dirt road. An old black police car pulled next to his and skidded to a stop. Corporal Martinez jumped out while the dust was still swirling. He didn't look happy.

"Señor Abbey, you seem intent on ignoring my directions."

"What do you mean?"

"First you leave town and drive into the mountains and try to trespass on the Van Huessen home site. Now I find you apparently abusing his niece, who is in mourning."

"I have abused no one. I'm heading into town and plan on meeting you in the morning as directed to recover my passport. Mrs. Plarez and I have had a very nice conversation. You can ask her."

Martinez looked briefly at the building and then back to Abbey. He thought for a moment and then nodded his head as if in agreement. "We will make sure we meet in the morning. Please follow me back to town. I am placing you in custody for tonight to make sure nothing untoward happens before you leave."

"What are you talking about? You can't do this! I've done nothing wrong. I'm an American citizen lawfully in Mexico. I have every right to go where I want and talk to whom I want. I left Mr. Van Huessen's land when he told me to, and I have certainly not abused his niece. As I said, you can ask her."

The constable pointed at Abbey and spoke angrily, "I will not bother her further. I can do this, and I am going to. As I said before, you are in Mexico, and in this part of Mexico, I set the rules," pointing his figure at his chest. "You are not the first person in recent weeks to visit us looking for the Van Huessens. Another man was here a few weeks ago. I understand he, too, had an encounter with Mr. Van

Huessen. Then, a few days later, Señora Plarez's husband was found dead under what I thought were strange circumstances. I am not about to have history repeat itself. You will come with me and be in my custody tonight. We will see what happens in the morning." He strode to Abbey's car, yanked open the driver's side door, and gestured for the professor to get in. "Follow me," he ordered, and strode to his own vehicle to lead the way.

Abbey had no idea what the corporal was talking about. But, as with the morning encounter with the policeman, he saw little choice but to comply. He got in his car and drove back to town following the corporal's car.

• • •

Maria observed the encounter, but she could not overhear the conversation. She thought it looked as if Martinez was arresting the professor. She knew Martinez was difficult to deal with, particularly with Americans.

She placed a call to Abbey's number on the card and spoke briefly with Marge, telling her that Professor Abbey appeared to be having some difficulties with the local police. Marge thanked her and immediately called Duprey.

"Mr. Duprey, this is Professor Abbey's assistant, Marge."

"Yes, yes. What can I do for you?"

"I'm not sure. I just had a strange telephone call from a lady in the village in Mexico where Professor Abbey is. She said he's having difficulty with the local police. She didn't tell me her name. It was weird."

"Oh, yes. Certainly. I think I know the problem. The professor and I talked recently. There's a difficult local policeman down there who doesn't like Americans. I think I can take care of things with a few phone calls."

"Should I contact anyone else, like the American Embassy?"

"No, no. Definitely don't do that. It would make matters worse. I'll take care of it."

"Will you let me know what's going on?"

"Certainly. I'll call you in the morning. I'm sure everything will be straightened out by then."

"Thanks for helping. I wasn't sure what to do."

"You did the right thing to call. Glad to help. I'll talk to you tomorrow."

• • •

At the police station, Abbey was booked in a fashion and shown to a dilapidated cell which didn't look strong enough to secure anyone. But he wasn't planning to test the security.

"I would like to make a call."

"Señor, this is Mexico, not the United States. There will be no calls this evening. Maybe in the morning."

I'm going to get out of this town in the morning, Abbey thought to himself. *And if I have to return, I'll do something to make sure this jerk doesn't bother me again.* He was fed a simple meal of beans and tortillas. *At least I don't have to find a room,* he thought wryly. After dinner, the corporal announced a visitor.

An old, weathered man walked slowly up to the cell door and peered between the bars at Professor Abbey. He appeared to be in his eighties, wearing faded jeans and a long-sleeved shirt with a leather vest. An old, battered cowboy hat was in his right hand. He grabbed one of the cell bars with his left hand and stared into the cell.

"Is this the man who bothered you this morning, Señor Van Huessen?"

"Yep, it's him. And I recognize that black car outside. That's the car he was driving."

"What about the man who visited you a month ago?" continued Martinez. "Is this the same man?"

"No," the old man replied curtly. "I told you, that man was dark and swarthy, with a mustache. He spoke broken English, like you Mexicans. And this man has both arms. I told you, the other had only one arm."

Abbey realized this was Mr. Van Huessen. *Might as well try to get some information,* he thought to himself.

"Mr. Van Huessen, I am Professor William Abbey, from the University of New Mexico. I didn't mean to offend you this morning. I'm sorry if I did. I'm simply researching the background of the original Baja settlers. I just wanted to talk to you."

"I don't like to talk to strangers, Professor . . . what's your name?"

"Abbey."

"Yes, Professor Abbey. I like to be left to myself."

Corporal Martinez re-entered the conversation. "I thought it strange that a second visitor comes in one month looking for you, Mr. Van Huessen. Last time, remember, your niece's husband was found dead three days later. You never saw his body. I did. It was not normal . . ."

"What do you mean, *not normal*, Corporal Martinez?" hissed Van Huessen.

"It looked to me like he had been hurt before he died. My supervisor told me to record it as an accident, which I did. But I'm not so sure . . ."

"Why didn't you tell me this?" snapped the old man.

Martinez shrugged. "I didn't want to disturb the family."

"But I told that stranger about my niece. I told him that neither I nor my niece would tell him anything about our family."

Abbey overheard the conversation with growing concern. *What's going on?* he thought to himself.

"This is why I hold the American," said Martinez. "I will not let history repeat itself. After you chased him off your property this morning, he went and bothered your niece. I found him at the museum. In the morning, I will decide what to do with him."

Abbey took one last stab. "Mr. Van Huessen, could you at least tell me whether you know anything about William Walker?"

The old man straightened up, let go of the cell bar, and looked intensely at Abbey. He paused and wrinkled up his forehead as he appeared to think.

"Who's he?" the corporal asked.

The old man turned to the constable and then back to Abbey, finally saying in a soft voice, "Only a name out of the past . . . the long ago past. Maybe someone my great, great grandfather knew, many, many years ago." Looking at Abbey, he said, "No, Professor, I cannot help you with any of your questions." He turned and walked slowly away, leaving the building without another word.

Martinez told Abbey he would be back in the morning, "first thing." Abbey still couldn't figure out why he was being blamed for some earlier visit by someone else. Once he was alone, he saw a few newspapers on the small table in his cell. He started reading them. Before he fell asleep, he noticed that a full moon lit the skies. He also remembered he had left his pills in the car. He didn't sleep well, tossing and turning restlessly on the sagging cot. He dreamed.

Son, we must move along.
Why? I've done nothing wrong.
They say we must.
But I'm not talking to them. I'm just watching them sing.
The police say that's the thing; their song. It's why we must move along.

• • •

Abbey woke with a start, a flashlight shining in his face. Two figures were standing in his darkened cell. He flashed back to those old movies of someone being pulled out of a jail cell for an interrogation – or a lynching. He hoped he was dreaming.

"Professor, it's me, John Duprey," whispered one of the figures hoarsely. Now Abbey knew he was dreaming.

"Don't worry," the shadowy figure said. "We're here to get you out. We'll get you home."

Abbey shook his head and rubbed his eyes. "What the hell is going on?"

"No time for talking," the figure whispered again. "We have to move quickly. We have a plane at the airstrip. We're going to fly you back to the States."

"You're Duprey? And I'm breaking out of jail? To fly to the States? What, are you crazy?"

"I'm definitely John Duprey," said the figure, turning his flashlight upward onto his face to illuminate it. "I learned from your secretary that you were here. She got a call late this afternoon saying you were in some trouble. Luckily, I had made arrangements to help you if necessary.

We've checked on this Corporal Martinez. He's a rabid anti-American. He's acting on his own. He has no authority for this arrest. But he'll likely make life very difficult for you if you don't get out of here. We've paid him some money. This isn't really a jail break. He knows you're leaving. He's not very happy, but there's nothing he can do. If we wait till morning, he'll have to make some sort of a report which will tie our hands. So let's hurry. Let's get out of here before things go any further."

Abbey was in a daze, confused, but he let himself be led outside to his car. The second man jumped behind the wheel. Abbey was pushed into the back seat, with Duprey jumping in beside him. They drove rapidly out of town and north on the road Abbey had entered on. The driver didn't turn on the headlights, but the moon shed a fair amount of light. Abbey was in the back seat bouncing around as the car climbed the coastal road. Suddenly, it slowed and turned abruptly right. Abbey could see two small lights a couple of hundred of yards in the distance, like another set of headlights.

Abbey tried to ask more questions, but Duprey turned, silencing him with his hands moving in a downward gesture, saying, "Just stay quiet for a moment. We're almost there. Everything's going to be fine." The headlights were a small plane parked on the old dirt runway. As the car approached, the plane's engine was started with a roar which reverberated about the empty field. The car pulled up to the open door and Duprey jumped out, motioning for the professor to follow.

"This is crazy," yelled Abbey over the engine.

"Goddamn it, Professor, this is the only way," yelled Duprey. "I guarantee, everything is all set. But we have to move out before all this noise wakes up the whole town."

"What about my car?"

"Don't worry about your car. It's safe. It's being driven back to the States by the other man. Please get in, and hurry."

Now fully awake, Abbey shivered uncontrollably. He couldn't talk. He sat huddled in the back seat. They pulled him out of the car and pushed him into the plane, and then to the back seat. There he sat with unfocused eyes, shaking his head from side to side. Duprey jumped into the right cockpit seat and turned to reassure Abbey again. "It's okay, Professor. Everything's okay."

The pilot immediately pulled the door shut and started taxiing to take off.

As they gained altitude eastward over the gulf, Abbey began to calm down. Looking down, he saw one or two lights in the small village and the looming Guardian Island in front of them. The pilot banked left and headed north. Abbey finally settled down enough to talk to Duprey.

"My passport . . ." he began.

Duprey handed it to him. After being repeatedly assured that there would be no record of any arrest or breakout, and that his trip through Bahia de los Angeles would go down as a perfectly normal one, Abbey told Duprey about his day. Duprey showed the most interest when Abbey mentioned the leather trunk in Van Huessen's library.

"How did she describe the trunk?" Duprey asked. "And where exactly is it in the house?"

"I think she said it was leather," Abbey answered indifferently. "In some library. What difference does it make? I probably can't go back now." Duprey told Abbey that he wanted to hear as soon as the professor received any information from Mrs. Plarez.

Seeing the coast approaching, Abbey asked, "How're we going to fly into the United States? There are all sorts of radar installations near the border to stop drug flights. And what about fuel? There was none at the airstrip."

"Don't worry," spoke the pilot for the first time. "I have a recorded flight plan from Denver to the Baja to take you fellows fishing and to return as soon as I drop you. I'm expected at the border. This is a Swiss-made, Pilatus PC-12 pressurized prop jet with a range of 2,300 miles without refueling. It's a real workhorse. We don't need any more fuel."

Soon, the pilot was talking on the radio to the border authorities, identifying himself and his flight plan. Once over land, it wasn't long before the plane started descending toward a small airfield. Abbey knew it was too soon for Albuquerque. Duprey explained that they were dropping him at a small airfield in Sedona, south of Flagstaff, Arizona, where there was no ground staff at this hour of the morning. Since their flight plan showed no stop before Denver, they didn't want to take the chance of stopping at the larger airport in Albuquerque.

As the plane wheeled to a halt, a car pulled up outside. The pilot reached over, unlocked the door, and swung it open. Duprey climbed out, with Abbey moving slowly behind him.

"I don't want you to worry about this," said Duprey. "I guarantee that everything is okay in Mexico, although you're probably right that you don't want to go back to the village right away. Let things settle down. Keep working the project from Albuquerque for the time being. And let me know as soon as you hear from Mrs. Plarez. It's probably best not to talk to anyone about this return trip."

"It's pretty tough not to worry, Mr. Duprey. I think you've turned me into some sort of criminal."

"No, not at all. There will be no report filed. You simply left town. No one will know how or why."

Duprey climbed back into the plane, and it took off immediately, heading northeast. Abbey was driven to his condominium in Albuquerque.

• • •

In the morning, Duprey kept his promise and called Marge.

"Marge, this is John Duprey."

"Yes?" she answered with a hesitant tone.

"Just want to let you know that everything's fine. Professor Abbey should be back in Albuquerque today. Everything's resolved in Mexico."

She gasped. "Oh, I'm so glad to hear that! I thought he was in some trouble."

"No. None at all. I'm sure he'll see you soon. He'll explain everything."

Abbey did come to his office later in the day. Marge told him about the warning call and her conversation with Duprey.

"What happened, Professor? How'd you get back so quickly?'

"Just a misunderstanding in Mexico. I drove all night to get back," he said, not wanting to divulge the plane ride.

"Thought it best to return right away. Everything's fine. Your call to Duprey was very helpful."

A few days later, Maria Plarez phoned Abbey. She first asked whether he had worked things out with the corporal, continuing in a questioning voice, "You certainly left in a hurry."

"Yes," he responded. "Got called back very suddenly. Corporal Martinez became much more reasonable. Just some sort of misunderstanding." He went on to explain that he had a newly issued passport which had caused some confusion.

She reported that she had talked to her uncle, but without much success. "My uncle said there was another man a month ago asking the same questions as you. A foreigner. Is there some connection between you and the other man?"

"No, none at all," he answered. "I don't know anything about any other man. But what about the trunk? Can I look at it?"

"I don't think so," she said. "My uncle said no one will see his family jewels before his death. He also said something else . . . that I should be wary of strangers. His words were, 'Keep your distance from strangers, Maria. Remember, you too are a Van Huessen.' I don't know what he meant."

"I don't, either. But I really do appreciate your calling. I'll let you know how my research goes. Hopefully we'll meet again." He decided not to mention the conversation he had overheard in the jail, something about her husband having been hurt. That conversation between Martinez and Van Huessen had made no sense. No reason to upset her.

He reported everything back to Duprey. To his surprise, Duprey seemed pleased with the report. He told Abbey to put the Van Huessen search on hold for the time being and to instead pursue the Walker descendants. By then, Abbey's car had arrived back in Albuquerque. He hoped the debacle in Mexico was behind him. So he sat down with John Modesta to talk about William Walker, remembering that the old man Van Huessen had seemed to recognize the Walker name.

CHAPTER 13

JUNE 1 – JULY 15
DENVER

Two months later, John Duprey sat at his desk, feeling satisfied with himself and with the progress on the assignment. Within three weeks of his reporting to his New York contact about Abbey's trip, Van Huessen's leather trunk arrived at Duprey's office in Denver. It was delivered by two men from a delivery service with a note explaining that the trunk had been obtained from Mr. Van Huessen. Duprey assumed it had been purchased. He was a bit surprised that one of the delivery men was one-armed. Seemed to him like a tough line of work for that handicap.

The lawyer also received a brief report from Professor Abbey explaining that some references to Van Huessen in the early nineteenth century had finally been found. Abbey's assistant John Modesta uncovered the name among early wagon train records in the Museum of the American West in Los Angeles. Van Huessen was among the names of the members of such a caravan which had reached southern California in 1821. The information was sketchy, but Jonathan Van Huessen had been one of the early pioneers to reach southern California.

As soon as the delivery men left, Duprey lifted the trunk onto his side table to review its contents. It wasn't heavy. Two feet wide and eighteen inches deep, the container stood about one foot high. It was brown leather, with metal studs around the edges, and it looked very old.

The leather was faded and cracked and shiny where hands had rubbed it for many years. The metal studs had lost their luster. The trunk had a fairly simple latch lock which had been pried open before it reached Duprey.

The contents were to some degree what Duprey expected to find, but he still found them extraordinary. On the top were handwritten copies of the original letters from Jonathan Van Huessen to the Mexican government in the mid-nineteenth century complaining about incursions on his land. More than just the three letters Abbey had discovered years ago in the archives in Mexico City.

Under the letters, Duprey saw an old parchment envelope tied with a blue ribbon. He lifted it carefully with both hands and moved back to his desk. Placing it on the desk, he opened it very slowly, sliding his letter opener under the flap and trying not to crack the seam as he lifted it open. Inside was a cracked yellow parchment. It was folded as a letter, but larger than letter size. Once again, he carefully unfolded the document and gently pressed it flat, holding the edges down with a book and a paperweight from his desk. It appeared to be the original of an official United States land grant to Jonathan Van Huessen, dated May 13, 1820, signed by a scribbled and undecipherable signature carrying the designation, *Secretary of the Treasury, as authorized by the Congressional Committee on Public Lands.*

This Van Huessen must have had powerful friends at the highest levels of the new American government to have received the grant, thought Duprey. He remembered that part of Abbey's report had touched upon American land grants to pioneers in the Southwest and elsewhere during the early 1800s. As an example, Abbey had described one granted to the Frenchman Marquis de Lafayette by the American

Congress in 1824 in appreciation for his assistance in the American Revolution. Now, looking at these documents, Duprey wondered whether Jonathan Van Huessen had been another European providing assistance to the colonies two centuries before. In any event, and for whatever reason, forty years after the war Van Huessen had received the Baja grant. *Maybe this was a son? Thanks delayed?* He went back to the trunk.

The trunk also contained a copy of the Treaty of Hidalgo of 1848, which did include the footnote 7 and the seventh explanatory note in the addendum. They couldn't be missed, because someone had circled them both with a bold, black pen. Duprey read the language of the seventh note slowly:

> *As for the Baja Peninsula Territory, nothing herein shall have any effect whatsoever upon private property rights to tracts within the Territory which have been perfected by actual cultivation and livestock grazing for a period of at least twenty contiguous years.*

He went back to the original 1820 grant to Van Huessen and read that language slowly and carefully. The grant was of a huge territory lying south of San Diego, beginning at a stone marker on the Pacific coast at Tijuana, turning south along the west coast of the Baja Peninsula to the 27th parallel of latitude, then turning due east and following the parallel to the east coast of the Peninsula, where the boundary turned again and ran northerly along that coast to the town of Mexicali. Then it returned due west to the "point of the beginning." It included all islands whose "closest point proximate to the coast is within twenty-five miles."

Duprey was neither a real estate lawyer nor a cartographer, but he knew enough real estate law to read the land grant description to include all the northern half of the Baja Peninsula – what was today the Mexican state of Baja California Norte. He wasn't sure of the significance of the treaty twenty-eight years later, but his quick reading of footnote 7 suggested that something had been held back from the treaty's grant to Mexico.

Looking further in the trunk, he found a number of old maps which plotted the land grant description, and a note and receipt from the California Registry of Deeds in San Francisco, suggesting that the grant had been recorded there many years later in November 1861. There was also a copy of an 1854 deed to William Walker containing the same description, which looked to have been recorded at the same time as the land grant in 1861. Duprey compared the Van Huessen signatures on the letters to the one on the deed to Walker. They were identical to his eye.

It looked to Duprey that the Van Huessen family had owned a substantial amount of land in Baja Norte under the 1820 land grant. All of it appeared to have been conveyed to Mr. Walker in 1854. Walker's estate had probably found and recorded the land grant and deeds after his death in 1860. If that land was excluded from the Treaty of Hidalgo in 1848 under the footnote language Professor Abbey had discovered, it was possible that Walker's descendants still owned some or all of Baja Norte, including all islands within twenty-five miles of the coast. Duprey realized that this discovery was immense. It was what he had been hired to find.

He picked up his phone and called New York:

"Mr. Silverman, this is John Duprey. . . . Fine, thanks. Actually, very fine. I've just gone through the Van Huessen trunk. I think it contains exactly what we're looking for. . . . Oh. You're aware of the documents. . . . Yes, of course. I'm going to take it a step further. . . . I'm on it as we speak."

Duprey immediately hired a San Francisco real estate firm to research the land grant, its apparent recording, and the significance of footnote seven in the treaty. Promising an extra fee for expedited service, he received back an opinion letter in two weeks. The letter stated that the 1820 land grant was regular in all respects and consistent with the form of lawful land grants from the early nineteenth century. It also opined that some or all of the grant might have been excluded from the later treaty grant by footnote seven. The San Francisco earthquake of 1906 and resulting fires had, however, destroyed almost all of California's pre-1900 recorded documents. The lawyers could find no public record of the land grant, but they advised Duprey that the absence of a public record was not in itself unusual.

As for the deed to William Walker, once again the registry records were of no help. He was advised, however, that the recording of a deed was not required for it to be effective. Actual notice of a conveyance was equivalent to the constructive public notice accomplished by a recording at the Registry of Deeds. The San Francisco lawyers advised that the Van Huessen letter to the Mexican authorities in 1854 might constitute sufficient notice. If so, Mexico knew of and was bound by the deed to Walker. As stated in the letter:

"If Baja Norte was excluded from the treaty grant by footnote 7, and if Mr. Van Huessen, the owner under the prior

grant, put the Mexican government on notice of his ownership by his letters, Baja Norte appears never to have been effectively conveyed or granted to Mexico."

Goddamn lawyers and their ifs, muttered Duprey to himself as he read the letter. He called the lawyer who had signed the letter for the San Francisco firm, who he was sure had done little of the background research.

After the opening pleasantries. "Look, John, I want you to drop the equivocation in the letter. . . .I know . . . You're being well paid. We're paying for an opinion – not a waffle. I want you to redo the damn letter and say Mexico does not own Baja Norte. . . . Sure you can do it. I bet that's what your associate told you, and you just watered it down. . . . Fine. Go over it with your people. But I want a better opinion letter. . . . Thanks. I'll be waiting."

He got the new opinion letter.

•   •   •

Back in Albuquerque, Abbey's efforts continued to focus on William Walker. There had been a lot written about Walker in the 1850s. The newspaper accounts of his southern expeditions were numerous. Abbey's assistant John Modesta had gathered many of them. In one account in the *Sacramento Times,* Walker was quoted upon his return from the Baja: "Not only did I conquer the Baja, I bought it!" Duprey chuckled when he eventually saw that part of Abbey's report. *You're damn right, Mr. Walker. You bought it. So let's find out who owns it today.*

The search for William Walker's descendents by Professor Abbey and his student assistant yielded results. Modesta reported to the professor that Walker had been killed in 1860, leaving a widow and two children back home in

Sacramento. Through internet access to the Mormon genealogical records in Salt Lake City, and other historical records, the Walkers were traced to a number of living heirs. There was no indication that any of them knew of their nefarious ancestor. The professor assumed that he would be contacting the heirs, but when he reported the Walker information to Duprey, the lawyer told him to hold off for a while so the client could decide what to do next.

• • •

Duprey knew what to do next. He decided that he would be better than Abbey to devise a scheme to contact the Walker descendants. The list which Abbey had generated included fifty-five names. Duprey sensed that Abbey might be a bit too straight-laced for the task he envisioned. So the lawyer took over the job and devised another ruse to attempt to obtain release and quitclaim deeds from the Walker descendants.

Each received a certified letter advising that the recipient had been selected to participate in a lottery for a vacation home in a new retirement community being built in Mexico.

YOUR NAME HAS BEEN PRESELECTED!
YOU COULD BE THE PROUD OWNER OF A
LUXURY VACATION HOME IN MEXICO!
DO NOT DELAY!
PLEASE RESPOND IMMEDIATELY!

The letters explained that the only persons who could win were those who did not already own land in Mexico. So to qualify for the lottery drawing, each had to sign a brief confirmation that they owned no property in Mexico. Each letter also contained a check for five hundred dollars.

Since apparently none of them knew anything about their ancestors, or thought they owned anything in Mexico, almost all signed and returned the confirmations to Duprey. He laughed to himself as each came in. He had artfully drafted the confirmations so that they were really deeds transferring any and all land in Mexico, and, in particular, any, "in that area and territory above the 27th parallel known as Baja California Norte." The grantee was Baja Properties, "or its nominee." He thought the language he had devised was clever. "I hereby confirm . . . and I therefore also convey and quitclaim . . . any and all real property or interest therein . . . ." After a month, he had fifty-two deeds in hand. Three were missing.

John Farese from San Antonio, Marcia Mobel from San Francisco, and Michael Knowles of Boston all ignored the solicitations. Duprey telephoned each of them.

"I'm a representative of Baja Properties," he began. "We recently sent you a notice of your prize of winning a retirement home in Mexico."

"Okay . . ."

"Do you remember our notification?"

"Not really. I throw that kind of stuff out."

"Mr. Farese, you're a potential winner in this raffle. You will definitely receive five hundred dollars. Your name survived the first elimination. You could win a Mexican retirement home."

"What's the catch? I don't want to buy anything or listen to any pitch."

"No, sir. It's nothing like that. This is a real raffle with a real prize. It's our way of advertising our new development."

"Look, I don't go for this kind of stuff on the phone. Send the package again. I'll look at it."

"There are only ten days till the final draw . . ."

"Then you'd better send it right along. I'll look at it. Good-bye."

Duprey had similar conversations with the other two individuals. He sent three new packages. The three missing deeds came in.

• • •

Duprey still didn't know too much about his clients, other than that they were extremely rich. The initial call had been from a New York investment group for which he had done some work in the 1990s. He remembered that it was an international group with very deep pockets to invest in the skyrocketing American stock market. In his current assignment, his firm's fees had been substantial, and he had seen the money paid to others. He really believed that he was representing an investor group planning to build the described retirement and resort community. He was used to complicated deals and unusual clients with great wealth who required secrecy.

Soon after he reported to his New York contact that he had all the deeds, Duprey got a call from New York.

"Mr. Duprey, we're very pleased with your results."

"Thank you," he replied with a bit of smugness in his voice. "Some real creativity has been necessary, but I think we're just about there."

"We now have to concentrate on the Mexican government," continued his contact. "We have to get some land from them. The land will be an island, the Isle Angel de la Guardia – known as Guardian Island – just off the coast of Bahia de los Angeles. I think you've been there." The man laughed.

"Just briefly," answered Duprey with a chuckle. "And I'm not sure I want to go back. There's a certain police officer down there . . ."

"No problem," said the voice, cutting him off. "Should be no need for you to go back. But we think you'll need to spend some time in Mexico City. We need to hire the best government lobbying firm in Mexico to help convince them to sell us this island."

"I can do that," answered the lawyer. "I have some good contacts there. I don't think it'll be difficult to purchase development rights on one of their islands."

"There is a bit of a twist," Mr. Duprey. "We want more than development rights. We want sovereignty over that island. Absolute sovereignty."

Duprey paused, thinking a moment before responding. "What do you mean, sovereignty?"

"Just what I said, Mr. Duprey. We want sovereignty. Just like our own little country." He added hastily, "Mexican law is too restrictive on coastal development. We need to be free from those restrictions. People will be much more receptive to investing large sums in a community which is independent of the corruption and unreliability in Mexico."

"Why in the world would Mexico give away an island?" Duprey said nervously with a half laugh.

"We're not looking for a gift, sir," was the response. "First, we'll pay very handsomely, both to the government and to whomever we have to deal with. But, perhaps more importantly, we'll give them back Baja Norte, which we think we now own, less this little island. We have purchased all remaining interests under the original Van Huessen title. All we want is the island. *They'll* be getting the gift."

Duprey suddenly realized the importance of his previous work and that of Professor Abbey. As an attorney, he knew enough real estate law to agree with the statement. His client now had strong and viable claim of ownership to Baja Norte – at least, enough of a claim to disrupt titles and development for years.

The man continued, "The island is nothing to Mexico. There're only a few turtles on it. We'll develop it in such a magnificent fashion that we'll change the Mexican economy. There will be hundreds of millions of dollars spent in developing the resort and supporting the community. It will become a Mecca for thousands of Americans looking for safe, luxurious, and affordable retirement living. But we will only do it if we rule that island. That, Mr. Duprey, is your assignment."

Duprey was used to unusual assignments. He had his marching orders. And he now thought he understood what was going on. He went looking for a Mexican lobbyist.

CHAPTER 14

AUGUST 3

MEXICO CITY

After talking to a number of his contacts in the United States and Mexico, Duprey approached the law firm of Alvarez & Cox in Mexico City. He first checked it out in the legal directories and on line and determined that it was the right firm for the job. It was one of Mexico's largest law firms, and it also engaged in lobbying activities. By American standards, it was small, with six partners and twenty younger attorneys. But it had a good reputation in Mexico and in the United States. It was unique in combining a Mexican and American staff. Charles Cox was an American expatriate who had moved to Mexico City from a large law firm in Austin, Texas, about ten years ago. Evidently, a bitter divorce had left him alone and fed up with the American legal system. Michael Alvarez was a respected attorney with years of experience in Mexico.

Duprey's initial meeting was with both Señor Alvarez and Mr. Cox. It took place in a conference room at their offices in Mexico City near the capitol buildings. The two Mexican lawyers began the meeting with a somewhat indifferent attitude. As they realized the possible extent of the assignment, and the likely fees, their attention became more focused.

"So, as you see," said Duprey, "my client needs to test the waters about the reception they will receive if they propose a large new development in northern Baja." He had decided not to tell them about the sovereignty twist till later; it would probably upset them. "The scope is huge. It entails as many as fifteen thousand residential units, with the accompanying infrastructure of roads, an airfield, seaport, and all necessary support facilities. It will be a high-end community. Our financing is in place. What we need is full support and cooperation from the Mexican government."

Up till then, both Alvarez and Cox had listened without many comments. Duprey knew that Michael Alvarez was the elder of a long-standing Mexican family who had managed to move in and out of Mexican politics and remain associated with whomever was in power. Charles Cox had always been a very competent lawyer, and, after ten years in Mexico, he had gained respect for his abilities on both sides of the border.

Cox asked, "What's the extent of your client's financing?"

"I'll only say that we are prepared to spend over one billion dollars to do this project. That is with a B, gentlemen. That includes land acquisition and construction, and, of course, fees and expenses necessary to obtain all required approvals. Naturally, we'll pay your firm's normal fees and expenses. If we are successful, we are prepared to provide each of you a free home in the development – a sort of 'contingent fee,' as we say in America."

"What exactly do you need from us?" asked Alvarez.

"As I mentioned, the Guardian Island at Bahia de los Angeles is the location my clients have chosen. It meets all of our needs on the ground, and it is close to the border, which is important. Many of our new residents will be the American retirees we hear so much about – the baby boomers. Unfortunately, the island happens to be a national park. We can do nothing unless Mexico is willing to remove that designation and make the island available for development. If you can accomplish that, we will discuss the necessary payments and technicalities involved in purchasing the island from Mexico and setting up a new retirement community. Your first assignment is to do what is necessary to make that island available to us for development."

"It might be easier to pick another location that isn't a national park," commented Alvarez.

"Maybe," replied Duprey. "I'm not the developer, just the lawyer. They say it's there or nowhere."

"Are we to understand that this is an American group which is proposing this community for American retirees?" asked Alvarez.

"No, not really. The developers are very much an international group. The funding is largely from outside the United States. We expect many of the eventual residents of the community will be Americans, but it will be open to all."

"Let's look at the maps and studies you have and bring in our senior associate for real estate development," said Señor Alvarez. "I think I should personally handle the early efforts to get governmental support. Our associates can work on the real estate acquisition details. Obviously, there will be some complexities involved in purchasing property from the government. It's more complicated than a purchase between private parties."

"Oh, I'm sure it will be," agreed Duprey, thinking, *if they only knew of the real complexity – the need for sovereignty.*

Mr. Cox added, "As you might expect, we'll need a retainer for a project of this magnitude."

"No problem," said Duprey. "My client has provided me with a check payable to your firm for one million dollars." Handing the check over to them, he continued, "As you can see, this is a serious, well-funded project. This will be your retainer and will cover startup expenses. We wish to move forward as quickly as possible."

Alvarez and Cox glanced at each other and tried not to show surprise. It was the largest fee and retainer that the firm had ever been paid. They sensed that they were onto something big.

Duprey went on, "This money is to move the project forward. We know how things are done in Mexico. If you need to make payments for support, these funds allow you to do so. We don't need a detailed accounting of how the money is spent. You may also bill against it as a retainer. I will, however, be very interested to hear your progress. I would like to receive weekly reports." He handed them another document. "I also have a fairly standard confidentiality agreement for you to sign to protect the identity of my client and to emphasize that, until we are ready to go public, we want no publicity."

"All of our client matters are confidential," said Alvarez huffily, as if he were insulted by the suggestion that he would be asked to sign such a document.

"I'm sure they are. I'm not suggesting otherwise. My client insists on the agreement. I had to sign one myself. It's required."

The lawyers swallowed their pride and signed.

The three men spent more time going over the details and bringing in the appropriate associates to answer questions and to briefly meet Duprey.

After Duprey left, Cox and Alvarez talked about the new client and the assignment. They realized that they didn't know much about the actual client, other than that it appeared to be a wealthy real estate development group with American and international participation. They agreed their first step was to organize a Mexican shell entity to have a name and business base to deal with. They needed a name, and Duprey had not given them one. They picked *The Baja Project*. The file was immediately opened under that name. All the staff at Alvarez & Cox received notice in the next weekly update memo that a new client was aboard. The memo named both senior partners and three associates as the lawyers working on *The Baja Project*. The staff read that as meaning *big*.

CHAPTER 15

JUNE 15 – JULY 1

ALBUQUERQUE

After receiving the last report from Professor Abbey about the Walker descendants, Duprey told him that it looked like most of Abbey's work had been accomplished.

"Successfully," he added. "Your work has given us what we need. Your role is probably over, but we need you to remain available as we proceed with land acquisition. We thought this would take quite a few months of effort by you, but you appear to have gone right to the heart of the matter on your first trip. We managed to obtain the Van Huessen records, and they are precisely what we were looking for. Your research and suspicion about a missing deed were correct."

"I don't feel like I've done much to justify all your costs," Abbey commented, wondering whether they were going to want at least a partial refund of the handsome endowment.

"Don't worry, Professor, we're satisfied. We paid to get a job done. No one else had your unique information and entrée. We're moving full speed ahead." He asked Abbey to send him all of his notes and all the paperwork he had generated. Duprey said he knew it sounded silly, but his client had this phobia about secrecy. They wanted to be sure that there were no possibilities of even inadvertent leaks. Abbey thought it a strange request, but he complied. They technically owned his work product, and they had certainly paid handsomely for it.

A few days later, Abbey was thinking of his experiences in Mexico and realized that he probably owed Maria Plarez at least a closing phone call. Her phone number was still in his Palm. As he thought about what to say to her, he heard the cranes lifting large adobe slabs into place for the façade of the new Overton Faculty and Administration Building. *Tenure and a new title, a new office, and some pretty interesting experiences*, he thought as he placed the call. Although he still had misgivings about what he had heard from Martinez and Van Huessen that night in jail, he tried to put those concerns out of his mind. It had nothing to do with him.

"Hello, Maria, this is Professor Bill Abbey from Albuquerque."

"Professor Abbey," she replied in a cutting, sarcastic tone, "I wondered if I'd hear from you again."

He was taken aback by her voice, but he continued. "I wanted to let you know how things are going and check a few more family details, if you don't mind."

"Well, I do mind," she yelled. "Why? Why did you have to steal it?"

"What are you talking about?"

"You know very well what I'm talking about. Within a week of our meeting, your thugs broke into my uncle's house and stole his trunk. I've been told maybe you had something to do with my husband's death. And now I'm hearing that you people are going to take my island." She was sobbing now. "I helped you. I told you things I shouldn't have . . . I also made the call which I think protected you from Corporal Martinez."

Abbey didn't know what to say. He stammered that he hadn't done any of those things, that she was mistaken. "What can I do to make you believe me?"

"There's nothing you can do. You've already done enough. Just leave me alone, and don't ever show up here again!" she screamed, slamming down the phone.

Abbey was dumbstruck. None of what she said made sense. Why make such accusations? Maybe Martinez was doing a bit of payback for having lost his prisoner. Abbey had received no official contact from anyone, so Duprey had probably been right that the escape had not broken any law. They could easily have found him if they had wanted. But the trunk? Martinez knew nothing about the trunk. He wouldn't have taken it. Only Abbey and Duprey had known about the trunk. Duprey had seemed pleased to learn of it, and he later said he had obtained the papers. Once he had learned of the trunk, Duprey had more or less closed down Abbey's part of the project. *What did Duprey do? Did he steal the trunk? The island? What about the island? And a dead fisherman?*

He had to contact Duprey. He placed the call and introduced himself to the receptionist.

"Mr. Duprey is out of the country on business," she explained. "May I ask the nature of the call? I'll be hearing from him."

"Yes. I did a project for him a few months ago, and he and I just talked last week. There are some open items that I need to talk to him about. I'm sure he'll know who I am."

"If you'll give me your number, I'll make sure he gets the message."

The next day, Duprey returned the call. "Professor Abbey, how are you? This is John Duprey."

"I thought I was okay, until I talked to my contact in Mexico, Maria Plarez, who was quite distraught and making a number of strange accusations."

"You what?" Duprey sounded alarmed.

"I said she's making statements that I stole her uncle's trunk and other things . . . "

"No, stop. I don't care what she said. Why in the world were you talking to her?"

"I thought I should call, since she had been helpful . . . "

"Stop right there, Professor. I don't want this call to proceed. Nothing more on the telephone. You are under a strict confidentiality agreement. I told you that your work was finished. I don't want you to talk to anyone else about this. You haven't, have you?"

"No," stuttered Abbey, suddenly feeling sheepish.

"I will be there tomorrow. First thing in the morning. In your office."

"Fine. I'll see you then."

"And Professor . . . do *not* talk about these things with anyone."

· · ·

As promised, Duprey was at Abbey's office at nine o'clock the next morning.

"I'm sorry I was short on the phone," Duprey began, "but some things are best not discussed on the phone. This is a very competitive world. People go through each other's trash to learn what a competitor is doing. Phone calls are easily tapped. Now tell me exactly what this lady Maria said to you."

Abbey related the conversation as best he could.

Duprey listened and paused for a moment to think before replying. "Professor, I pause to try to understand what you've said. You must understand that you're not the only one working on this project. There were and are others in Mexico and elsewhere. We did receive information from the trunk, but it certainly wasn't stolen. Keep in mind, this Van Huessen's a fruitcake. He's nuts. He almost killed you. I'm sure we obtained our information lawfully and properly. I have no idea what he might have said to Maria, and I really don't care.

"As for her husband's death, I have no idea what she's talking about. No one killed anyone. This is a real estate development. What most concerns me is that you took it upon yourself to contact this lady. That breaks our agreement. You're not supposed to be contacting anyone. I really don't want to call President Overton and ask for the money back, but I will if anything like this ever happens again."

Somewhat relieved by the partial explanation, but also shaken by the reminder that the huge endowment might be in jeopardy, Abbey didn't know what to say. He mumbled that he had thought the call was innocent enough and might even have provided additional helpful information.

Duprey stood and lectured the professor, pointing at him with a jabbing finger as he spoke, "That might be so, but that is not your decision to make. Let's make one thing crystal clear. Your work is completed. We do not want nor need any further information from you. There is no reason for you to talk to anyone about any aspect of your work. Your efforts were helpful. We are moving forward. And if we succeed, we will not forget the promise of a home for you. I will be in touch with you at that time. But other

than that, our relationship has ended. Don't take it personally, but I'd just as soon not hear from you again. Do we
understand each other?"

"Yes, I understand," responded Abbey in an obedient
tone.

"Then I will be going. Good luck with your career."

Duprey left, leaving Abbey in a troubled state of mind.
He thought he should get more answers, but he'd been directed to stay out of it. Against his better judgment, he
decided to follow the directive and do nothing.

CHAPTER 16

JULY 2 – SEPTEMBER 1
MEXICO AND TEHRAN

Michael Alvarez knew what to do once he received the assignment from Duprey. He had one of his associates begin research on the history of Guardian Island. Why and when was it designated a national preserve? What, if anything, was special about it? Most importantly, who were the national representatives from that section of Baja Norte? What were their interests? He himself was scheduled to attend a small dinner party at the presidential mansion Los Pinos with the Mexican president the following week. He would initiate some discreet inquiries about the reception that a large new development project in Baja Norte would receive. He thought he already knew the answer. Most Mexicans couldn't care less about the peninsula. It was an undeveloped waste desert in the north, other than the Tijuana strip and an American tourist outpost at its southern tip. He didn't think it had ever really been considered part of Mexico.

He found the dinner party fruitful. President Chavez raised no objection to a sale of the island, and in a private conversation after dinner, Alvarez set the hook.

"Mr. President, on another note, our firm is expanding our lobbying group, but we lack someone of real stature to head it. We would like to talk to you when your term expires."

"Certainly, Michael. That could hold real interest for me. Let's talk at that time."

They shook hands as the lawyer left, each smiling to himself for a different reason.

Within a few weeks, Alvarez and his associate had put together a plan. The information they developed was as Alvarez had thought. No one cared much about the island, other than some environmental types who thought it was a very special place for turtles to nest and live, unbothered by man or civilization. The island was fairly large, approximately sixty miles long north to south and ten miles wide. It contained two small mountains and a rocky shoreline on its easterly side. The mountain to the north end was 4,000 feet high, and the southern, smaller peak about 3,000 feet. The island's westerly shore was fifteen miles from the mainland, with sandy beaches running along the entire western side. On the southern tip was a natural harbor with deep water access to the gulf's sea lanes. This beautiful island guarded both the Bahia de los Angeles and the northern gulf access to the United States.

Since there were a number of additional nearby islands, which had no national park designation but which were also homes for the turtles, Alvarez decided to pursue a trade: move the turtles to the other islands, with enough money to make the other islands truly eco-sensitive, and put money into facilities on the mainland to create a top-notch marine research center. He learned that there was already a decrepit turtle museum in the town of Bahia de los Angeles. Their proposal recommended using the present museum as a base for a new, modern environmental center. He foresaw that the environmentalists would raise some objections, but they would come across as unreasonable. After all, the new island turtle preserves would be largely flat and exactly the type of areas the turtles used. They didn't need the mountains of Guardian Island. The lawyers chuckled as they joked with each other that the wrong island had been chosen for the turtles in the first place. That would now be corrected.

Two months after receiving the assignment, the Mexican lawyers reported back to Duprey that they were making good progress. He then decided that it was time to disclose to Alvarez and Cox the twist concerning the type of ownership which was going to be necessary and the ace in the hole about Baja's back title. He thought it was important enough to call for another face-to-face meeting. Duprey invited Cox and Alvarez to Denver for an important meeting with him and his client. He told his contact in New York that the client really had to make an appearance. He had carried the ball by himself as far as he could. He had to have some real people from this investment group to put forward.

·   ·   ·

General Mussahrah was alone at his desk in the Defense Ministry when he received a call that a meeting in Denver was planned and that someone had to attend. He was glad that he had foreseen this development and made some plans. He pulled out a folder with résumés and background checks on the three men he had chosen.

First was an Iraqi expatriate who had been very senior in the Hussein dictatorship. Major Rahman had fled when the government tumbled and had been the eight of diamonds in the famous American deck of cards of wanted individuals. As an Iraqi information officer, he had been a minor player in Iraq, but a much more major one in Iran, where his loyalties actually lay. He had turned himself in to the Americans after Saddam's capture and was soon repatriated as one of many who had undergone a change of heart and now supported the new government. Mussahrah knew that, as a Shia, Rahman really supported Iran. He had been left in Iraq to await an appropriate assignment. Although considered fully trustworthy by the general and his cousin the Ayatollah, Rahman was not told the true nature of the project. He had instead been advised that this was a mechanism to launder and spend millions of dollars of American currency which had been smuggled into Iran before the fall of Iraq. Mussahrah smiled as he remembered that cover story, knowing that there was actually a bit of truth to it.

Two other figureheads were in the file: former Mexican president Juan Gonzalez, and a Cuban immigrant who had made millions in real estate in south Florida. Both gentlemen had run into problems in their careers, which had made them receptive to the solicitations they had received about joining this grand new development team. Gonzalez had been defeated four years previously by the candidate Chavez, running on an anti-American theme. The former president had been unable to secure significant employment in the private sector, and the usual soft position in the government for ex-politicos had not been forthcoming. The Cuban expatriate Carlos Santez had made the mistake of building condominiums in southwest Florida with concrete he had purchased at below-market prices. Getting what he paid for, the structures did not hold up. His business had largely been ruined by the resulting lawsuits. Both were in need of money, and they were offered quite a bit, along with a free retirement home of their choosing.

After one last review of the file and a brief conversation with his cousin the Ayatollah, General Mussahrah made the final decision to send the three men to Denver. He issued the necessary instructions.

• • •

Before the meeting, Duprey had a fire to put out. It involved his associate Wendy Outlander, whom he had hired away from a Los Angeles firm two years before to run his firm's divorce practice. She was attractive and aggressive. Duprey had just received a copy of a letter in which one of her clients had complained to the judge that she had sold him down the river because he had declined her advances.

Walking into her office, Duprey glanced at the large stuffed tiger doll he had given her after her first year. It glowered at him from the corner.

Holding up the letter, he asked, "What's with this complaint?"

"Look, the son of a bitch tried to make it with *me*," she exclaimed to Duprey. "I told him I was his lawyer and not his fucking whore. And I damn well did force a quick settlement then. But the terms were the same as if I had dragged it out for six more months. I'm the one who lost money with the quick settlement. I'd be glad to talk to the judge about it."

"Okay, Wendy, calm down. I don't want you talking to the judge. I'll bring the guy in and calm him down. What was your fee?"

"I really nailed the bastard. Since I lost about ten thousand in fees by closing it quickly, I added ten grand to the final bill. I was goddamned if he was going to cause me to lose any money."

Holding out his hands to calm her, he said, "I think I understand. I'll offer him a reduction in the bill. That's what he's really bitching about. Don't worry. I'll cover your portion."

"He doesn't deserve a cent!"

"I know, but we want the problem to go away. Just let me handle it. But Wendy, I need a favor from you. I have two lawyers from Mexico and an international client group coming in for an important meeting, a bunch of guys. After the meeting, I have to take them to dinner. It'll be deadly. I need you to come along. Be your usual beautiful, sexy self."

She started to frown.

He added quickly, raising his palms in denial, "Just dinner. You'll add a little life to the group, that's all."

"You'll owe me . . ."

"Owe you? I'm going to get the client and the judge off your back, and I'm paying you a thousand dollars you don't deserve. Give me a break."

She shrugged. "Okay. When is this gala affair?"

•   •   •

The three representatives from the investor group flew into Denver and met with Duprey before the Mexican lawyers arrived. They arrived generally familiar with the project, and they learned more in the preparatory meeting. It was agreed that Duprey would do most of the talking. Of the three, it was clear that Rahman had the ears of the investor group and was in charge.

Cox and Alvarez flew into Denver on a United Airlines flight and were driven by limousine to Duprey's office in downtown Denver. The limo took them to an office building on Lincoln Street. They went up to a suite on the fifth floor which overlooked the capitol building. They noted that it was not opulent, but decorated tastefully in a western motif, with a large conference room. They were ushered into the room, where a large Remington print stared down from the wall behind the side table. It was huge – almost nine feet across – showing the American west with cowboys roping cattle on an open range and mountains in the background.

After introductions, the discussion started with the usual pleasantries. Señor Alvarez pointed at the large painting and commented that Mr. Remington could have painted the scene either in the American Southwest or the Baja Peninsula, since the terrain was so uniform and similar from the Four Corners of the American Southwest all the way to the tip of the Baja. It had been particularly so in the nineteenth century, he added, when Remington had painted his famous landscapes.

Duprey used that light discussion as a segue into the business at hand and began his presentation.

"Actually, the main reason for today's meeting finds its origins in Mr. Remington's time. We want to talk about historical events of the nineteenth century, which will have a direct impact on our acquisition of Guardian Island from Mexico. To help in our discussion, I have put together a binder of documents and analyses and some legal opinions." He handed each lawyer a brown, three-ring binder with *The Baja Project* emblazoned on its cover in large white letters.

Cox and Alvarez took the binders and began to skim them as Duprey continued to talk.

"These papers reflect a major part of the background work and due diligence we conducted before we chose this island, and before we hired you. The bottom line is discussed in the conclusion section on page forty-seven. We believe there are substantial outstanding title problems to large sections of Baja Norte. There is a question whether Mexico ever obtained legal title to that section of the Baja in the original Treaty of Hidalgo in 1848. Most view that treaty as the basis for Mexican sovereignty over the peninsula. These questions also apply to the islands along the coast, including Guardian Island. We think much of Baja Norte remained in private ownership after 1848 and was never effectively transferred to Mexico."

"Well, this is very interesting," said Cox slowly as he listened and skimmed the documents. "But so what? Are you suggesting that we can't get good title if we accomplish our task? If so, what are we doing all of this for?"

Cox and Alvarez waited as Duprey continued, "We're doing this because we want more than to simply own the island. We want sovereignty over it."

Cox and Alvarez exchanged surprised glances at this statement, arching their eyebrows as if they thought Duprey were a bit crazy.

Duprey ignored their expressions and continued, "Think of Guantanamo in Cuba, or Hong Kong before the British gave it up. There are many examples around the world of a country carving out a small area within its borders to be owned and governed as a separate state by someone else, with separate laws and government. Here it is necessary to do the same to avoid the old-fashioned and restrictive reach of Mexican law. Although claiming to welcome foreign investment, Mexico really does not. It places huge restrictions on the ability of foreigners to fully own coastal lands. It changes its fees and taxes on a whim. With all due respect, gentlemen, Mexico remains a third-rate, third-world country because it is one. Our investors are not going to invest millions of dollars in such a country. Nor will wealthy retirees put their life savings at risk there. The only way this project can proceed is if we own and control and actually rule this island as a separate state."

Almost as if on cue, the three investors murmured their assent and agreement to this position. "That is what we must have," added Rahman. "Independence and sovereignty."

Alvarez spoke first. "Since I have the political connections, maybe I should respond first to this surprising announcement. Let me understand. You say you want Mexico to cede sovereignty over this island to your group. You want to be your own little nation, free from all Mexican laws and control. You actually want to be exactly what Guantanamo is in Cuba."

"Correct," responded Duprey crisply.

"With all due respect to you and your group, Mr. Duprey, you're crazy. Mexico might be a third-rate and a third-world country in your view, but it does have some national pride. It is not going to simply hand over some of its territory. If we had known of this requirement, we would have tried to dissuade you from such an outlandish position from day one. We have just about concluded our efforts, and we have created substantial support for the project. We have almost everyone on board: the government, the local people, the turtle lovers. This will kill the project."

"I think not," responded Duprey calmly. "You haven't really had a chance to read the materials I just gave you. They are absolute dynamite. They show almost conclusively that Mexico does not own the northern half of the Baja Peninsula. It has been acting as sovereign over that area for over a century, but the original grant was defective. The area remains in private ownership. We have traced the descendants of the original private owners, and we have deeds from all of them. Just as one cannot obtain title by adverse possession against a government, a government cannot do so against a private citizen. The passage of time has not turned Mexico's control over the area into ownership.

"So, as I said, our clients today own Baja Norte. We are prepared to give almost all of it back to Mexico, minus one small island. And we will pay handsomely for the honor. It is for you, gentlemen, to figure out how to accomplish this task. You will see in the papers that our position is supported by opinions from scholars and attorneys of impeccable reputations. I apologize for not disclosing this position to you at the outset, but it would have been a waste of time to do so if your initial efforts had met resistance in Mexico. Your reaction today also shows that disclosure to you would have created a huge roadblock in your minds.

Duprey continued. "This is really a minor detail if presented properly. I think the Mexican authorities will be much more concerned about losing the tens of thousands of square miles of Baja Norte than a six-hundred-square-mile island. There doesn't have to be emphasis on the issue of sovereignty. We don't require any publicity on the subject. We will agree to whatever protective covenants are necessary to ensure that we do not infringe on the rights of Mexico in nearby lands and waters. We simply want the

rights of any sovereign nation, to be free of outside interference, and to be able to protect ourselves from any such
interference. It's really just a detail of the title transfer."

"And have you thought of what you might call your
new nation?" asked Cox, with a trace of sarcasm in his
voice.

The Iraqi spoke: "Yes. We will call it Parsa." When the
others looked perplexed, he added quickly, "It was the name
of ancient Persia, when the Persian Empire was the envy
of all and known for its arts, its educated people, and its
strength. We mean to recreate a bit of Persia in the West."

The meeting suspended for a time so that Alvarez and
Cox could review the paperwork in detail. Lunch was
brought in as they went over the documents in private.
After about an hour and a half, Cox closed the folder and
looked at his partner. "They might have something here,"
he said.

Alvarez nodded. "They might. But I'm starting to feel a
little bit used. I don't like to be spoon-fed the details of an
assignment this way. Let's just make sure the spoon is full
this time – full of money, for us. I'm not going to hand over
a country without being paid for a country."

When the meeting resumed, the Mexican lawyers said
it might be possible to obtain the required sovereignty. Alvarez spoke first: "This is a very complex situation. His-
torically and factually, what you say in these papers might
be true. But I have to deal with the realities of the current
situation. Mexicans are simply not going to believe all of
this. They're going to think you're trying to steamroll them
into giving up part of their country. They'll fight this proposal."

"That might all be so, Mr. Alvarez," said Duprey. "That's why you have to present it so the pressure is coming from others. If we publicize these facts about the missing deed, there will be a crisis in Baja Norte about who owns what. We don't have to prove we're right. The news alone will create a chill on real estate titles. Look at all the development underway today in Tijuana. That work will come to a grinding halt. Blame it on Van Huessen, or William Walker, but not on us. We think we're actually offering a good solution to a bad problem."

Alvarez and Cox glanced at each other, and then Alvarez spread his hands, saying, "My partner might have something to add."

All heads turned to Cox.

"We will do our best. If anyone can pull it off, it's my partner, Señor Alvarez. He's too modest to say so himself. But, if we are successful, we would expect a bonus fee. We suggest five percent of the purchase price."

"As you say in America," added Alvarez, "a sort of contingent fee."

Duprey glanced at the Iraqi and received a small affirmative nod from him. "That's acceptable," Duprey replied, "if you can close the deal within sixty days. My clients tell me that time is of the essence. Now let's go to dinner. I'll give you a taste of old Colorado at the Buckhorn Exchange. It's the oldest restaurant in Denver, a bit of the Old West. My partner Wendy Overstreet will join us. She's more into divorces than international deals, but I think you'll enjoy her company."

CHAPTER 17

SEPTEMBER

IRAN AND MEXICO

Ishmael Makad was in a quandary. Stationed at the Natanz nuclear enhancement facility in Iran, he was reading his new orders to redeploy to the area of Jask, on Iran's southern coast. He had been sending encrypted messages to Israel for ten years by wireless internet at Natanz. He knew there would be no wireless capabilities in Jask. He wasn't sure whether his coding technique of writing messages in a reverse mirror image would survive close examination if transmitted through a wired modem.

He hunched over his work station, glancing over his shoulder to make sure no one else was in the area. He also propped his small mirror on his cubicle wall so he could see anyone approaching. He knew he had little choice but to continue if he was to fulfill his blood oath to his dead parents . . . and prevent a world catastrophe. He used the mirror to compose his current communiqué. The name *Jask* became *ksaj*. He wrote *waterproofing* as *gnifoorpretaw*.

He still remembered his parents, and how they had been dragged from their home in Tabas after the aborted American hostage rescue mission in 1980. He was sure they had done nothing wrong. They had been branded traitors simply because they were teachers. He never saw them again, and later in life, when he was approached by an agent, he decided to work against the regime of their killers. He was the Israeli deep cover agent.

Makad knew his computer-programming skills were what made him important to the government. He had advanced steadily, and had eventually been assigned to computer programming at the Natanz nuclear facility. To attempt to protect his wife and children, he had settled his family as far outside of Natanz as possible, telling his wife that he wanted to get closer to the desert experiences of his youth. Now, pressing his lips together and grimacing, he hoped their home was far enough from the facility to avoid the likely epicenter of a retaliatory attack.

Apart from the new location of Jask, which he was disclosing in his message, he was sending other information. He wasn't sure whether it was important. He had noticed that much of the large machinery and components of the nuclear device were being boxed and packaged for shipment. That was not surprising. But he thought the packaging unusual. The equipment was being wrapped in large black rubber tarps, which looked like the thick rubber material used for roofing. The seams were being sealed carefully with a sealant. It looked like the wrapping was to be waterproof. He knew the new facility in Jask involved an overland trip, and there was very little rain in the Iranian desert, so why were they waterproofing the equipment? Ishmael could not figure it out. He sent the information along, leaving it to others to determine its importance.

• • •

At the same time, in Mexico, one of the Alvarez & Cox associates was reporting to the two partners what he considered to be a brilliant idea on the sovereignty issue. It had to do with the Panama Canal Treaty.

"In 1903," he said, "there was great opposition in Latin America to ceding sovereignty over the canal zone to America. So the negotiators created a new concept, simply made it up out of whole cloth. It was called 'quasi sovereignty.' The language of the Panama Canal Treaty did not transfer the zone to America completely. America was ceded, in perpetuity, such power 'as if it were' the sovereign over the canal. The new country of Panama saved some face, and President Roosevelt got what he wanted. It's terrific precedent. And in Latin America!"

Alvarez nodded thoughtfully. "Very good . . . very good idea. We might even go one better. Maybe we don't really need perpetual rights. I'll talk to our client."

Alvarez and Cox had prepared a written brief for the Mexican government, focusing on the Baja title issue. The Mexicans were astounded at the suggestion that Baja Norte might not be owned by Mexico. They conducted their own research in the archives at Mexico City. It was discovered that the unusual footnote 7 that Professor Abbey had found only in the English version of the treaty did, indeed, appear in some of the Spanish versions. In the final analysis, it was unclear whether footnote 7 was in the treaty or not. The advice to the Mexican leaders from the Legal Ministry was to take the claim seriously. There was great value in clearing up the matter. Otherwise, if the claim was made public, there could be years of unsettling lawsuits and title claims which would wreak havoc with real estate transactions throughout the Baja.

There was one possible loophole to Duprey's presentation which did receive attention.

"Mr. President, the treaty provision requires actual cultivation and cattle or sheep grazing for twenty years. There's no evidence that the Van Huessen family fulfilled that requirement prior to the treaty being signed in 1848."

"What is the evidence?" asked President Chavez.

"Well, we're not sure. The Van Huessens were in the Baja since the early 1800s. They certainly grazed some livestock, but not throughout the entire territory. The treaty language only exempts 'tracts' on which grazing and cultivation took place."

"And what is the accepted definition of 'tract'?" Chavez pressed his legal minister.

"Once again, far from established. A tract can be a piece of real estate of almost any size, but the term is seldom used for an entire territory."

"What again is the precise language of the note in the treaty?"

The advisor read: "'Nothing herein shall have any effect whatsoever upon private property rights to tracts within the territory which have been perfected by actual cultivation and livestock grazing for a period of at least twenty contiguous years.'"

One of the president's assistants interjected, "We must remember, most of the ranches in the early 1800s were in the same areas of Baja Norte which today have villages and small towns. We're not talking about waste desert areas. It's where people today live and work."

After a few moments of silence, the president spoke. "Gentlemen, we are beating a dead horse. First, there is no real opposition to developing this island. Other than Senator Ortiz from the Cabos area, everyone's aboard. And since his unfortunate death last week, even his opposition will now disappear. His replacement is supportive. It's a tremendous economic opportunity for the region and for the country. I myself have no problem with the so-called sovereignty request. It's not really sovereignty, anyway. As we've been told, it's *quasi* sovereignty. The development team appears to be responsible and well financed. It even includes our President Gonzalez. They have agreed to covenants which protect our surrounding resources. They will pay a handsome price. And none of you gives me any confidence that their title claim is unsound. I see no possible downside, and it solves these title issues. Does anyone see any problem?"

No one spoke. All shrugged in apparent agreement.

• • •

General Mussahrah and the Ayatollah scheduled a private luncheon with President Talabani after they received the report from Mexico.

"Tariq, we wish to bring you current on our nuclear program," spoke the Ayatollah. "As I think you know, you are about to play an important role. It is time for you to know everything."

President Talabani leaned forward and listened intently as the Ayatollah continued. "Our agents in Mexico are close to concluding the purchase of an island from Mexico. It lies just south of the American border and will give us the location in the West which we need for our missile. The purchase terms are quite advantageous.

"We will purchase the island with what they call rights of quasi sovereignty. We will actually take a ninety-year lease, rather than a full purchase, and payments will be spread over those years."

Smiling and nodding, the general interjected, "Payment terms were a stroke of genius. We only need it for a short period, so we will pay very little."

"Yes," continued the Ayatollah. "Very little. The price is ten billion dollars, payable one hundred million each year for the term of the agreement."

President Talabani did some quick mental calculations, then raised a finger and asked in a soft voice, "But is that not short ten million dollars, my Excellency?"

The Ayatollah smiled. "Yes, Tariq. You are very quick. It is actually short one hundred million dollars. That is the payment to our agents – the lawyers. It comes out of the purchase price."

"And let's see them collect that," exclaimed Mussahrah.

"As Allah will provide," the Ayatollah added more diplomatically, before continuing. "Our new country will be called Parsa. It will be totally free and independent of Mexican law. We have given some meaningless assurances that we will not interfere with their surrounding waters or their country, but Parsa will be a sovereign and independent nation. The island used to be called Guardian Island. It will now become our guardian. But rather than a guardian angel for the Christians, we will make it our guardian warrior.

"By the end of the year, we should be ready. We are planning for you to give a speech at that time. We want to talk about your speech . . ."

CHAPTER 18

SEPTEMBER
WASHINGTON, D.C.

Colonel Longley was reading briefing papers in his den at ten o'clock in the evening when the call came in on his private line. He was used to being alone, although he often thought of his wife. She had left him three years earlier because of his many absences and her midlife decision to pursue a different, fuller relationship with a close woman friend. He hadn't contested the divorce. He knew the marriage was over.

"Hello. Longley here."

"Colonel Longley, this is Henre Morad."

"Oh, shit. Is this the call we talked about?"

"No, not exactly. Not the final call we discussed. Something short of that."

"I'm glad for that," said Longley with a sigh of relief as his heartbeat started to slow. For a moment, he had thought Armageddon was at hand.

"So what is it?" he asked.

"We have received some troubling information from our source. Enrichment equipment is definitely being shipped to a new secret location in Iran, and we think they have something else up their sleeve."

"What's that?" asked the colonel.

"We think they're planning to re-ship the equipment to yet another location. By sea."

"That's crazy! They don't need to ship by sea."

"I'm not talking about another shipment within Iran. As you say, no movement within Iran would require a ship. We think they're going to ship nuclear materials to another country."

"Where?"

"We don't know. Could be North Korea, or Afghanistan, or Somalia. Could be anywhere."

"We have to find out."

"Yes, we do. That's why I'm calling you. As I said at our last meeting, our resources are different from yours. We need to monitor the new facility and be prepared to track whatever ships they might use. Israel does not have those capabilities around the globe. You do."

"Okay, Henre. Tomorrow morning in my office, eight o'clock. I want to go over your information in more detail and assemble what we need for surveillance. I'll probably call an emergency meeting of the Iran Group. But let's you and I meet first. We'll do what's necessary."

"I'll see you then, Colonel."

Longley spent most of the night wrestling with this new information and trying to figure out where in the world Iran was going to send uranium enrichment materials. *What exactly are they sending? Cascade centrifuges? Fuel? Have they gone beyond that stage? Do they have a bomb?* All these thoughts raced through his head.

Colonel Longley was in his office at six o'clock in the morning to review the intelligence data which was coming in from Iran. He wanted to know exactly what information was available before seeing Morad. The data did reveal some patterns which supported the phone call. The main north-south highway running from Tehran in northern Iran to the southern coast had carried a higher volume of commercial truck traffic over the last ninety days than during the same period a year ago. Not a tremendous increase, but noticeable. There was also an increase in heat emissions from a mountainous area just north of the coastal village of Jask. The analysts had interpreted that increase as due to new petroleum drilling activities in the area. One analyst had noted, however, that this was not an area in which known petroleum reserves existed. All the data had come from the two satellites Longley had redeployed to the skies over Iran after his first meeting with Morad. He now ordered high-definition photographs of the area north of Jask, which would take twenty-four hours to obtain.

Henre Morad arrived at the Pentagon at eight o'clock sharp and was escorted into Longley's office. When he entered, he looked grim.

"Okay, Henre, what exactly do you have?" said the colonel, without bothering with a handshake or pleasantries.

"We have a message from our source with some information. It looks as if some of the enrichment equipment and materials, and also some of the scientific staff, have been relocated from Natanz to an area on the southern coast east of the Strait of Hormuz. There can be no reason for that move, other than an eventual sea voyage. The coastal area is largely undeveloped. By being east of the strait, the Iranians have direct access into the Indian Ocean without the close surveillance which occurs over any vessel going through the strait. We know that some of the equipment has been enclosed in waterproof packaging."

"Is the area near Jask, by any chance?" Longley asked softly.

"Yes, exactly. How did you know?"

Colonel Longley shuffled some papers on his desk as he responded, settling on one, which he held up in his left hand. "We have some suspicious data coming from that area. Until your warning, it didn't look all that important. But something is going on in the foothills north of Jask, and there's been an increase of truck traffic to the area. How much more information can we get from your source? It's important that we know exactly what is going to be shipped."

Morad shook his head with disappointment. "Unfortunately, we might receive nothing more. His report said that he will be out of contact for some time. We have no way to contact him. It's a one-way blind message route, set up that way for security."

Longley nodded. "Okay. If that's it, we'll have to deal with it. I've ordered enhanced photography of the Jask area, which I should have within a day. Forty years ago, we could detect missiles on the ground in Cuba. As you know, we are much better today. Our satellite photographs should tell us what's going on in Jask. I'll also have one of our electronic surveillance vessels repositioned from the Persian Gulf to the sea off of Jask. At the minimum, I want to know what vessels depart that port, what they're carrying, and where they're heading."

"I'm scheduling a full meeting of the Iran Group for tomorrow afternoon at three o'clock, by which time I'll have the photos. If you can develop anything else by then, I would appreciate it. Your information has been very helpful. The National Security Council meets next Monday. I'm going to put this on its agenda. It's time we let the big guys know what's going on."

The photography was delivered to Colonel Longley the following morning. It showed clearly that a large, warehouse-type structure had been constructed in the foothills north of Jask. By comparing it to historical pictures of the same area, it was clear that the building had gone up in the last six months. It might be related to drilling activities, but Longley saw no drilling rigs. *No one would put a rig inside a building,* he thought as he looked at the pictures. He also saw an unpaved road leading to the building. No signs on the building revealed what was inside. It was, however, well guarded by guard posts and sentries.

All of this information was discussed in the Iran Group meeting later that afternoon, which was attended by Morad.

Colonel Longley opened the meeting: "Sorry to call you together on an emergency basis, but we have new information. Mr. Morad has just been able to update his last information about another nuclear facility in Iran. In addition to staff being redeployed to another site in the country, it now looks like equipment from Natanz is being prepared for shipment overseas."

"To where?" asked General Boyer of the Joint Chiefs.

"We think first to Jask on the southern coast, and then by ship to some final destination, but we have no information about the final destination."

"I'll wager it's North Korea," said Director Johnson of the CIA with contempt in his voice. "They've been working together for years. Kim Jong-il is so incompetent that he can't build an operational nuclear weapon on his own, no matter what he says. He certainly can't deliver one over any distance. My god, he can't even feed his own people. He's been trying to buy, beg, or steal nuclear capability for years. We almost gave it to him at his supposed new power plant. This is probably a gift from Iran in return for his begging."

Everyone in the room started talking at once about the ramifications of this new information. Finally, Colonel Longley raised his hands, signaling for silence.

"Unless any of you have more than guesses," he said, "we have to stay with what we know. I'm going to bring this to the Security Council at its next meeting. Let me know anything new you come up with before then."

The Security Council meeting occurred a week later. He did not think his presentation went well. He was peppered with questions which he couldn't answer.

"How reliable is the Israeli source, Colonel?"

"I don't know."

"Do we know whether they have successfully enriched any uranium?"

"We don't know for sure."

"Neither Iran nor North Korea has any operable long-range delivery vehicle, do they?"

"Probably not, but we're not sure."

Most of the questions were posed by Secretary of State Patricia Clark-Brenner. Longley knew a bit about her. She had been appointed to the position after coming up through the ranks at the State Department over a twenty-year diplomatic career. She had impeccable academic credentials as a graduate of Stanford and then a Rhodes Scholar. Most of her appointments at the State Department had been in Africa, where she was viewed as having served with distinction. But, Longley knew, none of the conflicts in Africa, from Sierra Leone to Ethiopia to the Congo, had ever been solved on her watch. Apparently, Ms. Clark-Brenner had handled all of her assignments with diplomatic finesse, and her reports were superb, but in the final analysis, he viewed her as a highly-credentialed bureaucratic cipher.

His answers were not purposely evasive, but he sounded like he was fumbling. The president and her advisors stated that they were not willing to make the jump from what was known to what Longley and the Israelis suspected. The president was in the third year of her term. Natalie Menton was not about to start an international incident without much stronger proof.

Longley also knew the president's background. She was not only a first-term president; this was her first elected position. President Menton had been a successful actress in action films in her younger years, but rumor had it that the character roles offered to her as she reached middle age had not kept her interest. She then lost her husband to illness and never remarried. She had entered government in various appointed positions, first in California and then at the national level. The favored candidate before the last election had stepped down just before the convention when it was disclosed that he was infected with the AIDS virus. He preferred not to have to disclose the source of his illness. She was drafted as a last-minute compromise candidate, with the hope that her gender would help avoid an election disaster. She turned out to be an able campaigner, and she won the necessary electoral college votes by the narrowest of margins. The colonel had not yet formed much of an opinion about her, viewing her as a bit of an unknown.

The secretary of state noted that all the experts said Iran was years away from operational nuclear weaponry. Trans-shipment of enrichment machinery by sea was not a violation of any international accord or treaty. She closed, saying derisively, "If it's going to North Korea, the North Koreans probably won't even know how to get it off the boat." Most in the room chuckled, viewing the North Koreans with distain and not considering them to be a worthy enemy.

The members of the group treated Longley with respect and stated their appreciation for the advice, but the NSC said they were not going to spend much of their time on this matter. They were still focusing their attention on terrorism at home and attempted terrorist incursions into the United States. Airports were now relatively secure. Although railroads overseas had become the newest terrorist target of choice, American rail lines had escaped attack. Inbound freighters and their shipping containers were still considered vulnerable. The main concern of the council was the entry of individual terrorists to the United States from Mexico and Canada, because the borders were still porous. The relative calm since September 11, 2001, was not coincidental. Massive deterrent efforts had stymied terrorism in the American homeland. It had instead continued overseas. The consensus of the council was that, although what was happening on the shores of the Indian Ocean was important, it was not nearly as important as what was going on in this hemisphere. Longley thought that the president and her advisors were circling the wagons to defend only at home.

The colonel decided, however, that he was not going to put the matter aside. He was a marine by training, which made him a persistent type. After the meeting, he ordered an increase in surveillance over the southern Iranian coast near Jask, and he put a tracking directive into place for any ship over two hundred feet which departed one of the three ports in the area heading east. No actual interception on the high seas was to be attempted, but he decided he would at least damn well know when and if the suspected ship sailed for North Korea. The politicians and bureaucrats might be sanguine in their disdain for the North Koreans. He, however, dealt with lives on the ground after the politicians screwed up. He would not be asleep at the switch, and he would not underestimate an enemy rogue country. He knew that, for the moment, it was all he could do.

CHAPTER 19

NOVEMBER 1
ALBUQUERQUE

The fall semester was in full swing, and Professor Abbey was in his office preparing for his next lecture on Mexican border security when the call came in. The new Overton Faculty and Administration building was not yet completed, but he was pleased to have been told that he was slated for a larger office in the new building. He had already started to choose his new furniture. The office wouldn't be grand, but bigger and better furnished than his previous cubbyhole in the library. He was even getting a second window. Another associate professor had been added to his department. Abbey was happy with his teaching and research schedule and his many field trips to the deserts and mountains. Life was good.

He answered the phone after the second ring. "Hello, this is Professor Abbey."

A sobbing voice addressed him, "Professor Abbey, this is Maria Plarez from Bahia de los Angeles. I said I never wanted to talk to you . . . and I truly don't want to. But I don't know what to do. Something is terribly wrong. Something is going on down here, and I don't know who else to talk to . . ."

"Please calm down, Maria. Of course I'll talk to you. If I can help, I will. But what is the problem?"

"Everything's changing . . . changing so much. And all since you were here. My island preserve is gone. My turtles

are being killed. Hundreds of strange men are on the island. I'm told to stay out of it, and that everything is going
to be great . . . *mucho bueno*, they say."

"I don't understand. What island? What men? Slow
down and please explain."

"Our Guardian Island is no more – no longer a national
park, and no longer a turtle preserve. All my experiments
on the island have been destroyed. It is to become some big
American retirement community, they say. But they are not
Americans on the island. There are many foreigners there,
and they carry guns and put up fences. I went last night
to see for myself. Huge floodlights light up a construction
area on the south end of the island. I went onto the island
north of the activities, where my turtles used to lay their
eggs. I tried to stay hidden, but they saw me and shot at
me. I thought they would kill me! I just managed to get off
the island in my boat." She was crying again.

Abbey thought, *An American retirement community on
Guardian Island? Shooting at Maria? Could it be?*

"Have you talked to Constable Martinez?" he asked,
remembering his old nemesis, and also how much trouble
Martinez had given him.

"No. He is no longer here. He was just replaced by
a more senior federalist officer. A new police station is
being built. We were told that things would be much better and that Guardian Island was no longer to be home to
the turtles. It was to be developed. The turtles would nest
elsewhere. But all of my questions and inquiries have been
rebuffed. I am told this was all done at the highest levels in
Mexico City, and that I should stay out of it.

"I'm calling you because this all started with you, Professor. I know you had something to do with it. Maybe you

don't know how bad things have become. Maybe you can
help."

Hearing her words, but not really listening to them,
Abbey continued his questions. "What about your uncle?
Can he help?"

"No. He is gone. He died soon after I talked to you the
last time. I inherited his ranch and now live on it. He cannot
help. Can you help, Professor Abbey? Can you figure out
what is going on? As I said, it all happened since your visit.
Although I yelled at you and cursed you and blamed you for
the problems, you seemed to be a caring man when we met.
No one else cares. Maybe if you were to come back and see
what is going on, you would have some ideas. Otherwise,
I will just stay in the mountains and probably go crazy like
my uncle. Everything I worked for here is ruined."

"Me, come back?" Abbey remembered Duprey's last
instruction to stay out of it. "I don't know what I could
possibly do. I'm an American college professor who means
nothing down there. Last time, I even got arrested."

"Yes, but I know you have some importance. I talked
to Corporal Martinez after you disappeared. He said you
had important friends at high levels who convinced him
that he should leave you alone. I heard and saw the plane
that night. Only someone important does things like that.
I think in some way you caused these problems. Maybe
you didn't mean to, but I need your help to at least understand and maybe undo what you have done. I need you
here." She sobbed.

Abbey knew he had to do something, but what? Going
back to the Baja was not high on his priority list right now.
Besides, there was Duprey to think about. His last instructions had been quite clear: Stay out of it. Maybe he had

caused some of these problems. Those and other thoughts ran through his mind as he tried to figure out what he could do.

"Please, I need your help," Maria continued. "Remember, I helped you when you were in trouble here."

It had been Maria who had placed the phone call which led to his escape. He owed her something.

"I'll do what I can," he finally responded. "But first I have to figure out what's going on. Give me a couple of days to make some calls and get back to you. Should I call you at the ranch?"

"I have nowhere else to go," Maria said plaintively. "I'll be here."

After hanging up, Abbey sat thinking for a while. There was no way he was going to call Duprey. That was a non-starter. The claw-back threat of the money had been made. The more he thought about it, however, the less he thought the funds would ever go back. He was not violating any confidences if he simply looked into matters and spoke again with Maria. He was not about to disclose what he had done or what he might know about the new island resort. Actually, he knew very little. The more he found out, however, the less he liked. And then there was the free home that had been promised. He certainly had the right to look into his future retirement community.

He did decide that his name should probably not be involved in any inquiries. Duprey seemed to have a far-reaching web of contacts. From what Maria had said about the plane, his previous short visit to the Baja had not gone unnoticed, and his name was known in the area, at least to some degree. He turned again to his assistant Marge to make some preliminary inquiries. He had not told her much about his sudden return. As far as she knew, the Baja research had concluded.

He found Marge behind her desk. "Marge, I need some help on that old Baja project."

She raised her eyebrows. "Sure. I thought it was finished."

"It is, more or less. But there's a new resort being built near the village I visited, Bahia de los Angeles. I need to get some information about it, but I really don't want my name involved. The people I interviewed on my first visit might think I'm involved in the project, and I'm not. Could you make some calls for me?"

"Certainly. What's the name of the resort?"

He paused. "Actually, I don't know the name. But it's a small place. Can't be more than one resort being built there. And it's on an island . . . Guardian Island, right off the coast."

She shrugged. "I'll make some calls. Maybe I can get some marketing materials."

CHAPTER 20

NOVEMBER 2

ALBUQUERQUE

A day after asking Marge to look into the new resort, Abbey heard back from her.

"I haven't been able to find out much about the island resort," she said, "but it's definitely being built. The Mexican Tourist Bureau wasn't very helpful. They say there should be marketing materials soon, but until then, they know very little. The local people in Bahia de los Angeles know even less. So I called an old friend in San Felipe, north on the gulf coast. She says there's a lot of buzz and speculation about a foreign group building a huge new retirement community for the American baby boomers. That's about all I could find out."

"Well, that gives me some information. What's it called?"

"Baja Properties, is what I was told."

Abbey decided that he wouldn't learn much more without making another visit. He was curious, however, how an island which was a Mexican national park was now being developed. The maps all designated it as a park, and he had been told by Maria that it was some type of turtle preserve to protect the breeding grounds of the green and leatherback sea turtles. He called an old friend at the Mexican Department of Natural Resources to inquire.

"Miguel, this is Bill Abbey from the University of New Mexico."

"Professor, great to hear from you. Are you coming down on another of your research trips?"

"No, not right away. Had a couple of quick questions, and I thought you might be the best person to answer them. It concerns the Isle Angel de la Guardia off the Baja's northern gulf coast. Do you know that area?"

"I know it well. A lot's going on there. Until recently, the island was a national park. Some high-powered development group has orchestrated a complicated deal to permit the island to be developed. Don't know all the details. Basically, they convinced the government to remove the park designation and create new parks on other nearby islands. Then they paid quite a bit of money to actually buy the island. Billions, I understand. It's now some type of special Free Trade Zone, exempt from a number of the regular laws in Mexico. Happened on a very fast track."

"Who's the developer?" asked Abbey, assuming it was Duprey's client.

"Not sure. Some sort of international group, I think."

That surprised Abbey a bit, since he had expected to hear the name of some rich university graduate.

"Was there any opposition?" he asked.

"Not much. It went through so quickly that many of us weren't even aware of what was going on. It was years ago that it was made a national park, and I don't think many people cared one way or the other. Wasn't used much except by your American eco-tourist friends," he added with a laugh. "Most Mexicans don't give too much attention to the Baja."

"Well, I've heard that it's going to be a great retirement community and that I should look into it," said Abbey, trying to come up with some reason for the call.

"You're too young, professor. Give yourself a few more years. I think they've started some work on the infrastructure, but I'm sure it will take many years to build it out."

Abbey went on to talk about other matters they had worked on in the past, including trips he had made to the Mayan ruins on the east coast of Mexico, and his photography of Maya and Inca wall drawings. He had learned what he needed to know. After a few more moments, he said he would see Miguel on his next trip to Mexico City and ended the call.

He now realized that the island development had to be the culmination of his earlier investigation. He remembered Duprey telling him that others were working on the project. There certainly had been, and they had apparently been successful. But why was Maria so upset? And what of her talk about foreigners with guns shooting at her? He had to call her back. He had to try to help. But what could he do?

He picked up the phone. "Maria, this is Professor Bill Abbey."

"Oh, Professor, thank you so much for calling back. I knew you would help."

"I'm not sure what I can do. I've checked, and there is development taking place on the island. But it appears to be with full government approval. The island is going to become a large retirement community, evidently a very nice one. There's nothing evil or sinister about that."

"Professor, I went there to recover my turtle nesting cages and food trays and some other personal items after I heard what was happening. I saw huge fences with barbed wire and men patrolling with machine guns. Signs on the fences said trespassers would be shot on sight. I admit I ignored the signs and tried to recover my things. Suddenly, they were shooting at me. Not shotgun blasts in the air like my uncle. Many bullets hit all around me. No one on the mainland knows anything or will do anything. I need to recover my equipment to put it in new locations on other islands that they say are available. And I need to know what these men are doing on my island."

"How'd you get on the island?" asked Abbey.

"My usual way. Just took my boat directly across from our harbor and beached it in my normal spot."

"Is there some type of marina or dock area?"

"There is now. They're building a big marina on the southern tip of the island which looks like it will take large ships. But I just went to my normal beach north of the construction."

"Well, maybe you just surprised someone by looking like you were trying to sneak onto the island. Maybe you should go in through the marina area, announce yourself, and explain why you're there. What time of day was it?"

"It was dusk."

"See, you probably looked suspicious."

"I will not go back to that island alone. I'm afraid. I just can't do it. And no one else will go with me. They just say to stay off the island."

"So are you asking me to go with you?" said Abbey with a nervous laugh.

"I don't see what else to do."

He knew he had to do it. In some way, he had caused this situation. It couldn't be as bad as she thought. "Okay." he said. "Here's what I can do. I'll be in Tijuana on the border next week working on a paper on border security. I'd just as soon not take my car into Mexico again. As you know, my last departure was a bit irregular. If you'll drive to the border and pick me up, I'll drive down with you. We'll make a normal daylight visit to the island and explain what we need. I don't see why there should be a problem."

She gasped with relief. "You'll do that? For me?"

"Yes, I'll do it for you. And, in a way, for me, too. I have to find out what's going on to satisfy my own curiosity. If something's wrong, as you say, I need to do something. I'll call as soon as I can make some arrangements to leave."

After he hung up, he sat thinking for a few moments. His Duprey assignment was developing more complications.

CHAPTER 21

NOVEMBER 9

TIJUANA

As he had told Maria, Professor Abbey was working on his next research project: the Mexican exodus to the United States. His department had received a grant from the U.S. Immigration Service to conduct interviews of illegal immigrants to determine the key factors which had motivated their crossing the border. He and his students had already found and interviewed dozens of illegals. Finding them was not difficult. The interviews were always conducted with an iron-clad promise of anonymity. The results of the interviews were not surprising. Economic opportunity – jobs – and joining family members were the two reasons repeatedly stated for crossing the border. The interviewers found no terrorists.

Abbey had tabulated the results of the interviews and decided that he should also talk to American and Mexican border agents. So his trip to Tijuana was not just based upon his promise to Maria. Now, however, he planned for a longer stay, and it looked as if he would be going back to the village of Bahia de los Angeles. *At least Corporal Martinez will not be there this time*, he thought gratefully as he packed for the trip.

This time, he decided to take a short commuter flight from Albuquerque to San Diego, and then a bus to the border. He took his passport and packed a duffle with clothes for a week. As usual, he brought his camera equipment. He gave Marge the Van Huessen phone number.

He set out with some trepidation. Everything went smoothly until he presented his passport to the Mexican agent at the border. The agent punched the identity into his computer while Abbey stood before him.

"Señor Abbey, you have visited our country before."

"Oh yes," Abbey replied casually. "A number of times."

"But señor, you never left Mexico after your last trip. That was over six months ago. And now you wish to reenter when you never left?"

"Of course I left," Abbey snapped. "I'm here, aren't I?

"The question, señor, is how did you get here? Please wait in our holding room while I call my supervisor," he said, pointing to a small room with a glass panel facing the clearance area.

Abbey knew the problem. His passport showed him entering the country on his last fateful visit, but there was no departure stamp. His flight out by air had not gone through any Mexican security. He started thinking hard about what explanation he could give to the supervisor. He couldn't think of anything which wouldn't dig a deeper hole.

"Ah, what do we have here?" said the mustached agent as he walked into the room after having talked briefly with the man at the clearance post. He was carrying Abbey's passport and peering down at it.

"Entry on a thirty-day visitor visa, and with an automobile. But no record of ever leaving our great country. And an interesting code 3 on your passport."

"What do you mean, code 3?" asked Abbey.

"I will ask the questions, señor. Why is there no departure stamp on your passport? And where is the car?"

"I have no idea," replied Abbey, having decided that he would simply play dumb. "I don't do your paperwork. Obviously, I left Mexico. I'm a professor at the University of New Mexico in Albuquerque. I've been in Mexico a number of times over the years. My car is back home in my garage. If my papers weren't stamped properly, that's not my fault. And I don't understand your statement about some code on my passport. It's a normal and proper passport."

"You see this 03 here, don't you, señor?" said the official, placing the booklet in front of Abbey opened to the first page. He pointed to the bottom left of the page, where the numbers *03* appeared in small type.

"Yes, I see it. So what?"

"That, señor, labels you a money-launderer. Someone in America thinks you traffic in bad money."

Abbey was dumbfounded. "That's ridiculous! I've never heard of such a thing."

"But we have, señor. And taking a car into our country, and then not bringing it back, shows some truth to the code. Can you explain any of this?"

"No, I can't. None of it makes sense. I think I should talk to my embassy."

"You will have plenty of time to do that, señor Abbey, because you are not entering Mexico." With that, he took a rubber stamp from the table, pressed it on an ink pad, and slammed it on the open page of the passport. Abbey could read the imprint upside down: *REJECTED FOR ENTRY INTO MEXICO.*

"You will now leave and go back to your American side. You, señor, are not welcome in Mexico."

Abbey walked back the short distance with his bag over his shoulder. Once again, he found himself in Mexico and in a difficult situation. Or, almost in Mexico. He had to contact Maria. She was waiting for him in a small hotel just over the border. He found a pay phone and placed the call. Luckily, the receptionist at the Borderline Hotel was helpful, found Maria in the lobby, and put her on the phone.

"Hello, Professor Abbey?" she answered with a cautious tone to her voice.

"Yes, Maria. This is Professor Abbey. I've run into a problem. They claim my papers are not in order. They won't let me cross into Mexico. I'm at the border station. I'm not quite sure what to do."

"What do they say is wrong?" she asked.

"I guess I didn't get the proper exit stamps when I left so hurriedly last time. I assume I can get things straightened out, but it's probably going to take some time. We might have to reschedule this visit. I'm sorry, but I don't think I can do much about it."

After pausing for a moment, Maria said, "There might be another way."

"What do you mean?"

"I have full Mexican citizenship papers. I can cross and re-cross the border pretty much at will. I just drive across in my car. Sometimes they stop me briefly and ask where I'm going. A quick shopping trip is always a sufficient answer. They seldom even look at my papers entering the United States. Coming back is even easier. My papers show me to be a married woman. So today I drive over and pick you up, and you come back as my husband. They'll just wave me through. I don't know what the problems are with your papers, but believe me, Mexico seldom cares about Mexicans driving back into Mexico from the United States. Let's do it!" she said excitedly.

Abbey was not quite as excited. Having snuck out of Mexico once, he wasn't sure he now wanted to sneak back in. From his phone booth, he could see the border crossing. Maria was correct that the cars with Mexican plates, driven by Mexicans, were simply being waved through. He did have to get this trip behind him.

"Maria, why don't you drive across the border, and we'll meet and talk about it. No promises. But we should at least sit down and talk, since we're so close. I'll wait at the coffee shop at the Gringo Café, which is just over the border on Route 1, on the right side driving north. How long will it take you?"

"Only five or ten minutes," Maria answered with excitement in her voice. "Oh, Professor, thank you so much. You are the only one who is willing to help me. I'll be right there."

When she arrived, he saw that she was even more attractive than he remembered. Dark hair and brown eyes, with some Anglo blood mixed with Mexican, gave her a slightly lighter complexion and a more angular face than he would expect in a Mexican. She was about five and a half feet tall and slender. And she was persuasive. They sat at a small table and ordered coffee. They talked for a while before she grasped his hands in hers and turned serious.

"Professor, it will only take two days, one down and one back. I'm sure they will let you enter the island. You're an American professor, while I'm a simple Mexican. You can talk better than I. You can explain how we won't interfere with their work. Maybe they'll even tell you what they're doing and why all the secrecy."

He saw the plaintive look in her dark eyes. Taking a deep breath, he finally said, "Okay, I'll go."

Maria jumped up, ran to his side of the table, and hugged him, saying, almost in tears, "Thank you so much. Thank you." They headed for her vehicle, which was a four-year-old Ford F-150 pickup. He got into the passenger side, and they drove across the border as husband and wife. Maria was right; they attracted no attention whatsoever. They were waved through, and they were soon traveling south on Mexico's Route 1.

Within half an hour, they were again talking of his Mexican studies and her turtles. The conversation then moved to their respective backgrounds. Maria explained that she was truly alone. Her parents had died years ago, leaving her an only child, her mother from illness and her father in a car accident. She had been raised by her uncle. A small life insurance policy had enabled her to attend the university on the mainland, but she had returned to her bay and married a childhood friend.

"My husband Jaime and I had explored and fished all over as children," she explained. "I guess I was a bit of a tomboy, as you Americans put it. I had never thought of him in a romantic way. But after I returned, we got together again. Marriage seemed to be the expected thing. We had a good marriage, but not long enough. No children," she added, shrugging her shoulders. "It just didn't happen."

Abbey told her about his parents, who still lived in northern California. He, too, was an only child. He explained that he had been particularly close to his mother since his father had been away often.

"Guess I've been too busy for marriage," he added. "In addition to my teaching, I spend a lot of time taking pictures of old Indian wall drawings."

She then told him excitedly that she knew of some wall drawings in a special place high in the mountains behind her uncle's ranch.

"It's a cave Jaime and I discovered when we were young. I think it might even be on my uncle's land. I don't think anyone else knows of it, and it has some scratching on its walls. Some we put there, but some looked very old. Maybe I can show it to you."

"That'd be great. I'd love to see it. Let's visit the island first. Then I should have some time. I brought my camera." *I like this woman,* he thought.

By then, it was getting late in the afternoon. Maria said she knew of a small inn just east of Rosario which would be a good place to stop for the night. They took separate rooms. After a light dinner, they sat outside on the front porch for a while and talked further. Abbey explained what he was doing at the university. Currently, he was trying to understand why so many Mexicans were fleeing to the United States, and what could be done to stem the tide. Maria explained that many of her friends had gone north. As for her, she had been happy in Mexico, until recently.

"What do you think is really going on at the island?" Maria asked as their evening drew to a close.

"I think it's just as I said. A new development. A gated retirement community, and they want to keep the locals out. I can't believe they were shooting to really hit you. I think they were trying to scare you, get the word out to stay away, like when your uncle warned me off. But, Maria, what is it that's really bothering you so much? It has to be more than turtle cages."

She gazed off into the dark night. "Not really much more. Some personal things, but, mostly, I'm just mad. My uncle told Jaime and me that the Van Huessens once owned the island, many years ago. He actually told us that our family once owned a lot of land in the Baja. When I went that night, I went to get my things, but I also took a vase with Jaime's picture in it and some flowers. I was going to leave it as a sort of remembrance. As I ran for the boat, it dropped and broke. I can't just leave it there, broken in the sand."

He could see she was crying. After a few moments of awkward silence, he said good night.

In the morning, Maria stopped at what she said would be the last gas station before they turned south off of Route 1 onto Route 12. She filled her tank and also filled four six-gallon gas containers from the back of the pickup.

"For the generator," she explained, when Abbey asked about the extra gas.

After pulling out from the gas station, Abbey decided that they had to turn their talk to the matter at hand. He explained that, on his first visit, he had been doing exactly what he had said – looking for the Van Huessen family line. He had been hired to do the research without knowing exactly why, but, yes, there had been talk of an eventual resort and retirement complex. He told Maria that he had learned little more about the project once he reported that he had found her uncle. If, as she had said, someone stole the papers from her uncle, he knew nothing about that. He was very upset to hear that it had happened. He had had no involvement with the matter since his departure from the village over a year ago.

"I believe you," she replied. "So now we will work together to find out what is happening."

He nodded his assent, realizing that Maria was pulling him deeper into these matters than he really wanted. He told her he didn't want another suspicious evening arrival at the island. Since they would not reach the village before afternoon, they decided to go to her uncle's ranch for the night and get an early start the next morning. As they approached the ranch, Abbey noted that Maria had taken down all the warning signs which had accosted him last time. There were no shotgun blasts. He hoped that would remain so for their visit to the island the next day.

The ranch was old, a fine example of a Southwestern ranch from the early nineteenth century. It was in a beautiful setting at the end of a small valley, with rolling hills extending in almost all directions. A small stream flowed down the middle of the valley toward the gulf. There were no utility poles, so Abbey assumed there was no electricity other than by the generator she had mentioned. As they entered, he was surprised at how much cooler it was inside because of the thick adobe walls. He saw a kitchen, a modest-sized dining area, and a large beamed sitting room. Maria directed him to a door leading to what had been her uncle's bedroom.

"Why don't you stay in my uncle's room?" she said. "I've never been comfortable there. I sleep in the guest room. I still feel like a guest here."

As he looked around his assigned room, he heard a generator begin to rumble behind the building. Soon, there was electricity and running water. It was still afternoon.

Maria left to go into town to pick up her dog, which she said she had left with a friend.

While she was gone, Abbey took himself on a brief tour. Sure enough, there was the library, where the trunk of documents had supposedly sat. He noticed a mobile phone which appeared to be one of the new satellite reception instruments. That explained the phone service. There was a small barn behind the house, but no evidence of any live-stock. In the barn were old tools, which he knew were for sheep shearing, and two empty horse stalls.

He was sitting on the front porch when Maria returned with her dog Lucky, a golden retriever which seemed glad to be home. After dinner, they took a walk into the foot-hills with Lucky. They agreed to be up early so they would reach the island by late morning. She said her boat was at the dock in the village. It had been Jamie's fishing boat.

CHAPTER 22

NOVEMBER 10–11

BAHIA DE LOS ANGELES

The prevailing westerly winds created a light chop as they headed out in her boat the next morning. It was a twenty-six-foot Mako with twin 225-horsepower outboards. It took about an hour to reach the southern tip of Guardian Island. Even knowing of Maria's previous problems on the island, Abbey didn't foresee any difficulties. It was a nice day, and he was cruising in an open boat with a beautiful woman. He was sure he could talk and reason with whomever was on the island.

As they approached, Abbey saw a dock structure jutting about fifty feet into the small harbor. It looked like it was still being built, and there were signs of construction activities on the island itself. A number of tents and small shed-like buildings were scattered around the beach near the dock. He pulled his camera out of the bag and began to take pictures.

They couldn't miss the signs. Large signs on buoys had been placed about 100 yards offshore at approximately half-mile intervals as far as they could see in both directions. As with the signs which had confronted him at the ranch on his last visit, they were in both Spanish and English. But these had been professionally lettered.

THESE ARE RESTRICTED WATERS
NO ONE IS PERMITTED ENTRY
VIOLATORS WILL BE SHOT!

Abbey had a feeling of déjà vu, as he remembered his first approach to the Van Huessen ranch. He suggested that Maria sound the small horn, which she did. He waved as they approached the dock under minimum headway. They could see that their boat was drawing some attention. A man in a uniform, who looked to be carrying a rifle, walked to the end of the dock. He held a megaphone to his mouth. "You in the small boat. You must obey our signs. You are not welcome here. Turn about and depart immediately."

Abbey had to try to get within earshot. He yelled, "We need some help. We need to talk to you for a moment. We will not come ashore." The boat crept closer. They saw the man unsling his weapon. "My friend here has things on the island." He pointed with his left arm. "Five miles up the western side. We only wish to recover her possessions. Then we will leave immediately."

He must have been heard, because the man responded, "What things?"

"Turtle traps and cages and nests for turtle eggs," shouted Maria. "I've had them there for years. They are very important to me. I need to get them." They were now only yards from the dock, but Maria wisely kept the engine idling and did not attempt to bridge the gap.

"You will not come onto this island. If you do, you will be shot. We will do as those signs say," pointing at the warning signs.

"But why do you threaten in this way?" asked Abbey as politely as he could. "It will take us at most an hour. It is my friend's property. She's Mexican. We're in Mexico. It won't hurt you in any way."

The uniformed man looked briefly at Maria when she was mentioned, and then turned his attention back to Abbey.

"Sir, you are not in Mexico here. We have purchased this island from Mexico. Mexican law no longer applies here."

Abbey thought for a moment. "Well, then, what are you?"

"We are the island nation of Parsa. We are building a new island state which will be the envy of many. Who knows? You may choose to live here someday. But until we finish our work, you will not enter the island. We paid Mexico for this land. If your friend has property here, she should take it up with Mexico. Maybe they will pay her. But before you leave, your film, sir." He held out his left hand while the gun remained cradled in his right arm.

Abbey looked down at his camera bag and hesitated for a moment.

"No delays," the man said. "Give me the film. Now."

"Just a second. I have to get it out of the camera." Reaching down with both hands, he lifted the camera body, flicked open the rear, and pulled out a long lead of film. He leaned over the side to hand it to the man.

"Just throw it in the water. I don't need the pictures," sneered the man. Abbey did as he was directed.

None of this made any sense. Maria was seething. She was being treated as an intruder in her own country, on the island she had used for many years. She saw that there were no boats of any type docked or beached in the area. These intruders might control the island, but they did not yet control the sea.

As she began to turn the boat, she yelled over her shoulder, "So we will leave. But you, señor, can go to hell!"

She roared away, and they both held their breath, looking straight ahead, praying no bullets would follow.

"I'm not sure that was the smartest thing, Maria."

She said nothing and headed toward the mainland, already planning how she could return. When they reached her slip at the village, they discussed what to do next. Abbey wanted to go to the authorities, but Maria reminded him that that could be very awkward since they would certainly ask to see his papers, which carried the *No Entry* stamp. They were on their own. She mentioned that there had been no boats in sight. She knew the island very well. Her traps were five miles up the shoreline from the dock. She wanted to return, go ashore quickly, recover what she could, and depart before they could be noticed.

"Maria, turtle traps and nesting equipment, and even your husband's memories, don't justify risking your life. I'll buy you new traps. We've tried. That's an impressive operation on that island. Even if you didn't see any boats, that doesn't mean you should be crazy."

"I might be crazy, but I lost my husband in these waters, and my uncle in this village. I am the last Van Huessen. I am not going to be pushed around like a piece of Mexican trash. I will get my property, with you or without you."

She was visibly angry. After a few moments, she calmed down. "In fairness to you, Professor, you are right. It is not worth the risk for you. You have done more than your share in coming here at great risk to help me. You have a great life and career in front of you. You should go home. I, on the other hand, have very little to risk." There was a look of determination on her face . . . and, he saw, sadness when she made the last comment.

"What are you going to do?" he asked quietly.

"I will go back tonight. I will not wait until they get boats, because they certainly will someday. In the morning, I will drive you back to the border. Tonight, I will leave you my keys. If I am not here in the morning, please take my truck and simply park it at the border. You will have no problem."

"You're serious, aren't you?"

"Yes, I'm serious."

He looked at her and said softly, "I wish I had your strength. I don't think I do. I think going back is a mistake."

She shrugged. "That's okay. You have done enough."

CHAPTER 23

OCTOBER 1 – NOVEMBER 11
IRAN

The work on Guardian Island had been underway for two months when Maria and Abbey had their confrontation with the man at the dock. The man was Major General Mohammed Ashkan of the Quods Force of the Iranian Revolutionary Guards. He was a close confidante of General Mussahrah, and he reported the brief dockside encounter to Mussahrah in his daily report. In the same report, Ashkan updated what he had accomplished on the island over the last four months.

General Ashkan had come to the island on the initial ship with a construction crew and a cargo of supplies and building materials. Offloading had been difficult before the temporary dock was installed, but luckily the small bay at the southern end of the island had good depth all the way to shore. By using a boom crane on the ship, the crew had been able to move most of the cargo to the shore. The ship's crew was Iranian, as was the construction crew. Once the dock was installed, additional ships delivered more equipment and materials and more workers and soldiers. There was a workforce of seventy-five men and a security force of twenty-five on the island.

In Tehran, General Mussahrah read Ashkan's report with interest. Mussahrah thought this small dockside incident proved the correctness of choosing the island. Outside incursion could easily be detected and stopped. The island had been carefully selected. The small mountain range running down the east side of the island from north to south was like a curtain masking their activities. At the southerly end was a valley on the gulf side which ran to the shore.

It was in that southern valley that most construction was taking place. From the valley, there was a clear, unobstructed path at sea level to the American border three hundred miles to the north. The general knew that the buildings, which had been prefabricated in Jask, had been erected. Most importantly, the eight-foot-high wall of pre-poured concrete sections was almost complete. It surrounded an area about the size of a football field. Because of the climate, foundations were not necessary, and everything was going up quickly. The structures were not expected to be used for long.

There was nothing fancy about the site. The men lived in tents, and all provisions were brought by ship. Electricity was provided by a large, oil-powered generator stationed on one small ship which remained in the harbor. The project did not in any way resemble the beginnings of a high-end retirement community. Its only purpose was to provide a launch site for the missile waiting in Iran.

The Iranians' schedule called for construction work on Guardian Island to be completed by December 1. On that date, the ship which had been selected was to depart Jask carrying the missile and its launching equipment. It would take almost three weeks to steam easterly from Jask to the island, concluding with a Christmas delivery. General Mussahrah was proud to have developed the schedule to take advantage of the Americans' laxness at their special holiday time. After delivery, it was important that everything be in place by late January. In Iran, everything was ready. They were waiting for notification from the island that the work there was completed.

General Mussahrah had explained to the Ayatollah and President Talabani the historical as well as tactical significance of this site. Any missile launched from the island would streak north across America's border and over the White Sands testing site, where the first nuclear bomb had been exploded by the United States over fifty years ago. The border could be reached within ten minutes, making interception almost impossible. The populated centers of California were only minutes away.

As Mussahrah told them, "The Americans wish to keep the bomb out of our hands so that they can dictate international rules based upon the weapons they already have. They started all of this at White Sands. Then they dropped the first bombs in Japan. Now we will join their nuclear club, whether they like it or not."

CHAPTER 24

NOVEMBER 11–12

BAHIA DE LOS ANGELES

Maria and Abbey spent the afternoon preparing for the coming incursion. He thought he could at least try to make it as safe as possible for her.

"How do you think they detected you the previous time? You were five miles up the coast from where their activities seem to be centered."

"I think I figured that out," she answered. "I beached on the small, open beach I always used. I saw a low fence, like a wind fence, which had been strung along the top of the entire beach, about two feet high and held together with wire. It really made me mad, because it trapped the turtles which were already upland of the fence, and it barred turtles from the water from getting to their nesting sites. So I ripped it up and left it in a pile. It was not long after when I heard vehicles approaching from the south, along the beach, and then I ran for my boat while being shot at. I think the fence was wired. When I tore it down, I caused some type of signal to be sent, like a motion detector.

"This time, I will leave the fence alone. I won't touch anything but my things. I'm not going to be crazy. I'll be careful. I think I can be in and out in about twenty minutes. Might take four trips to get my things to the boat, but I'll be quick."

Abbey nodded his agreement. Her explanation about the fence made sense. "How're you going to navigate and get there in the dark, undetected? You can't use any lights."

She was standing on the dock next to the boat. While coiling a line around her arm, she answered, "I've been going there for years, often at night. I have a point on the coast just south of here which is well marked. From that point, I follow a 110-degree magnetic course for fifteen miles. It takes me right to my beach."

She seemed to have the answers, he thought, as he poured gas into her extra tank. She had rigged up some large carrying sacks from fishnet which she said would hold the gear she was removing from the island.

By late afternoon, everything was ready. They bought some sausage and bread from the store and had a snack on the shore. After eating, she walked to a small gear shack on the dock and rummaged inside. She came back carrying a pistol and put it into a compartment in the dash of the boat.

"Is that necessary?" Abbey asked.

"I hope not. My husband usually carried it to kill large fish before bringing them into the boat. He taught me how to use it. It's a .45-caliber that he brought home from the army. I'll have it if necessary."

When the sky began to darken, she said, "Well, I guess it's time." They were standing on the dock above her boat. She dug into her pocket and pulled out her keys, removing one from the ring and handing it to him. "Here's the truck key. I'm going to go slow to keep down the engine noise, so it'll take about two hours each way. Maybe faster coming back," she laughed with forced cheerfulness. "Hopefully I'll be back here soon after two in the morning. If I'm not here by daylight, you know what to do."

He turned to her with his hands clasped together. "I can't let you go alone, Maria," he said.

"We've been through all that. You've done your part. Now I'll do mine."

"No. You have four sacks. They'll be too heavy to carry more than one at a time. With me there, we can cut the time ashore in half. I said I'm scared to go, but I'm also scared for you to go alone. So if you're going to do this, I'm going with you." He jumped into the stern of the boat quickly, as if he had to do it before he changed his mind.

She was at the bow line on the dock. She looked pensively at him. "You're sure?"

"Let's go before I change my mind."

She cast the line into the boat and stepped aboard. Sitting facing him, she looked into his eyes and grasped his hands in hers. "We will keep each other safe. Thank you again for helping me. I knew you were a good man, a strong man. Maybe stronger than you realize."

She turned and started the engine. They were off, moving southerly towards her landmark. The sun had just set over the western mountains, and with almost no moon, it was dark. No boat lights were visible, and only a few glowed on the shore. She pointed at the one which was her landmark.

• • •

Abbey was scared. Sitting in the stern of the boat, he shivered with nervousness. He could hear his heart pounding, and he was sure Maria could hear the thumping and detect his fear. She stood behind the wheel, making slight steering adjustments as she peered down at the glow-ing compass. After about an hour, he saw a growing dark mass in front of them. It was the island.

As they approached the shore, they saw lights to the south and heard machinery and construction noises. It was clearly not a nine-to-five job site.

"Luckily, they seem to be fully occupied elsewhere," Abbey joked to calm his nervousness. Maria smiled grimly.

She beached the boat on her little strip of sand an hour before midnight. The crossing had gone just as she said, although it was very dark, and Abbey had no idea where they were most of the time.

Once the boat ground to a stop on the sand and she had lifted the engines, they jumped out onto the beach, each carrying two of the sacks. They pulled the bow a few feet up on the sand. Maria walked the anchor line about twenty feet up the sand and set the anchor in the beach sand. They each dropped one sack next to the anchor and continued carrying one. They would pick up the two empty sacks when they returned for the second trip. Maria took Abbey's hand to lead the way. Hers felt warm and dry, while his was damp with sweat. He saw that she had stuck the pistol in her belt. He trembled as he looked nervously side to side, and stumbled in the sand to keep up with her purposeful strides.

The beach was only seventy-five yards wide, with small rocky outcroppings at each end. The fence had been re-placed. It appeared to stretch completely across the beach at the top of the sand from one rocky point to the other, although it was difficult to see either end of the fence through the darkness. As she had said, it was only about twenty-four inches high. They stepped over it gingerly after first throwing the sacks over to the other side. Abbey risked using a flashlight to quickly examine the fence. There appeared to be an electrical wire running along its length, confirming Maria's suspicion that she had tripped some type of alarm on her previous visit. Maria grabbed his hand again and whispered that it was only another hundred feet to her gear. After only a few yards, she took his light and scanned the ground with it. "I think this is where I dropped the vase," she whispered. But there was no vase. Nothing but sand and dune grass.

They had to use the flashlight again when she stopped. Piled neatly on the ground were about twenty small cages which looked to Abbey very much like lobster traps. There were also a number of wicker-like baskets filled with sand and grass. Abbey couldn't recognize the other items which were scattered about. He started to quickly stuff as much as possible into his sack, while Maria stepped a few feet away and scooped some sand out from a narrow depression. She removed something from the sand and stuffed it into her pocket before continuing to fill her sack with turtle gear. They worked quickly. Although it was a cool night and the physical effort had been minor, Abbey was sweating and breathing hard.

After loading most of the items into the sacks, they moved quickly back towards the beach.

"Oh, shit!" whispered Abbey as they reached the fence. To the south, they could see a small spotlight sweeping the shoreline and moving toward them. It was clearly from some type of guard boat. They then heard the sound of an outboard engine. The engine was revving slowly, with no urgency to the speed of the boat or its sweeping spotlight, so it appeared to be a normal beach surveillance patrol rather than a response to any type of alarm. Nevertheless, they were trapped. If they tried to depart, their engine would be heard. If they stayed where they were, their boat would be seen. The spotlight would reach their beach within minutes.

Abbey stood frozen, not knowing what to do.

"Let's get to the boat," whispered Maria with urgency. "Then jump into the water and help me move it."

"How? We can't start the engine."

"Just do what I say. We're going to walk the boat to the north end of the beach. There's a small cave there in the rocks. We can hide in the cave. They'll go right by us and never see us."

They jumped the fence, ran to the water line, and threw the sacks into the boat. Abbey waded into the water while Maria retrieved the anchor from the beach. Because of the drop-off, they had to both stay on the beach side of the boat to walk it toward the rocks at the north end of the beach. Abbey kept looking over his shoulder at the approaching light. Abbey was near the stern, with Maria in front of him. With their left arms hooked over the side of the boat and their right hands pushing on the hull, they pushed and walked as fast as they could. It was going to be close.

When the spotlight reached the southern end of the beach, they were still in the open. Abbey and Maria strained to move quicker in the resisting water. His legs burned as he tried to lift them quickly against the pressure of the water.

Finally, they reached the rocks. Maria slid back and whispered in his ear that they would have to swim the boat around the corner because it got deeper. Holding onto the side with one hand and doing a sidestroke with the other, they moved the boat slowly around the rocks. Just as they turned the corner, they looked back one last time. The spotlight had reached the middle of the beach, where it was frozen in place. It illuminated clearly the depression in the sand where the boat had been beached and their footprints in the sand. Ten feet from the depression were the two empty sacks which they had left behind for their second trip. They were detected.

Maria directed him a short distance further, where a small crevice between the rocks led to a tidal pool. After swimming into the pool, they pulled themselves into the boat. They were masked from the sea, but it probably made no difference. An alarm was certainly being sounded, and it would not be difficult to find them. Maria climbed out of the boat, onto the rocks, and slowly to the top to view what was going on at the beach. The rocks rose about fifteen feet above the water.

She saw a rubber Zodiac beached next to their boat's depression. One man was in the boat, moving the spotlight around the area. She could see that he was talking on some type of radio phone. A second man was up by the fence, shining a hand light over the fence. She slid back down to where Abbey stood in the boat, holding onto the rocks.

"There's a way to escape," she said with urgency. "But we have to move quickly before others arrive."

"They'll see us – and hear us," he whispered back.

"They might hear us, but I think I can make sure they don't see us. I'm going to climb back to the top and shoot out their spotlight. Let's first swing around so the boat is pointing out to sea. As soon as you hear my shots, start the engine. I'll be back in the boat within seconds, and then we'll get out of here. Quickly!" She looked back at the engines, seeing they were still lifted out of the water, and showed him how to lower them.

"We're only fifty yards from them," Abbey said. "They'll be able to fire at us and chase us."

"Okay. They're in a rubber boat. I'll also fire into the side of their boat to damage it. What else can we do? Wait to be shot?"

"I guess it's the only way," he answered meekly.

Maria still had the pistol in her belt. She hoped the sea water wouldn't stop it from firing. It held seven rounds, and she wanted to save at least a few. Once back at the top of the rocks, she momentarily considered shooting the man in the boat, but she couldn't bring herself to do that. She took careful aim. Although it would be easiest to first shoot at the boat, she knew that would leave her vulnerable to the spotlight. She had to kill the light first and hope she could then hit the side of the rubber boat in the darkness.

It took three rapid shots before the light splintered and went dark. Maria then moved her aim down slightly and placed three more shots into what she hoped was the side of the boat. Almost immediately, bullets were hitting the top of her rocky post, just as she was sliding down to the boat. Abbey started the engine as directed when the first shot was fired. As soon as she was in the boat, Abbey pushed the throttle forward as far as it would go. The boat leapt out of its hiding place, and he wrestled the wheel to the right as it left the rocks. Soon, the rocks were between them and their pursuers.

The Zodiac had been hit, but it was constructed to survive loss of air pressure, and the rubber sides had a self-sealing capability. As soon as the man on shore jumped back into the boat, they tore after the departing engine noise. Without the light, they fired their weapons at the engine noise, not being able to see their prey.

Maria's boat was faster than the Zodiac. Her two large engines were at full throttle. The Zodiac, although much lighter than her boat, had only a single sixty-horsepower engine, and the shots into its sides had put it out of trim. As the Zodiac rounded the rocks, some of the shots started hitting the water near the speeding Mako. Abbey and Maria saw the florescence caused by the bullets hitting the water, even though they couldn't hear the impact over the engine noise. There seemed to be a stream of lighted water droplets following them and getting closer. Abbey and Maria dropped to their knees, trying to stay below the sides of the boat, while still steering with an open throttle. They heard splintering fiberglass on the right side near the stern as some of the bullets found their mark.

Soon, however, they were out of range. They prayed that no larger, faster boat would pursue them as they sped back to the mainland. Luckily, the damage to the boat appeared to be minor. No water was coming in.

Their trip back was much quicker than the earlier trip to the island. They pulled into Maria's slip just before one o'clock in the morning. After quickly tying up the boat, they threw the sacks into the truck bed and drove back to the ranch. Neither had spoken since the island encounter. The engine noise had made conversation difficult, and talk seemed unnecessary.

As they drove, she said with bitterness, "I never even had a chance to find my vase, or the picture. But this time I won't go back. They weren't just trying to warn us. They were trying to kill us."

"I agree," Abbey said, almost to himself. "You're right. Those weren't warning shots."

They were exhausted when they reached the ranch. They went to bed in their separate rooms, and each fell asleep almost immediately. Later, before daylight, Abbey felt someone enter his bed. Maria whispered in his ear, "May I stay with you tonight? I'm afraid to be alone." He welcomed her presence. They slept on, exhausted, holding tight to each other.

He dreamed again of his mother. *This woman is yours for a while*, she was saying. *Love her deeply; love her smile. Take care of her, because it's here where you will finally lose your fear.*

• • •

When Abbey awoke soon after daylight, Maria was snuggled against his back, with her arm over his shoulder. He was groggy for a moment, not sure where he was. Then he felt her breathing, slow, rhythmic, and cooling on his back. He turned toward her and gently pulled her body against his. She came eagerly, and he was soon aroused. She stroked him larger and whispered in his ear, "I need you . . . I want you."

They made love, first with wild passion and excitement, tumbling and groping each other's bodies. Her body tasted salty and earthy from sweat and saltwater.

Maria got up and brought back a small basin of water, saying, "Let me wash you." She cleansed away the night's sweat and salt, and then he did the same for her. Then they coupled again, this time tasting and smelling clean, with a hint of sandalwood.

"Slowly, this time," she said. "Love me slowly."

He did, and they finally crescendoed together with arched backs and deep gasps.

As they lay side by side afterwards, he said, "Maria, you're a strong lady, but also a tender one. I'm glad you talked me into coming."

The night before seemed like a dream. They knew they had almost died. Apart from that, Abbey knew that he had a new woman in his life. Maria was becoming important. As he later worked over breakfast in the kitchen, she came up behind him and hugged him tightly.

"Professor Bill, you are a wonderful teacher."

"I think we taught each other," he murmured as he turned and kissed her deeply. "And you, too, have a wonderful teaching style."

She laughed lightly, as the tension from the night before dissolved.

• • •

After breakfast, they drove down to the village to pick up Maria's dog, which she had left with a friend, and to check out the boat. As they approached the docks, they saw trouble. A familiar-looking Zodiac water craft was tied up at the dock with a man sitting in it. Two other men were on the dock, kneeling and looking closely at Maria's boat. One was the uniformed foreigner who had barred them from the island yesterday. The other wore the uniform of the Mexican national police. Maria quickly pulled her truck behind a building, out of sight from the dock. She told Abbey that the Mexican was Lieutenant Gonzalez. He had replaced Corporal Martinez and was the local policeman in charge. Their first inclination was to head back to the ranch. But, as Maria said, the officer knew it to be her boat and would probably soon follow.

"You're in the country illegally," Maria said. "We can't have them asking you questions. You have to stay out of this. I'll go down and talk to them. I'll come up with some story. I don't think anyone can identify us from last night. They never saw us."

"Yes, you're right. I'll stay in the truck. But if there's any trouble, yell for me. I'll come, whether I'm legal or not."

She smiled and kissed him lightly on the cheek before getting out of the truck. She walked around the corner of the building and strode casually toward the dock.

"Gentlemen, what can I do for you?" she said.

"Señora Plarez, I believe," said the Mexican policeman. "We are looking at what appears to be some damage to your boat."

"Really? Let me see." She walked to the boat and knelt down on the dock to examine what she had not really seen the night before. The right rear side of the boat was shattered, at the top above the water line, which explained why no water had entered. "Yes, you are right. Some splintered fiberglass. I don't think it was there yesterday."

The foreigner spoke. "Yes, señora, yesterday. I believe I had the honor of talking to you from the dock on our island yesterday." His voice was not friendly. "You and your friend. You were not happy about being barred from our island. Did you perhaps return last night?"

"Of course not," she exclaimed. "Why should I go back where I'm not wanted?"

"But someone did come back. And I think they came back in your boat. They shot at my men. My men naturally had to defend themselves and fired back. The condition of your boat suggests that it was hit by bullets last night."

"As I said, it was not me," Maria said sharply. "Maybe someone took my boat."

"Maybe, señora, but I have two men who can probably identify who was there. I would like you to accompany me to the island so they can see your beautiful face. Maybe they will agree with you that it was not you."

"Señor, I can promise you one thing. I will not accompany you to your island or anywhere else. As you said yesterday, I am not welcome there. As I said yesterday, you may go to hell. You have come here and created a great disturbance next to our quiet village. I do not like you or whatever it is that you're doing on the island."

The Mexican lieutenant quickly interjected, trying to soothe the situation. "Maybe you should cooperate, Mrs. Plarez. These are our new neighbors. We have to live across the water from each other. If it was not you, I will investigate who might have taken your boat."

Maria knew they were not going to simply drop the matter. She thought quickly and said, "Señor, why don't you bring your men to our police station tomorrow morning? I will be there. I am sure they will say they did not see me on your island."

"And your friend, señora?" smiled the Iranian.

"He left last evening. He was simply visiting the area and took a boat ride with me. He's gone." Then she suddenly realized that whoever the Iranian brought back tomorrow would certainly say she was the one, whether she had been seen or not. She came up with an idea. "Maybe we can all save some time, señor. I see you have a radio phone. Why don't you call your men right now and ask them for a description of who they saw? I am sure they will not describe me."

"Ah, if only I could. But my men are working on the other side of the island, and the mountain is between us. I cannot get through to them now. We will come tomorrow, as you suggested."

Lieutenant Gonzalez said that the arrangement seemed reasonable. They would meet at his office at ten o'clock in the morning.

Maria thought quickly, "May we do it at noon? I have to be in town anyway at that time. I'd just as soon not make two trips."

"Certainly, señora."

"And Lieutenant, I would like you to examine this man's papers and those of his men when he returns tomorrow. I'm sure if you ask for them now, the papers will be back on the island on the other side of the mountain. If they are coming into Mexico, they must show us who they are. So I will see you tomorrow at noon, and I will expect to see satisfactory identification papers from these foreigners."

"As you wish, madam," the foreigner said through clenched teeth. He was not happy to be spoken to like that . . . especially by a woman.

• • •

Maria turned and strode away. Once she was out of hearing range, the lieutenant laughed nervously. "You have maybe heard of our Mexican women?" he said. "They are hot-blooded."

"Yes, I see. But on another more friendly point, I have no transportation here on the mainland. Would it be possible to purchase a vehicle? Maybe do it today? I have both pesos and dollars."

"I would suggest you talk to Pedro over by the general store. He always has old cars he's trying to sell. Can't promise anything very special. But it will work."

"Anything will do. And where did you say the señora is coming from tomorrow, that she must come so late?"

"She lives up in the mountains, at the old Van Huessen ranch."

"Thank you, Lieutenant. I will see you tomorrow. Now let me find this Pedro."

• • •

As Maria turned the corner to where her truck was parked, she glanced casually to her left to make sure she was not being followed. Then she hurried to the truck.

"Professor, I have to get you to the border and be back here by twelve noon tomorrow," she said. "We must hurry!"

"What do you mean? What's happening?"

"The foreigner claims his men saw who was on the island last night. He wanted me to go back with him to the island for them to look at me. Naturally, I refused. But I had to offer something, so I said I would meet them in the police station, here, tomorrow. I don't think they saw us last night. They're lying. I don't think they'll show up. But I'm not concerned about them. We have to get you out of here. We have about twenty-four hours for me to drive you to the border and return. We can do it if we drive all night. There's no other way."

Abbey nodded with resignation. "You're right. But I don't want you to be here alone with these folks."

"Don't worry. I have a friend who will go with me. He was my husband's closest friend, very strong and resourceful. I'll be okay."

• • •

While they were talking, General Ashkan made his deal with Pedro for an old Honda which had seen better days. He also obtained directions from Pedro to the Van Huessen ranch as he peeled off fifteen one-hundred-dollar bills to pay the Mexican. He drove the car to the outskirts of town, parked it, and returned quickly to the Zodiac, in which one of his men, Hamid, waited. Hamid had been one of the two men in the Zodiac the night before. On the way back to Guardian Island, Ashkan explained his plan to the man.

"You and Kazam will be going back to the mainland tonight. Here are the keys for that old Honda I left at the north end of town. You can see it there. The white one." He pointed at the vehicle. "There is a lady, a Maria Plarez, who I am sure was in the boat last night. I know you didn't see the person, but it was her boat, and she is too angry in her denial. She is also insulting and rude. She lives alone in the mountains. I have the directions. I think it might also have been her who visited that same spot two weeks ago. I want you to find out from her why she is coming to our island and what she has seen. Then I want her dead. I want to silence her before she talks to people. Return her body to the island, where we will dispose of it. I want no one to be suspicious about her disappearance, so I don't want any body to be found. Understand?"

"It will be my pleasure, General. I have a score to settle from last night."

CHAPTER 25

NOVEMBER 12–13

BAHIA DE LOS ANGELES

Maria and Abbey drove back to the ranch and gathered his personal belongings. She put the gas cans back into the truck, and they moved the sacks to the barn. While taking the two sacks from the truck, Abbey remembered the small package Maria had pulled from the sand.

"What was it you dug out of the sand last night?" he asked.

"Oh, you noticed? They were letters from my husband. I read them on my small beach after his death and left them there. As I told you, we had a good marriage. I have been very alone since he died." She hesitated, then added, "You are the first man I have been close to since then. I'm sorry it took bullets and all these problems to do that."

"Well, I was getting a little bored being just a teacher. You've certainly changed that."

They left quickly. This time, she would leave Lucky at the ranch. She would be back in the morning. Maria began as driver, saying that the first fifty miles of Route 12 were the worst. They had to make good time, and she had been driving the road for years. After about fifty miles, they switched so she could get some sleep. It was going to be a long night for her.

Abbey got to the intersection with Route 1 and turned north. Finally, pavement. He drove for about an hour. It was dark when he saw a vehicle in the distance with someone waving a flashlight. He slowed and saw that it was a woman, with a child standing beside her. They were waving as if in some sort of trouble. Abbey slowed to pull over behind their car. The change of speed woke Maria, who sat up straight with a jerk.

"What's happening?"

"Just checking on someone who seems to be in some trouble. Just be a second."

She looked around. "No. This is a mistake. It could be bandits. This is one of their favorite routines in the middle of the night when they see someone driving alone. Keep the headlights on and the doors locked."

"Señor," yelled the Mexican woman, "can you please help? We need some petrol."

"Don't open the door," said Maria. "Wait for a moment to see if anyone else appears."

Sure enough, within a few seconds, two figures came stealthily around the rocks to their right, about fifty feet off the road. Maria yanked open the glove compartment and pulled out the pistol she had left there the night before. She opened her window and shouted, "Don't come closer, or I'll shoot you!"

Without waiting for a response, she discharged the one remaining bullet over their heads and yelled at Abbey to leave. "Quickly! Get out of here quickly!" The sound of the gunshot crashed about the inside of the cab, almost breaking their eardrums. Abbey took off, spinning gravel and dust at the woman decoy and her helper. He accelerated and sped down the road, looking in the rear view mirror to see if they were being chased.

"Don't worry," Maria said. "I doubt if they'll chase us. It's almost a form of begging. They're poor, hungry, and desperate. Of course, desperate people can be dangerous, but probably not these. They assume I have more bullets. I doubt if they even had a weapon."

Nevertheless, he kept going fast and looking in the rear view mirror. "Why am I always the getaway driver?" he muttered nervously.

"Because you are so good at it, Professor Bill," she said, leaning over and snuggling against him.

"Hopefully that will be our last escape from trouble," he mused. His quiet teaching life was changing by the day.

A few miles before Rosario, Maria suggested that they stop for gas at the same station they had used before. "I don't want to have to stop there alone in the middle of the night on my way back," she explained.

After gassing up, they continued north without incident until they reached the border area at Tijuana just after midnight.

On the way, she told him how she had demanded identification from the foreigners for the meeting tomorrow. Abbey thought that was a good idea, but he cautioned her about pushing these people any further. "They're not nice people. At some point, they'll strike back."

"I'll be careful," Maria assured him. "I will not push further. I promise," she said with a smile and a reassuring pat on his arm. Because of the late hour, they decided that she should not cross the border with him. She would leave him on the Mexican side. As he got out of the truck, Maria came around to say goodbye. They embraced and held each other tightly for a moment.

"Please call and let me know you're safe," he whispered.

"I will."

"Wait!" he said. "I want your picture. It'll keep me company till we can be together again."

She posed by the border sign, and he took a few exposures. Then he showed her the digital images. As they skimmed through the images, he came to several of the signs and the dock from Guardian Island.

She looked up at him with a perplexed expression, pointing at the images. "Where did those come from? He made you throw out your film."

"Oh, in all the excitement, I forgot to tell you. I wasn't using film at the island. I pulled out an old roll of film from my other camera body. I still have the digital pictures from the island."

She laughed. "And you tell me I take chances. How did you think of that so quickly?"

"I really don't know. The idea just came to me. I think he asked for my film, not my memory card, so that's what I gave him. The film actually had some nice shots from a cave in Joshua Tree Park. Hopefully you'll help me get new ones."

They embraced again, and he walked to the border crossing with some trepidation. Every time at the border, he seemed to run into some type of problem. But there was no problem departing Mexico. At midnight, he appeared like any other American leaving the city after a night of fun and frolic. U.S. customs, however, noted the *No Entry* stamp on his passport and the *03 code*, and started to ask questions about where he had been. He was evasive in his answers.

"I don't have to explain my whereabouts. I'm an American citizen and have every right to enter the United States." They let him through, but Abbey realized that he was going to have to talk to someone about his passport problems – and what was happening on the island. Mexico did not appear to care. It was permitting an armed camp of foreigners to exist within its borders. Maybe he could get some advice on his side of the border. He certainly wanted to go back to see Maria.

• • •

Maria made it back to her ranch by ten o'clock in the morning. Once she realized that she would make it on time, she pulled off Route 12 and slept for a few hours. Driving up to the ranch, she was surprised that her dog Lucky didn't run out to greet her. Then she saw why. The dog was lying on the front porch, frozen still.

Jumping out of the truck, she ran to the porch, where she saw the dog lying in a pool of dried blood. As she dropped to the ground to embrace the body, she saw a horrifying wound on his face. Someone had cut out the dog's tongue and pinned it to the wooden floor in front of his mouth with a knife. Maria screamed hysterically, until she was sobbing to catch her breath. How could someone do that to a dog, an innocent animal? And the tongue . . . the universal sign of silence. She was being told to keep silent. Her dead dog Lucky had been used to deliver the message.

Maria finally fell silent. Sobbing quietly, she gathered the body in a small tarp to be buried later. She would not miss her meeting with these animals, and she wouldn't be silent. She had little else to live for. They had taken just about everything from her.

She took the pistol out of the truck and went into the house where her husband kept the ammunition. Snapping seven new rounds into the clip, she was determined to make the man pay. She didn't think she would hesitate to shoot a person this time.

However, as she had predicted, no one showed up. She told Lieutenant Gonzales about her dog and how she was sure the foreigners had done it. To his credit, Gonzales was shocked. He immediately called Ashkan on the number which had been left with him.

"Sir, we are waiting for you at the police station."

"Oh, yes. I am so sorry. I apologize. As the woman thought, my men were not able to see who was in the boat. The meeting would have accomplished nothing. They were supposed to call and cancel our meeting. They must not have been able to get through the mountain."

"Well, we also have another problem," continued the lieutenant. "The lady's dog was killed and brutally butchered last night. She thinks you are responsible."

"Did she observe me or my men do such a thing?"

"No. She was not there."

"She should not make such accusations without having seen anything, Lieutenant."

"Maybe not. But I think you should not come to our village again until we get to the bottom of this. And that might make the new car unnecessary."

General Ashkan was finished playing with these people. "We have no plans to return, and our need for the car is no more. Maybe give it to the lady as my gift. A remembrance of sorts. Goodbye, Lieutenant."

Gonzalez and Maria went to inspect the car and then checked with Pedro. It had been driven twelve miles since its purchase the previous day, precisely the distance to and from the Van Huessen ranch. They had Pedro disable the car so that it couldn't be used again. Lieutenant Gonzalez tried to console Maria about her loss, but there was very little more he could do. His orders were that the island was to be left alone. He had no jurisdiction there.

CHAPTER 26

NOVEMBER 14
ALBUQUERQUE

Soon after Abbey got home from Mexico, he heard from Maria about her return to the ranch and her slaughtered dog. He was relieved that she was safe, but it might only be for the moment. He thought she was in danger, and he told her so.

"Maria, I don't know what you can do," he said. "At least stay away from the ranch for a while. I have plenty of room here."

"But this is my home!" she protested.

"I know, I know. I might do the same if I were you. I might also stay. At least talk to that friend of your husband's. Please, be careful."

Abbey wracked his brain trying to figure out what to do. Something terribly wrong was happening at Guardian Island, and he had played a role in getting it started. President Overton would be no help. Overton wanted to protect the gift at all costs, and Duprey had already made his position clear. The professor knew he had to break the confidentiality agreement, whatever the consequences. But who should he talk to?

He remembered that Professor John Meadows of the archeology department had occasionally talked about his brother, "the FBI agent." He knew Meadows slightly from faculty conferences involving their mutual interests in ancient peoples and places. He called Meadows.

"John, this is Bill Abbey."

"Hi, Bill. What's happening in Hispanic studies?"

"Just trying to understand our southern neighbors. Nothing really new. But I do have a bit of an unusual request."

"Sure. What can I do?"

"I'm researching and writing about border security, and I'm trying to get some input from law enforcement types. I remember that your brother is in the FBI. I'm wondering if you could make an introduction so that I could talk to him. He might be of help, or he might be able to direct me to someone else. If I just call someone cold, I'll probably get the brush-off."

"No problem. I can give you his number in L.A. I'll call him later today so he'll expect your call."

"That's great," replied Abbey. "That would be very helpful."

The brother was agent Charles Meadows. Abbey took down the number. He called the next morning.

"Agent Meadows," answered a crisp, professional voice.

"Hello, sir. This is Professor Bill Abbey from the University of New Mexico. Hopefully your brother told you I would be calling."

"Yes, he did. Glad to talk to you. But I have to warn you that we're very restricted in talking about security and law enforcement matters. I might not be able to help you very much."

"I understand," said Abbey. "I'm actually looking to talk to someone about what might be a serious criminal matter. I don't know anyone in the FBI, and it's somewhat delicate, so I wasn't fully candid with John about why I needed to talk to you. I guess I reached you under false pretenses. It's important, though, and I hope you'll be willing to listen to me."

"My job is to investigate criminal matters, so certainly I'll listen to you. Should you talk to an attorney first?"

"No, no. It really isn't so much about me. There are certain things I've observed in Mexico, though, that are very troublesome."

"Mexico's a little out of our jurisdiction," commented Meadows. "Maybe I should direct you to the appropriate Mexican officials."

"Maybe," said Abbey, "but I don't think the Mexicans are going to be much help. I'd like to first tell you about the problem."

"Okay. Keep in mind this conversation is being recorded."

Abbey gave the agent a somewhat sanitized version of the events over the last six months and the recent events at Guardian Island. He didn't disclose Duprey's initial involvement, nor the payments, but instead just said he had been doing the investigation for academic reasons. He explained that something was wrong with his passport and that he had been accused of being some type of money launderer. Meadows took it all in without comment. Abbey concluded by saying that it certainly didn't appear to be any retirement community which was being built on Guardian Island. Rather, it appeared to be something military-related. He also told Meadows that he had pictures from the island.

"What do you think?" Abbey asked after finishing his story.

"I think you're lucky to be alive," Meadows answered. "I'm not sure what the FBI can do. I'll certainly be able to look into the passport issue and have the right people contact you. I'll put in a report about this Guardian Island to our international division. I'm sure they'll make some inquiries. But I'm not sure anyone will get back to you on that. If it becomes an investigation, our policy is usually no comment. In the meantime, I'd advise you and your friend to stay away from the island. At the minimum, it appears to be private property, and they do have the right to keep you out. I'm not sure about the use of deadly force, but it's Mexico and not the U.S. Can you add anything else?"

"No. That's the story. I just feel relieved that I've told someone. I'll wait to hear about my passport. Thanks very much for listening to me. And I'd appreciate it if my little ruse to your brother was not disclosed. It would be embarrassing."

"Don't worry, Professor. We protect our sources."

• • •

Meadows made an immediate report and some inquiries. The Guardian Island matter was well beyond his jurisdiction, but he sent the information along to his superiors. Maybe this guy simply had a vivid imagination. Maybe it was that Mexican tequila. Immigration did confirm, however, that Professor Abbey was a suspected money launderer. Agent Meadows told immigration about the call from Abbey and added that the professor seemed to want to try to clear the matter up. He then decided that he had fulfilled his filial obligations to his brother and returned to his regular duties.

CHAPTER 27

DECEMBER 2–22
JASK, IRAN, AND OTHER PLACES

On December 2, the Israeli agent Makad was monitoring incoming electronic messages at the communications desk in Jask when he saw the message: *Parsa is now ready for its Christmas delivery.*

He knew what it meant. The missile site was ready.

He also knew about the missile and the delivery ship.

The missile was the Shahab-4, a medium-range guided ballistic rocket which Iran had developed in cooperation with the North Koreans. It had a range of over twelve hundred miles. Publicly, Iran had been describing the missile as a telecommunications satellite launch vehicle, with no military application. It was small, only seventy-five feet long and two feet wide, and easily concealed inside the cargo hold of a small freighter. Makad knew that two missiles and the nuclear weapon material sat packed and ready in a warehouse that had been constructed north of Jask.

The ship was the Birania, which was anchored off Jask in the Gulf of Oman. She was a fifteen-year-old break-bulk freighter with a large open center cargo hold and two loading cranes. The open cargo hold permitted bulky cargo to be placed deep within the ship, out of sight of prying eyes in the sky. Eight hundred feet long, and rated at 50,000 tons, the ship could cruise at twenty knots.

The Iranians had leased the Birania on a bare-boat basis from an international shipping company without a crew. Its engines and mechanical systems had recently been completely overhauled, although the hull remained rust-spotted, with dirty brown streaks running down its sides. The captain was a Russian, Ivor Sanovich. He had more than thirty years of navy and civilian maritime experience and had captained the Birania on the first trip to Guardian Island three months before. Makad knew that Captain Sanovich would now bring the Birania into port.

· · ·

Captain Sanovich had been anchored off Jask, waiting impatiently for sailing orders.

"These Iranians," he said aloud in his empty cabin. "First they have me outfit this ship to be a first-class freighter. Then they have me sail across the Pacific on what they say is a trial run, and now I'm just sitting at anchor." He didn't like the crew which had been provided, although they did as directed – but with an attitude. Now, suddenly, he had received orders to be underway. He read the fax: *Be dockside at nightfall. We will attend to nighttime loading. You are to depart at daybreak. Your destination is the same as before.*

His course would take him straight east across the Indian Ocean, through the Polynesian islands, and then on a northeasterly circle route to the southern tip of the Baja. For this trip, he was also given some special instructions. He was told there was very special cargo in the hold . . . a cargo that terrorists would like to hijack. The ship would be guarded, but he was also given a small transmission device and was told that he should activate the device if anyone boarded the ship by force. It would destroy the cargo but not sink the ship. Under no circumstances could he permit anyone to seize the cargo. All of the instructions were given to him at dockside by a General Mussahrah, who acted like he was a man of some importance.

As ordered, the freighter approached the docks in Jask in the middle of the night. Trucks from the new warehouse in the foothills had started leaving the warehouse at 6:00 p.m., and they were at the dock by midnight. Cranes moved the missiles and crates holding the bomb materials into the hold while it was dark. By daylight, the loading activities had concluded. The plans had been well thought out to avoid observation by satellite. General Mussahrah supervised everything.

• • •

Even though the loading activities were shielded by the cover of darkness, Colonel Longley received an immediate report that they were taking place. Although observation was more difficult in the dark, the new infrared technology was amazingly good. The fact that cargo was moving at night from the warehouse to the docks, and then loaded during the same night, had been detected. The type of cargo could not be determined. By daylight, the cargo was out of sight, and Longley was advised that the ship sailed at daylight.

Longley's surveillance had reported five ships of interest sailing from the Jask area over the past two months. That was a fairly large number of ships for the port. Each had been tracked as it headed east across the Indian Ocean and through the Polynesian islands. None had turned north towards North Korea. All had continued east across the Pacific, which Longley found a bit puzzling. Since he had only been concentrating on shipments to hostile foreign nations, he had not been worried about the cross-Pacific route. *All friends on this side of the Pacific*, he thought. Now he ordered that this newest ship, the Birania, be followed all the way to its final destination. Maybe a diversion was being conducted, and maybe the ship would eventually circle to the north. He was going to find out. It was December 8.

• • •

On December 22, in late afternoon, Longley was interrupted by an aide and told that Henre Morad was in the reception area of the Pentagon waiting to see him. The matter was urgent. Morad was shown in.

"Henre, what can I do for you? I'm glad you came in person rather than calling. A phone call would have suggested urgency."

"Hello, Colonel. I would have called, but I was waiting in your reception area to receive clearance to show you our most recent message from our source. The message came in last night. It's very disturbing." He took a copy of an email transmission from his pocket and handed it to Longley without comment. It was not long. Longley read it while still standing:

I am now in Saqqez. This will be my last message. There will be another message on January 26. As Paul Revere signaled, they are by water. I am prepared to die <u>here</u>.

"It was sent through normal email without encryption," said the Israeli. "He clearly was hurried and is trying to tell us something, and the something involves Saqqez. It's his underlining."

Longley sat down with a puzzled look on his face. "First he says this is his last message," he murmured. "Then he says there'll be another. And this Paul Revere stuff, and dying? I don't understand."

"It is confusing," said Morad, who was still standing. "But he doesn't say the January 26 message will be from him. He has always been very precise with his words. We think he's trying to tell us that he's been uncovered and not to expect or trust any future messages. The underlining must mean that Saqqez is important. Saqqez has never aroused our suspicion. Isn't this Paul Revere someone in American history?"

Longley nodded. "Yeah. He warned the Americans in Boston of the coming of the British at the start of our Revolution." Pausing to think, he queried, "So your agent is warning us that the Iranians are coming? What the hell does it mean? Where *is* Saqqez?"

The Israeli walked to a large world map on the wall and tapped his finger on the northern section of Iran. "Northwest Iran. A largely undeveloped area. It's about as close to Israel as you can get in Iran, six hundred fifty miles. Jask was almost fifteen hundred. We don't like it."

Longley stood and walked over to the map. "What do you suggest, Henre? We can't simply bomb them because of this email."

"I agree. I'm also here to see if you've learned anything new."

Colonel Longley told him about the suspicious nighttime loading in Jask and that the freighter had left two weeks before and was being tracked. It was in the middle of the Pacific right now. He pointed at the various locations on the map as he spoke. He promised that it would be followed to its destination and that he would inform Morad immediately when he received more information.

"What about the National Security Council?"

"They don't seem to care," Longley answered. "This is not enough to get their attention. Maybe the next message will, the one on January 26."

"Any significance to that date, Colonel?"

Longley walked to his desk and turned his calendar pages, looking for the date. Since he hadn't yet inserted the pages for the new year, he couldn't find it. He buzzed an assistant:

"Anything happening on January 26? . . .That's all you have? . . . Ok, thanks. . . . No, just curious about the date – no – I certainly don't want to go."

Turning to Morad, Longley explained, "Nothing special about January 26, other than the date for the president's State of the Union address, which some of the brass have to attend. Happily, not me. Nothing else of importance that I know about. May I keep a copy of this?" he asked, holding up the email message.

"No, I'm afraid not. My authorization to show it to you came all the way from the prime minister. Our intelligence people are apoplectic that the CIA or someone will get it and use it to uncover our source. I apologize. I would suggest, however, that you remember the wording and see if your people are able to figure it out. Particularly the reference to Paul Revere."

Colonel Longley studied the message for another moment and then handed the sheet back to Morad. After a few more moments, their meeting ended. Longley then added Saqqez to the areas to be surveilled by satellite. Since it was so far north of Jask, even more satellites had to be repositioned. Looking again at the map, Longley noticed that Saqqez was close to the border with northern Iraq, the area controlled by the Kurds. He initiated some inquiries to his previous command staff in Iraq as to whether a team could cross the border into northern Iran and determine what was going on at Saqqez. He was told that it was possible but that it would require higher authority than his own to send such a mission.

CHAPTER 28

DECEMBER 24 – JANUARY 6

WASHINGTON, D.C.

It was Christmas Eve. Colonel Longley was still in his office at the Pentagon at four o'clock in the afternoon. He had missed the office party. Since his divorce, there was little to draw him home, and he often worked late.

The report, with maps and aerial photographs, had arrived at his office late in the morning. The freighter Birania had not turned north toward North Korea. It had continued easterly and crossed the Pacific. Right now it was rounding the southern tip of the Baja Peninsula and heading north into the Gulf of California. He measured on the map and determined that the ship was only seven hundred miles south of the American border. It was continuing to move north at a speed of fifteen knots. The charts showed that the water depth remained almost 1,000 feet all the way up the gulf, so shallow water wasn't going to stop the ship. There were some ports along the coast of mainland Mexico, but they were fairly small, and there was no apparent reason for a freighter from Iran to be going to any of them. Neither Longley nor his staff could figure out what was going on.

Colonel Longley tried to raise the chairman of the Joint Chiefs and the head of the National Security Agency. Neither was available on this holiday except in a dire emergency. Their deputies suggested this was not such an event. The White House was largely shut down for the holiday, with the president at her home in Bel Air, California. She, too, was incommunicado. Longley had to make some decisions on his own. Although frustrated and confused by the situation, there were some things he could do.

He ordered jet flyovers of the freighter to commence at daylight with planes from Edwards Air Force base in southern California. Satellite surveillance was increased, and he ordered the trailing electronics-loaded spy ship to approach and make visual contact. He wanted to make sure that whoever was on that freighter knew that they had been detected and were being watched. Remembering his promise to Morad, he called the Israeli and notified him of the position of the ship.

Morad's response: "They are now very close to you. We might now both have the same problem. Don't let your guard down."

• • •

The following morning, Iran time, General Mussahrah received an urgent communication from Captain Sanovich advising that American jets were overhead and a trailing ship was closing the gap between them. Mussahrah was concerned, but he knew that nothing visible on the decks would cause suspicion. Just the evening before, he and the Ayatollah had talked about how the Americans appeared to have no suspicions about Guardian Island.

"Probably just normal border patrol activities," he advised the captain. "Stay with the plan. Continue northward to the island. But remember, no one must be allowed to board the ship."

"Yes, sir," answered the captain, masking his growing doubts about this mission.

• • •

Longley finally made it home at eight o'clock on Christmas Eve. He tried to call his children, but he only got through to their answering machines, wishing them Merry Christmas by wire. He had a couple of whiskeys and a simple dinner of leftovers, remaining in telephone contact with the surveillance sources throughout the night.

On Christmas day, the freighter continued its steady northerly course. None of the surveillance could detect anything unusual.

At 9:00 p.m. Christmas day, Pacific Time, Longley received a call telling him that the ship was pulling into its apparent destination: an island known as Guardian Island, in Mexico, right off the Baja Peninsula. The flyovers and visual surveillance from the trailing ship had stopped for the night, although satellite views would continue. The American spy ship reported that nighttime unloading activities were underway, but surveillance was unable to observe exactly what was being unloaded.

The next day, late in the afternoon, the ship departed the island, heading south. Colonel Longley received another package of aerial photographs. As he scrutinized the pictures, nothing ominous stood out. A great deal of construction activities had clearly taken place recently. There were areas of freshly dug earth where no vegetation was yet growing, and small, tracked vehicles and cranes were parked at the southern end of the island. A number of tents and small buildings were grouped around a docking facility at the southern end of the island. That was where the freighter had docked, he was told. A little further north, along the east coast of the island in a small valley, there were also signs of pathways and cleared areas. Longley ordered the highest possible resolution photographs and assigned the top analysts at the CIA to decipher them. Because of the holidays, that took a few days. On January 3, he met with the analysts.

"There's something being hidden on the island," the chief analyst reported.

"What do you mean?"

"Look at this valley area about a half mile north of the docks. See the slight difference between the color of this area and the surrounding vegetation?" The analyst pointed to the photo. "And see these very faint straight lines going out a few feet from that middle area?"

"Yes, I see," responded the colonel.

"That's almost certainly a large camouflage net. It's pretty well done. It's a net to conceal something underneath. The straight lines are ropes tying the net to the ground."

"Has it just gone up?" asked Longley. "That's important. Was it there before December 26?"

"Impossible to say," replied the man apologetically. "This area was considered so unimportant that it was not the subject of high-resolution photography before now. We don't know when the net was erected."

"Okay, this is Mexico, right?" continued Longley. He turned to his deputy. "Contact our Mexican liaison officer in the Pentagon immediately. I don't even know who he is. Have him reach the Mexican diplomats and the military. Find out what the hell is going on at Guardian Island. And I want the answer now."

• • •

It took two days to get the answer, and Longley didn't like it. Mexico advised that Guardian Island was the site of a new development. The developer had been given almost complete autonomy in building and running the project. The Mexican authorities had no oversight over the project and very little idea what was going on. They did pass along that the developer was using a Middle Eastern work force for the first phase of the project. Perhaps that was the reason for the Iranian ship?

"What the hell is going on?" Longley stormed to his staff. "A Middle Eastern work force, building an unknown project, three hundred miles from our border, and concealing it with a camouflage net? An Iranian freighter delivering possible nuclear materials to the site?" He turned to his assistant. "You call our National Security Council contact and set up an emergency meeting for tomorrow morning. Contact Admiral Neal and tell him I need a contingency plan for a team of SEALs to get on that island and find out what's under that net. Advise NORAD that there is the possibility – and for now, I repeat, only a possibility – of an Iranian missile on that island. Convene the Iran Group here at seven a.m. Invite Morad."

The meeting of the Iran Group confirmed everything Colonel Longley had initiated, but they had no new information. They agreed unanimously that this was a crisis. Two hours later, Longley made his presentation to the National Security Council. When the name Guardian Island first came up, the director of the FBI beckoned an aide and whispered something in his ear, and the aide left the room. The president asked the first question.

"Is there any possible innocent explanation for all of this?"

No one could come up with one.

"What type of missiles does Iran have?"

Johnson of the CIA was the first to respond: "They have a number of short- and mid-range missiles with ranges up to about three hundred miles. But those are unguided and don't carry much of a payload. The most likely missile with a longer range, and the capacity to carry a heavy payload, would be the Shahab-4, which they developed in cooperation with the North Koreans. It has a maximum range of about twelve hundred fifty miles. It's guided, and it can carry a heavy payload. They tested it about a year ago, and our intelligence reports that it was on target over a one-thousand-mile distance."

"Can it carry a nuclear bomb?" asked Longley.

"Probably. Obviously, we don't know the details of their nuclear technology. But I would say yes, probably, it can deliver a nuclear weapon. Even what is considered a small weapon, such as the fifteen-kiloton bomb we dropped in Japan, has an almost total destruct radius of a half mile from ground zero and a human kill radius going out over one mile, not counting the radiation spread. They don't need a big bomb."

"How far is this Guardian Island from Los Angeles?" asked the president.

"About five hundred miles."

"How much time between a missile launch from the island and the missile reaching our border?" she asked.

"Less than fifteen minutes, ma'am," Longley responded solemnly.

"What about interception by the Patriot missiles?" asked the president.

"Very difficult at that short distance," responded the Air Force representative. "We're moving batteries into intercepting positions, but we're facing a much faster missile than the Patriot has ever gone up against. We do have the ship-based Aegis missile defense system, and we're moving those ships to appropriate positions as we speak. One is redeploying all the way around the Baja Peninsula and north past this island to be under any likely trajectory. The ship is en route, but it will take four days. We think we've done everything possible defensively, but we've never really planned for a nuclear missile to be this close."

The room was deadly silent for more than a moment. During the silence, the FBI aide re-entered the room and handed the director a slip of paper.

"We actually have some more information," the director said quietly, almost to himself, as he read the note. He looked up at the group. "When you mentioned Guardian Island, I remembered that I had recently seen that name in a weekly report. Six weeks ago, an unsolicited informant contacted our L.A. office and reported a number of strange occurrences on an island off the Mexican Baja coast. He called it Guardian Island. It has to be the same island. It was a strange story, but suffice it to say that he and a companion were shot at and almost killed when they tried to go onto the island. He reported that the island was being guarded by armed foreigners – not Mexicans – and that one of them told him that the island was no longer part of Mexico. He's a professor at the University of New Mexico, William Abbey. His record also suggests some involvement in international money laundering."

"Mr. Director, I suggest you find this Professor Abbey and get him to Washington right away," said the president.

"It's already in motion, Ms. President."

Admiral Neal spoke up and said he had already formulated a planned incursion onto the island by the Navy SEALs, at the request of Colonel Longley. "We can put them ashore covertly just north of the suspected site," he explained. "A team of six will be dropped a half mile offshore and will travel with underwater propulsion devices to a rocky cove, where they should be able to go ashore undetected. I can have them on the island by morning. Should I proceed?"

Everyone in the room nodded and murmured in the affirmative.

"Put them ashore," the president directed.

Longley then reported the recent message from the Israeli informant and the possibility of Saqqez being involved in some way. He didn't think to mention the date of January 26, or the reference to Paul Revere.

"I have requested that a Delta Force team be ready to cross the border from Iraq into Iran to see what is happening in Saqqez. Should they proceed?"

The president turned to General Boyer, Chairman of the Joint Chiefs. "What do you recommend, General Boyer?"

"I say hold on that avenue and concentrate on the Mexican site. We'll have time to deal with Saqqez later if we need to."

The meeting suspended, to reconvene in one week or earlier if necessary. It was January 6.

CHAPTER 29

JANUARY 6
ALBUQUERQUE TO D.C.

On the opening day of winter term, Abbey was giving a morning lecture on the Maya civilization of Mexico and Central America when he saw two men enter the rear of his classroom and remain standing. They looked older than the average student and wore dark suits and ties. Since it was the beginning of the term, he assumed they belonged to some review or auditing team from the university, or one of the accrediting bureaus.

This was his most popular course, named "Por Que?" He had created it to focus on why the flourishing and highly developed societies of the Incas, Mayas, and Aztecs had all suddenly failed and disappeared. His last lecture in the spring had become a standing-room-only affair. In that last class, he asked whether the youngest Western society – America – was destined to follow the pattern of its predecessors. With analogies and comparisons, Professor Abbey showed that current American society was not unlike the earlier ones. He presented the last lecture in a bit of a tongue-in-cheek fashion, but today was straight history. His final comments described the demise of the Mayas in the ninth century.

"Recent research suggests that the Maya civilization did not just disappear overnight for unknown reasons. Instead, it was attacked by outsiders. Not being able to defend themselves, the Maya people were wiped out."

With those final words, he closed his notebook and prepared to leave. The visitors walked quickly to the front of
the classroom. Two others appeared inside the door at the
side of the lectern. They displayed badges and identified
themselves as FBI agents. The man in charge told Abbey he
was being taken into custody as a material witness. He was
told that no handcuffs or force would be necessary so long
as he came along quickly and voluntarily.

"Material witness to what?" he exclaimed.

"That is the only information we have, Professor. Please
come along without any disturbance." Some remaining
students stood nearby, gaping at the scene. Abbey could
only imagine what they were thinking. This was probably
about his passport. He had better go quickly and not create
a public scene.

"Okay, I'm coming. Just let me grab my books." He
was shuffled out quickly and proficiently, with an agent on
each arm and one more in front and behind. Outside, two
dark sedans waited at the curb. He was moved quickly into
the rear seat of the first, and the car sped away. He saw the
second car head toward the library.

"What's this all about?" he demanded. "My passport?"

"Don't know anything about your passport, sir. We've
been directed to transport you to Washington, D.C., immediately."

"Washington? Who wants me in Washington?"

"The president, sir."

"The president . . . of what?"

"Our orders are from the President of the United States,
sir."

Abbey sat stunned. They drove to the airport and onto
the runway, where a small plane stood ready with its en-

gines running. The logo on the tail said it was a Cessna Citation X. Two agents accompanied him onto the plane, where two more agents were already seated. The plane was taxiing before he sat down. He thought about how simple his life had been before that visit from Duprey a year ago.

"Can I at least make some calls so people know where I am?" he pleaded.

"No, sir. Our orders are that you talk to no one until some people in Washington talk to you."

What have I gotten myself into? Abbey thought to himself.

In Washington, the plane landed at Andrews Air Force Base, where most of the Iran Group and its staff were assembled in a conference room in a nearby hanger. It took only a few minutes for Abbey to be driven to the building. As he was escorted into the room, he looked around and was shocked at the number and apparent grades of the people present. There were over a dozen men in the room, and he saw many stars and stripes on their shoulders and sleeves. They were senior officers, almost all older than him. All sat in metal chairs around folding tables, which looked to have been hastily assembled into a large rectangle. No one stood as he was escorted into the room. There were no introductory pleasantries.

• • •

"What do you know about Guardian Island, Professor Abbey?" began Colonel Longley.

"I – I've already told the FBI what I know," Abbey stuttered as he tried to keep his composure. "What's this all about?"

Longley ignored the question. "Yes. We've heard the tape. But it leaves a lot unanswered. We want you to tell us the whole story. You will not leave this room until you do." By now, the full dossier on Abbey had been assembled and reviewed by the group. They knew of the initial payments and of his first trip to Mexico, from which he had never officially returned. They knew he had been barred entry but had apparently entered anyway. The FBI team at his condominium had located the Guardian Island photographs on his computer, and they were being analyzed. They knew others were involved. He could not have done all this on his own.

It was clear to Abbey that he had to tell all, so he got started. Once he identified John Duprey, Longley turned to the FBI agent who had remained. "Get him," he ordered. The agent left the room. The story took two hours, with interruptions and questions. Abbey left nothing out. They were most interested in what he had observed on the island. Since he had never approached the enclosure on the eastern side, they were disappointed that he could shed no light on what was inside the enclosure and under the camouflage net.

"If you're telling us the truth, Professor, you might not have much to worry about. At worst, you exercised some bad judgment and showed greed," Longley said after the questions ended. "But if you're lying, I'll see you hung. You will remain in custody here until we get those questions answered. Next will be a polygraph test. In the meantime, give my assistant the names of people who might miss you, and we will make appropriate calls to them."

"What will you tell them?"

"Very little. But they'll know you're alive and safe and in the custody of the FBI. I'm advised that we've now located Mr. Duprey. He's on his way here. Your friend Maria is a bit more complicated, being in Mexico. We will have to decide what to do about her. Hopefully for you, Duprey will confirm your story."

"Shouldn't I be talking to an attorney? I seem to be under arrest."

"Professor Abbey, let's get one thing straight," spoke one of the older men with five stars on his shoulder, pointing his finger at Abbey. "As far as we're concerned, you are a prisoner of war. You have no rights, and you will be granted no rights. You have admitted to acting as an agent for a foreign country in an apparent attempt to attack this country. Someday you might hire the ACLU or someone else to sue. But in the meantime, don't bother us with such questions. We'll do what's necessary to protect this country."

"I want to protect the country, too, sir," Abbey exclaimed. "I'm just confused as to what's going on."

Longley jumped in to try to keep the line of communications open. "Let's first talk to this Duprey. He'll be here soon. Once we finish with him, we'll try to answer some of your questions."

Abbey was ushered out to a holding area.

While he was out of the room, a report came in on his pictures. A speaker phone was activated, and a CIA analyst addressed the group over the line.

"The island is pretty much as he described it," he reported. "Most troubling is the armed man on the dock whom Abbey briefly mentioned. There's a distant shot of the man in one of the digital frames. We've done some extensive enhancement. There's a pin on his left shirt lapel. It looks like a raised fist holding an automatic weapon. That's the logo of the Iranian Quods Force – their Special

Forces. We put his face into our computer base, and the results aren't good. We think he's Major General Mohammed Ashkan. The head of Quods. After General Mussahrah, he's probably the second-ranking military officer in Iran. If all of this is so, the Iranians have someone very senior on this island. And very dangerous."

• • •

Duprey was a harder nut to crack. Although he went with the agents peaceably when they took him into custody at his office, he physically resisted boarding the plane waiting to take him to Washington. He was subdued and put under restraint by the agents and carried onto the plane. In Washington, he immediately invoked the attorney-client privilege and his fifth amendment privilege to remain silent. He refused to say anything and threatened all sorts of lawsuits against this Stalinist behavior.

"Who the hell do you think you are?" he thundered. "This is the United States! You can't simply snatch someone and fly them across the country. I'm going to sue your asses for every cent you even think you have, and then I'll go after the rest."

A CIA-directed interrogation was briefly considered, but they were in the United States, and he was a citizen. Instead, they decided to release him but to keep a very close watch on his activities.

After twenty-four hours, Duprey was returned to Denver with wiretaps on all of his phones and close surveillance on his movements. His name was flagged in the TSA and immigration computers to stop him from flying or attempting to leave the country. Abbey was released at the same time with similar watches on his activities. Longley explained to Abbey that there appeared to be military operations on Guardian Island which were hostile to the United States. He could not tell him more. Abbey told him that he would cooperate and help in any way possible.

"We're going to fly you home," Longley explained, "but we will expect your continued cooperation. I recommend that you keep this all confidential." He did not tell him that wiretaps had been placed on his phones.

. . .

As soon as Duprey was back in Denver, he tried to contact his New York source for the Baja Project. Based upon the interrogation he had undergone, that was certainly what had prompted his seizure. He found the phone to be disconnected. He placed more calls, but he was unable to reach anyone who could help.

. . .

Once he was home, Abbey called Maria. He had already told her of his disclosures to FBI Agent Meadows in Los Angeles. She had been relieved to hear that.

"Maria, this is Bill."

"I was hoping to hear from you today," she answered brightly. "You probably don't even know. It's my birthday!"

"I'm sorry. I didn't know . . . Guess I'm not very good at that kind of stuff. "Happy birthday," he said with little enthusiasm.

"What's wrong?" she said, detecting the strain in his voice.

"We're involved in something much bigger than we realized. The FBI just returned me home from Washington D.C., where I was essentially taken by force two days ago and put through a third-degree interrogation. It's clear they think something very wrong is going on at the island and that we're involved in it."

"What? Were you arrested?" she asked in horror.

"I don't know. It felt like it. I told them everything . . . Even your name. I had to. They might contact you."

"So you're home now?" she said with relief.

"Yes, I'm home. But I don't think we've heard the last of this."

"Well, I would be glad to talk to anyone. There *is* something very wrong on the island, and I want it stopped. It's been like a second home to me for years. I worked there and relaxed there. I want it back."

"We'll see what happens," Abbey said. "I want to see you again, but I don't think I can go into Mexico right now."

"I want to see you, too, Professor Bill," she answered softly. "Maybe I could come there?"

"Yes, that would be great!" he said with the first enthusiasm she had heard during the conversation. "I give final exams and grade them over the next two weeks. Then I can take some time off. Could you come then?"

"Yes. Let's have a quieter time than our last visit. No more midnight excursions. No more guns. A quiet time."

"That would be nice," said Abbey. After they hung up, he thought of his night with Maria.

• • •

A few hours later, Abbey received a phone call from Colonel Longley in Washington.

"Professor, this is Colonel Longley."

"Yes?"

"We've decided that we want to speak to your friend Maria. She's the best local source about what has happened at Guardian Island. It's probably almost like a second home to her. We want your help in contacting her. We want her to be cooperative. No pressure."

Abbey was not stupid. Maria had just told him the island was like a second home, and now the same phrase from Longley?

"Colonel, I'm sure you know she should be here in a few weeks. And I'm sure you know that she will cooperate."

"Very astute, Professor. Yes, we have your phone tapped. We have a court order to do so. These are very important national security matters. We appreciate her willingness to cooperate. But we cannot wait weeks. We need to see her now."

"I'll call and see if she can come sooner," said Abbey.

"You don't understand. Now means *now*. I can have a plane at that local airstrip you're familiar with tonight. We want her to meet us at the airstrip. We will not take her by force. This has to be voluntary. She will be flown directly to Washington. If you wish, when we are finished, we will take her to Albuquerque. We need to learn as much as possible about Guardian Island as soon as possible."

"What's going on there?" Abbey asked again.

"As I said before, I can't tell you, Professor. Suffice it to say that your future and mine may depend on our solving this problem."

Abbey called Maria and arranged the pick-up. That night, he dreamed again:

Mommy, it's me. Back to see you.
Were you bad again, dear?
Only a little. Not really bad.
That makes me sad.

He woke after the dream and realized he had gone two days without his anti-seizure pills. He was starting to see a connection. Were seizures causing these dreams?

· · ·

Maria was apprehensive about the flight. Someone from Washington called her and scheduled the pick-up for that evening. She was told that it would be best for her to drive to the airstrip alone. Someone would return her vehicle to her ranch. She told a friend that her professor friend from Albuquerque was flying her to the States for a visit. Her friend thought it sounded very romantic.

She was surprised at the activity at the airfield. She saw several large helicopters, and what appeared to be American troops bivouacked in a number of large tents. At the eastern end of the field, Maria observed military trucks with racks of rockets and the name *Patriot* painted on the sides. She was told that the Mexican government had approved all of these activities and that they were training exercises.

She was at the field at six o'clock as requested. The plane was waiting for her. Maria had never flown over her beautiful bay or island. She watched with amazement as the land, then water, and then islands swept below her. It was dusk, but there was enough light for her to recognize some landmarks. She quickly saw how her Guardian Island had been changed by a scarred landscape illuminated by powerful spotlights at its southern tip.

In Washington, she was taken by military vehicle to the Pentagon. Awaiting her was an interrogation team headed by Colonel Longley. FBI agents were also present, along with the leader of the SEAL team who had just entered and returned from the island. She was treated with respect and dignity.

"Mrs. Plarez, we very much appreciate your willingness to be here and to help in these difficult times," the colonel began. "Our country is indebted to you."

"I will do anything to get justice and revenge," she answered quietly. "I think they killed my husband, and maybe my uncle, too. They have ruined my village, my island . . . my life."

"Yes, they have, ma'am. We've uncovered many facts in the last few days. We've located and spoken with Corporal Martinez. I'm sorry to report that it's likely that these men did murder your husband. They were trying to get information from him about your uncle's land ownership and his papers. They then stole the papers from his ranch. Your friend Professor Abbey was also involved, but we don't think he knew what was really going on. We don't think he had any knowledge of either the murder or the theft."

"For that I am glad," she answered. "I thank you for the information. It is as I thought."

He continued, "There is a military operation taking place on the island that is hostile to both Mexico and the United States. Your Mexican authorities are with us on this. Mexico has authorized the activities you observed at the air strip. We now need to know everything possible about the island. That is why you're here." He gestured to the SEAL team. "One of these men recently entered your island secretly and returned with some information. But it is your island. No one knows it like you. We need your help."

"Are you going to destroy the island?" she asked with fear in her voice.

"We might have to. To save many lives, we might have to. But we hope not."

"I hope not, too. What do you need from me?"

For the next three hours, they reviewed detailed maps of the island and every small lagoon, inlet, and rock outcropping. They told her that an aerial attack would be most likely, but a land incursion could not be ruled out. They needed to know how they could best get onto the island and move around. After that process, Maria was exhausted. She had jet lag, and her emotional energy was expended. They took a break for the day and offered her a guest apartment in the Pentagon. She was escorted to a simple room with an adjoining bath. Before she fell asleep, she noticed there was no phone in the room.

• • •

After another day of meetings, Longley and his staff decided that Maria had provided everything she knew about Guardian Island. They were ready to send her home.

"Mrs. Plarez," said Longley at the end of the day, "we're ready to get you home. You've helped a great deal. Your assistance will save lives. If you want, I'll make arrangements for you to go through Albuquerque."

Maria sat for a moment, thinking, before she responded. "In these times, Colonel, I think I belong at home. Eventually, I will want to see Professor Abbey, but not now. I hope and think that he is a friend, but most of my friends are in Mexico. I must be there to help them."

"I understand," he answered. "But please say very little to your friends. I promise to contact you before anything happens. Until then, it's important to maintain secrecy."

"Yes, I know," she said. "I will say nothing. But I would like to at least call Professor Abbey."

"I'll set it up," Colonel Longley said as he rose to leave. "Remember, the call will be monitored."

• • •

Abbey answered the phone and heard Maria's voice.

"Maria?" he said with excitement. "Where are you?"

"In Washington, at your Pentagon. But they're about to send me home. They said they would take me through Albuquerque to see you . . ."

"That's great!" he exclaimed with even more excitement.

"I'm not so sure," she said softly, but with determination. "I don't think this is the time for us. There's too much going on. I need to be at home. So I told them to take me directly home."

"Well, I guess I understand," Abbey responded in a disappointed tone.

A few seconds of silence ensued.

"But I wanted to at least talk to you," she added. "I hope this is not goodbye. I hope our time will come again, after all this trouble is hopefully behind us. So, goodbye for now, my professor William," she said in her still, soft voice.

"Yes, Maria. Goodbye for now."

CHAPTER 30

JANUARY 8
NATIONAL SECURITY COUNCIL

The information reported to the NSC after the SEALs'
visit to the island was not particularly helpful. Major John
Keiser had headed the team. After returning, and after
participating in Maria's debriefing, he personally reported
to the council in the White House Situation Room. The
SEAL mission had accomplished little. He had led a six-
man team to the island in two Zodiac crafts similar to the
rubber craft which had chased Abbey and Maria. Entering
the water just before dawn, the team had made it onto the
island undetected, but when they approached the suspected
missile site, they found the area around the camouflage net
heavily guarded. Since their orders were to enter and depart
undetected, there was no way they could find out what was
under the net.

Their monitors detected no radioactivity, but they
could not get closer than one hundred yards from the site.
They installed miniature radio transmitters around the
camouflaged area in order to triangulate its center. This
would aid in later precision bombing. To do so, they buried four transmitters in shallow holes one hundred yards
off the midpoint of each side of the netting. They brought
back photographs which showed a large concrete walled
area covered by the net.

Major Keiser reported that the guards spoke in the Farsi
dialect, the prevailing language in Iran. The guards were
heavily armed with personal and anti-aircraft weapons.

The weapons they observed were Russian-made AK-47 assault rifles and Strela SA-7 man-held portable anti-aircraft weapons. The report from the SEALs estimated the security force around the camouflaged area to be a platoon-sized force of approximately two dozen men. There were more personnel on the island in a tent grouping to the south, at the dock area.

The key question remained unanswered. What was under the net? General Boyer reported that, if Iran was trying to saber-rattle by putting some conventional weapons near America's border, it could easily be resolved. Likewise if it was setting up a site for future nuclear weapons. The council was still hung up by the experts' conviction that Iran was years away from nuclear bomb-ready capacity. The secretary of state led the consensus that there was a crisis but that there was time to solve it using due and deliberate measures, rather than an emergency military response. There had yet to be any communication from Tehran. The Iranians apparently didn't know that their plans had been discovered. They knew that the ship had been watched as it approached the island, but that in itself would tell the Iranians very little.

General Boyer of the Joint Chiefs explained, "Ma'am, we think it's a bit like North Korea. It's a prelude to some saber-rattling. We have missiles armed and targeted which can destroy this site in minutes. The difference is that the Iranians are quite smart. They seem to be almost inviting us to attack this target. Until we know what's under the net, it could backfire, just as the absence of WMDs in Iraq made us look foolish."

The secretary of state added, "We certainly have no basis under international law to take military action,

Madam President. Remember, Iran is a signatory to the Nuclear Non-proliferation Treaty. They may only withdraw on ninety days' notice. They have not withdrawn. We should pursue diplomacy."

President Menton was not going to overrule their advice. Continued monitoring was ordered. For two weeks, nothing changed.

CHAPTER 31

JANUARY 26

THE STATE OF THE UNION ADDRESS

The Constitution calls for an annual report by the president to Congress. That has become the annual State of the Union address. This year, it was scheduled for January 26.

As January 26 approached, Colonel Longley and Henre Morad stayed in close contact with each other. They discussed the various possibilities concerning the message which had been promised on that date.

"I have all our communication channels open and listening," Longley told Morad.

"As do we," said the colonel.

"Henre, why don't you join me at the Pentagon on the twenty-sixth in our communications center? We'll be ready for anything, ready to respond quickly."

The day wore into the evening, and the two men watched the State of the Union Address. It had been decided in the White House that the speech would make no reference to the threat, other than the annual complaint about Iran being a renegade in the family of nations because of its pursuit of nuclear weapons. Beyond that, Longley and Morad watched as President Menton gave a one-hour speech with the usual references to national and international accomplishments, closing with the oft-repeated statement, "In conclusion, I am glad to report that the state of our union is good."

Leaving the podium to healthy but far from overwhelming bipartisan applause, she had just reached the aisle and started her long exit walk down the middle of the chamber, shaking hands on both sides of the aisle, when the television transmission was abruptly interrupted. All television screens in the communications center went dark for five seconds. Longley looked around the room and saw that all screens were blank. Then the signal flickered on and off, and finally back on.

After several more seconds, a bearded, dark-skinned man wearing a white tunic suit appeared on every television screen. His face filled the screen. Behind the face was what Longley recognized to be the national flag of Iran. The man spoke in a low-key, conversational tone: "Citizens of America. This is a message for all Americans. I am Tariq Talabani, President of the Islamic Republic of Iran. May Allah be with you. I have an important message for you tonight. I wish to announce that my country has established a new island nation just south of your state of California border in the Gulf of California. We have purchased this island from Mexico. We wish to be good neighbors, and to live in peace with you. On occasion, however, America has spoken badly of Iran and threatened us with hostilities. We have therefore defended our new island nation with a nuclear device.

"We have no wish to use that device. We will, however, defend ourselves if necessary. We are delivering at this moment a more complete written statement to your government, because my time on this airwave is very limited. Be assured that our intentions are peaceful. Just as you once inserted Israel as our next-door neighbor, we have now become yours. Just as you say that we should live in peace with Israel, we hope that you will live in peace with us. Thank you for your attention, and, as I said and truly mean, may Allah be with each of you."

There was pandemonium in the communications center. As soon as the interruption had occurred, technicians had begun scrambling to try to determine what was happening. Longley placed an immediate call to the networks and ordered them to pull the plug.

"We've tried," they said. "We can't turn it off."

• • •

In the Capitol chamber, where the president was still shaking hands, few knew that anything was amiss. The director of the Presidential Security Division of the Secret Service was watching the address from the Capitol's security center. As soon as he heard the phrase "nuclear device," his training took over. He immediately sent to each security operative by radio and instant messaging the following order: *Evacuate . . . Bomb . . . Red! I repeat: Evacuate . . . Bomb . . . Red!*

He knew the order meant to evacuate the president from the premises with all immediate speed, using deadly force if necessary. A bomb explosion was imminent. The order had been rehearsed often, but it had never before been issued in a real life situation.

The security director could also see live what was happening in the chamber on the closed circuit system, which had not been corrupted. The president was continuing down the aisle, unaware of the speech or the evacuation order. Two agents immediately picked her up by her arms and elbows and ran her toward a nearby elevator, which was already guarded with the door open. A half dozen other agents appeared from seats they had been occupying as dignitaries and formed a moving protective ring with their guns drawn. The few senators and congressmen in their path were shoved aside without ceremony or apology, two of them tumbling to the floor. The director heard the president gasp, "What's going on?"

"We're under attack," shouted one agent. "We're getting you out of here."

"Oh my God," she murmured.

The elevator took them down to ground level, where the presidential limousine was waiting. Because the code word *Red* had been used, which meant a nuclear device, the president was not being taken to the White House. A short distance away, the presidential helicopter was landing. President Menton was driven to the helicopter, which took off immediately, heading west toward Camp David. The protocol was to wait for no one. All of her staff were left behind. She was alone in the helicopter with the pilots and her immediate security detail.

Just as the Iranian speech started, the security director also saw the Swiss ambassador walk to the secretary of state and hand her an envelope. Without diplomatic relations between Iran and the United States since the embassy hostage crisis, he knew the Swiss were usually used as an intermediary. The ambassador had been asked by Iran to deliver the envelope immediately after the president's speech concluded. The ambassador assumed it was a vitriolic protest over criticism Iran anticipated would be directed its way in the speech.

• • •

In the presidential helicopter, the president had not yet heard the Iranian speech. She didn't even know it had occurred. The head of the Secret Service was on the line with her immediately. He filled her in on the speech and on why he had ordered the evacuation. She didn't quarrel with him, but she noted that no bomb had yet exploded. If one was planned, it would have happened by now. She was sensitive to the fact that she was the first female president. She remembered that George Bush had made it back to the White House the night of September 11. She was not going to let herself be portrayed as running away. She ordered the helicopter turn around and head back to the White House.

From the helicopter, she called her staff and told them to schedule an immediate press statement – no questions would be taken – for 11:00 p.m. That would give her time to quickly consult with her advisors. She thought she knew what she had to say. While still on the helicopter, she reached the chairman of the Joint Chiefs, who had been in the chamber for her speech. He assured her that nothing beyond the speech was known. He said he assumed there was a missile in place. He couldn't add anything to the claim that it was armed with an atomic bomb.

At 11:00, President Menton appeared in the Press Room and read the following statement:

"My fellow Americans, I talk to you again tonight to assure you that there is no need for fear about the electronic trick you witnessed a few hours ago. We have known for quite some time that Iran was trying to create a facility off of our southern border. Their operations have been under close surveillance. Indeed, we have inserted troops onto the ground at their facility, and we have photographed it. We have nothing to fear from Iran. We have both the defensive and offensive military capability to deal with their threats. Over the coming days, we will provide more information, but be assured that Iran is no threat to us, just as we have never been a threat to them. Thank you, and good night."

Back in her office, she looked around at all of the advisors. The reports coming in said there was a wholesale, panicked departure from the American Southwest. Highways were full of cars heading north and east. Since it was close to midnight, there were only a few scheduled flights, buses, and trains departing, but mass transit was frozen. The president's message might do some good in calming the panic, but they all knew the exodus would continue, even if at a slightly less frenzied pace. She ordered the National Guard to be activated in California and Arizona, but she knew it would be morning before they reached their armories.

"I hope I was right in saying they are no threat. We'll meet with everyone at seven in the morning. Put the military and NORAD up to full alert until we decide otherwise. I don't think there's anything else we can do now."

• • •

Professor Abbey had been watching the speech. By the end of the Iranian interruption, he was shaking uncontrollably. *What have I done?* He ran to his phone to call Maria. He got no connection, other than a metallic voice saying, "The circuits are busy." He kept dialing, but with no luck. *They really played me,* he thought grimly to himself.

Maybe he could get a domestic call through. He tried Duprey's number in Denver. Duprey had some explaining to do. No luck. Then he thought of his cell phone. The call went through.

"Hello?" came a distant voice, as if through a tunnel.

"Mr. Duprey, this is Professor William Abbey."

"Yeah, hello, Professor," came the foggy response. "Why are you calling me at this hour?"

"Did you see the State of the Union speech?" asked Abbey in an accusatorial tone. "Did you see what you've done? What you made me do?"

"No, I didn't see the goddamned speech," Duprey answered, his voice rising also. "I don't watch that crap. What the hell are you talking about?"

"Turn it on," Abbey shrieked. "Turn on your TV and see what we've done!"

Duprey hung up.

CHAPTER 32

JANUARY 27
NATIONAL SECURITY COUNCIL
THE WHITE HOUSE SITUATION ROOM

The president opened the meeting at 7:30 a.m. sharp. "I assume you have all seen the side letter which was delivered to us and to the Israelis?"

All nodded.

As promised in the speech and observed by the security director, a letter had been delivered to the secretary of state. An identical one had gone to Israel. Although containing a lengthy diatribe about American and Israeli conduct over the past fifty years, there were four paragraphs of most concern:

"Iran's acquisition of Guardian Island from Mexico is fully lawful and in complete accordance with international law. Just as the West acquired various colonial outposts around the world over the last two centuries and claimed sovereign national status, we in the Middle East have every right to do the same. At least we have negotiated and paid for this island. The documents executed with Mexico make it clear that Guardian Island is now the independent state of Parsa. It is entitled to the same rights and privileges as any other sovereign state . . .

"Our claim that we have a nuclear weapon on the island is true. We invite inspection by the United Nations to confirm that fact. Our President will be visiting our new outpost in the near future. He would be glad to welcome a delegation from the United Nations, or from the United States, while he is on the island. Today, Iran formally nullifies its ratification of the Nuclear Non-proliferation Treaty and withdraws from that treaty, just as the United States has nullified and withdrawn from treaties which no longer suit its purposes . . .

"We also have a second nuclear device within Iran at a location capable of reaching Israel in a very few minutes. We are not prepared to disclose the location of that second device. Neither weapon should be considered an offensive threat. But if we are attacked at either location, both devices will be used to defend. Much as with the American Monroe Doctrine and its policy in South Korea and other places of interest to it, an attack on one location will be considered an attack on the other. We do not threaten with dozens of weapons, as possessed by America. We believe these two are sufficient to defend ourselves . . .

"Parsa is not only a military outpost. It is a beautiful island in a wonderful region. We hope to populate it with civilians. It would be a fine American retirement community, and Americans will be welcome if they choose to come. We are sure that it will grow into a popular Muslim community. Americans will be welcome among us so long as they respect our customs and traditions."

Turning to the FBI director, the president asked about the television interruption. "How did they pull that off?"

"Ma'am, we don't know yet. Our electronics people have secured all equipment used in the feed of your speech. The equipment is being disassembled as we speak. As soon as we know, we will advise you. In the meantime, the networks have replaced all transmission equipment here in the White House to assure it does not happen again."

The president continued, "Because of the letter threatening Israel, I have invited Mr. Henre Morad of the Israeli intelligence service to attend this meeting. That was at the strong recommendation of Colonel Longley, who is also in attendance. Colonel Longley appears to be the only one who called this correctly.

"I just met with the Mexican ambassador. He is a shaken man. He says he has been up all night on the phone with President Chavez and the leaders of their senators and deputies. The bottom line is that the Iranian statement that they own this island appears to be true." Murmuring broke out in the room among those who had hoped it was a hoax. "The Mexicans thought they were creating some type of grand resort and retirement community on the island. They say they didn't pay a lot of attention to the text of the documents, which essentially granted the developer sovereignty over the island. I'm sure a lot of money changed hands to encourage that inattention.

"Based upon the information we've received from this Professor Abbey and his photographs, their claim of a nuclear weapon is probably true. The CIA says Iran's second-ranking military man is on the island. "

The secretary of state spoke up. "Sounds like fraud and misrepresentation to me. Maybe the purchase of the island can be nullified." She looked at her assistant for international law who had accompanied her.

The young man looked uneasy as he responded, "Unfortunately, international law does not permit nullification as easily as in private commercial transactions. Otherwise, it would be too easy for new regimes to attempt to renegotiate land exchanges and border agreements of prior governments. Based upon the little that we now know, it is probably going to be difficult for Mexico to throw out this agreement. But our staff will continue to research the point."

"With all due respect, ladies and gentlemen," said Henre Morad, "the Iranians might consider such an attempt to be an attack on their island. In Israel, we certainly consider any attempt to change or reduce our borders to be an attack on us."

"Let's review our military options. General Boyer?" the president said, directing the question to the chairman of the Joint Chiefs.

"In some ways, this is very simple. We can easily take out the probable site of the weapon, or the entire island, for that matter. We can do it with conventional weapons."

"But what about such an attack detonating their nuclear bomb on the island?" asked the director of the CIA.

"Extremely unlikely. Essentially impossible," responded the general. "These bombs have very complex explosive mechanisms. A precise number of neutron particles have to be projected into the uranium core of the weapon. Detonation requires almost fifty carefully timed and directed small, preliminary explosions – much different from conventional bombs, which could be detonated by a nearby blast. Bombing the site would, however, cause a dirty-bomb-like explosion. It would be conventional, but it would disburse radioactive uranium from the core of the bomb into the air."

"How bad would that be?" asked the president.

"For us, not too bad. The initial dispersion radius would be about ten miles. The prevailing winds there are from the west. That would mean most radioactivity would blow eastward over the gulf, with some residual radioactivity reaching mainland Mexico."

"We're forgetting one thing," said General Boyer. "The other bomb in Iran, supposedly pointed at Israel."

Everyone turned to Morad, who responded with delicacy, "That is obviously an Israeli problem, and not so much yours. But we have worked cooperatively on many matters over the years, and we hope we can do so here."

"We don't even know where the Iran bomb is," commented the secretary of state.

"We think we do," said Morad softly. "We think it is in the town of Saqqez, in the northwestern section of Iran near the Iraqi border. We are prepared to take it out."

"What type of weapons would you use?" asked Longley, remembering their earlier conversation.

"That would be the subject of discussion at a much higher level than I hold. The weapon would, I'm sure, be of the appropriate type."

Colonel Longley added, "From the Iran Group's perspective, it would be a grave mistake to respond to this nuclear threat with nuclear weapons. That should be absolutely the last option. We don't want the Arab world to see nuclear weapons being used. It will incite them and whet their appetites for some of their own."

"Message heard and received, Colonel," said the president. "I will talk to the Israeli prime minister on the subject. How certain are we of Saqqez?"

"We are confident, but not certain," the Israeli responded.

"Remember," added Longley, "we still have the option of inserting the Delta Force and finding out for sure what's happening there. The plans are drawn and the personnel are in place."

"Might I suggest another option?" All heads turned to Morad. "Although your Delta Force is formidable, it might be detected. It would be considered a hostile act by Iran. Israel has a man in place in northern Iraq – a Kurd – who might be able to accomplish the same thing more quietly. Saqqez is a traditionally Kurdish area. He can melt into the population easily. Quite candidly, if, as I suspect, we pursue a joint operation, with us taking out Saqqez, it might be best not to have the Americans involved there. I fear that any force on the ground near Saqqez might not survive an attack. We do not want American blood on our hands if we destroy the Saqqez site."

"I think you make a good point, Mr. Morad," commented the president. "I will leave it to you and our military to work out those details. If your agent can obtain the necessary information, let's use him."

The secretary of state said, "What about this offer of a United Nations inspection? Maybe we should take them up on it to be certain."

The president turned to General Boyer.

"I don't think so," he replied. "At some time, we're going to take out this island. I don't want there to be prolonged negotiations about some inspection while they move in civilians as human shields and beef up whatever defensive weapons they do have there. I certainly don't want United Nations personnel on the island when we attack. We take them at their word. We don't want them there no matter what they have under that tarp. We simply have to plan how to best do it. We're planning as we speak. We actually now have at our disposal a local Mexican woman who knows the island very well and is giving us useful information. If you remember the names that have come before you previously, the lawyer John Duprey from Denver had a change of heart last night. He is now singing like a bird. I'm not sure how helpful he'll be, but we're still collecting a lot of information."

"May I, Ms. President?" asked Longley.

She nodded. "We should have listened to you before, so we're certainly going to now, Colonel. Go ahead."

"I believe that we should immediately get two things from Mexico. First, a complete nullification vote of the legislation which gave this island to Iran, signed by the Mexican president. Second, an unequivocal request to destroy this island."

"But we already explained that it cannot be nullified," said the secretary of state somewhat primly. "And Mexico is unlikely to invite us to bomb its own country. Besides, let's remember, Iran's purported withdrawal from the NPT is a nullity. The treaty requires a three-month notice period before a signatory may withdraw."

"I'll be sure to tell them that they have to wait three months," Longley responded with more than a hint of sarcasm. "I don't care what the lawyers say, Madam Secretary.

Whether it's effective or not, I think the Mexican nullification vote should be in place. And they'd better give us the invitation to attack the island before we ratchet up real pressure on them. I'm not suggesting that either the nullification vote or the letter be publicized at the outset. I think they should be in our back pocket, to be made public the day we eliminate this threat. As far as I'm concerned, Iran has declared war on us and on Israel. We have to move quickly and aggressively to defeat the threat."

The secretary of state glared at him. She was not used to being addressed in that fashion by anyone.

President Menton stepped into the silence. "We will work on all those things, Colonel. Now, I have to prepare for another address to the public. I understand there is a great amount of fear and confusion in the country," she said, concluding the meeting.

There was fear and confusion. The attempted exodus from the Southwest continued, and the night before, the telephone grid had locked down for the first time in history because of the volume of traffic. Fortunately, the television lead had still been locked out when the president was carried out of the Capitol chambers to the elevator, so that embarrassing scene was not televised around the world, but it had been observed by reporters and others and widely reported.

The vice president, Henry Caruthers, who was in attendance, was an old curmudgeon of American politics who had been chosen to add respectability and depth to the first female presidency. He spoke up quickly as the meeting was being adjourned. "Madam President, may I have one moment?"

Looking at her watch somewhat impatiently, Menton sighed. "Certainly, Henry. What do you wish to add?"

"Ma'am, I think it might be a mistake for you to address the nation again. Optics and public confidence are important. You spoke to the nation twice last night. That is already unprecedented. We don't want to reinforce the sense of crisis which is already spreading around the country and the world. You have a fine array of assistance in this room and elsewhere. I recommend that you go about your normal business and let your staff – probably General Boyer or the secretary of defense – deal with further statements. This is, after all, a military matter. Although presented to us in a way which suggests a crisis, it is presented by a country which we should not fear. At least, we should not show any fear. Your second statement last night was a masterpiece. Let that, at least for the moment, be your last one."

The president was already standing when he spoke. She looked pensively at him for a moment. "You know, Henry, I knew I was right in asking you to be my vice president. I think I agree with you. Furthermore, I think it's time for me to visit home. I can manage this situation from Bel Air as well as from here. We'll show those sons of bitches that they don't push around this country, or this president."

Eyebrows were raised in the room. The president had never before cursed in a public setting.

"General Boyer," she continued, "please prepare the appropriate statement for release by either you or the secretary of defense at the Pentagon. I will depart for California this afternoon. Colonel Longley, I want you and Mr. Morad to accompany me. We will meet again tomorrow morning at the same time in this room. I will be here on a television lead. And folks, please make sure I am not interrupted this time. I will talk to the Israeli prime minister this afternoon from Air Force One."

CHAPTER 33

JANUARY 27
AIR FORCE ONE

The president reached the Israeli prime minister from Air Force One. "Mr. Prime Minister, your Andre Morad has been of invaluable assistance."

"He is among our best."

"We need to be considering a joint operation."

"I agree."

"We are proposing to destroy this Guardian Island with conventional weapons. A small number of our cruise missiles will accomplish the task, followed up by a marine landing. I am assured that a nuclear response is not necessary."

"Yes, my military people tell me that you can deal with the island in that fashion. But if you do that, we have concerns for the safety of Israel . . ."

"What about you, Mr. Prime Minister? What is Israel proposing for Iran?"

"Our initial thinking is to destroy Iran, using our most potent weapons."

She responded with urgency in her voice, "The precedent would be terrible."

"It would be both bad and good," he responded. "Certainly the destruction on the ground and the thousands of casualties would be viewed as bad by some. But we are growing tired of these threats. We lost over ten million in the holocaust. That was because of international weakness, and because strong countermeasures were never taken. The Iranians are threatening another holocaust. If not Iran, it will be North Korea, or the Sudan, or the Palestinians. There will be another similar threat by someone. We think we have to put an end to these threats. There appears to be no other way. The world seems only to understand power and destruction."

"But Mr. Prime Minister, there has yet to be anything but words in this current crisis. I'm sure we both remember the playground rhyme that words alone will never hurt."

"I know the rhyme, Madam President. But we are not here talking of sticks and stones."

"We in America understand your concerns. I will not, however, countenance the use of nuclear weapons in this attack. If that is your final position, Israel will be going alone."

"I hear what you say, Madam President. I will talk to my people. We should talk again tomorrow. We do not have much time."

"No, we do not. We have less than three weeks. I have just learned that another ship has departed Iran, heading toward this new island state. It apparently carries some type of celebratory group to applaud this nuclear checkmate over America and Israel. We probably won't let it reach the island. We can destroy the island and its weapons, but I will not authorize coordination with a nuclear response from Israel. It is your decision."

"Yes, I agree, it is a hard one. Thank you, and we will talk again tomorrow."

• • •

Israel had no choice. Prime Minister Shalon and his military staff knew that their nuclear weapons were not necessary to destroy the facilities at Saqqez, or Jask, or Natanz, or all three of them. Conventional bombs could accomplish the task. These were not hardened underground bunkers, because any Iranian missile had to have a wide, unprotected opening to the sky. They also knew they had to coordinate with the Americans. A preemptive strike by either country alone would cause the bombing of the other. The prime minister sat, shaking his head, realizing that the diabolical Iranian two-pronged threat against both Israel and the United States was going to save Iran from a nuclear holocaust.

• • •

While still in the air, the president called Longley to her airborne office. She sat alone in one of the two armchairs next to her desk. She offered him the other chair with a small hand gesture. As he sat, he could smell perfume. He had never noticed that before. She was dressed casually in slacks and a sweater.

"I talked to the prime minister. I told him there was no way we would go along with any use of nuclear weapons."

"And?"

"He'll talk to his people. He'll come around. He pretty much has to." She sighed. "I guess we should have listened to you, Colonel."

He smiled grimly. "I just call them as I see them. I know there are other considerations beyond the scope of my job. I'm not sure what we could have done, anyway. No one ever believes the bad guys are really bad till they get punched in the nose."

"Well, I guess we've been punched." She looked at him more carefully. "So, tell me a little about yourself."

He shrugged. "Not a lot to tell. I'm a typical career marine. The corps pretty much took over my life. Lost my wife because of it. But it was my choice." Looking around the cabin, he looked back at the president. "I must admit I'm not used to these rarified heights." He acknowledged his double entendre with a grin.

A buzz on her phone abruptly brought them back to reality.

"OK, I'll talk to him," she said quietly. When she looked up, Longley was already standing. "Back to work. It's the Mexican president. Probably wants to apologize again. Thanks for spending some time talking. Maybe we can do it again."

"Yes, ma'am."

Before he reached the cabin door, Longley suddenly found himself flying toward the rear bulkhead of the cabin as the plane went into a steep emergency dive. A shrieking alarm blasted throughout the plane. All four engines pushed to full throttle and headed for the ground while turning wildly left, then right, while at the same time, releasing anti-missile chaff and flares.

Longley landed on top of the president on the wall behind her desk, almost in an embrace. She was face down, and he on top of her, with his arms stretched out on either side of her head. Luckily, the furniture was bolted to the floor, but books and lamps and small items cascaded about them. The Secret Service agent outside the door tried to enter, but she was pressed against the door jamb by the centrifugal force.

After a few moments, the plane pulled out of the dive. The alarm stopped, and the shaken agent pushed the door open with her weapon drawn. Longley was kneeling next to the president behind her desk. He was gently lifting her head when the agent braced him.

"Sir, move away immediately!"

"I'm trying to—"

"Now, or you're dead." She aimed at his face, only ten feet away.

He dropped his hands and slowly stood as he backed away. The president's head hit the carpeted floor, and her eyes fluttered open.

"What happened?"

"I don't know, ma'am. For some reason we went into an emergency dive." The agent's cell phone rang. She put it to her ear with her left hand, her pistol still in her right.

Over the intercom, the pilot said, "Sorry. We had a report of a missile fired at us from the island. I had to dive. Now I'm told it was a short-range anti-aircraft missile, probably aimed at a reconnaissance plane. I'm diverting from L.A. International to Edwards. More security there. We'll be on the ground in twenty minutes."

The agent holstered her weapon. Looking somewhat sheepishly at Longley, she said, "Sorry, sir. I wasn't sure what to do."

"No problem. You did the right thing. Think I'd better get back to my seat. And my seatbelt." He looked over at President Menton. "Are you okay, ma'am?"

"I think so. You go to your seat. We'll talk again later."

He left the cabin as more agents and medical technicians rushed in.

CHAPTER 34

JANUARY 27

GUARDIAN ISLAND

With the missile disclosure having been made, General Ashkan knew there was no longer need for secrecy or concealment. Indeed, the plan called for them to show off what they had. The camouflage netting was removed during the night.

American surveillance flights reported that there was a missile in place, apparently ready to be fired. It was a Shahab-4. The missile site was ringed by guards with shoulder-firing anti-aircraft weapons. One anti-aircraft missile had been fired during the night at an overflight. When the ascending rocket was observed, there was no way of knowing what type of missile had been fired. Thus the report to the president's plane and the evasive maneuvers.

Longley was put in charge of orchestrating a military response. An attack-class nuclear submarine was repositioned to the entrance to the Gulf of California off the southeastern tip of the Baja. Traveling underwater at emergency speed, the vessel was in place within twenty-four hours. The water was 1,000 feet deep at the entrance to the gulf, and there was a clear open-water approach to the island 700 miles north. The submarine had the capacity of firing a dozen Fasthawk cruise missiles, armed with either 1,000-pound conventional explosives or electronic disruption devices. Nuclear warheads were not being considered. Once launched from the submarine, the missiles would reach the island, undetected, in less than thirty minutes. The submarine's twelve vertical firing tubes could be quickly reloaded for additional barrages.

In the afternoon, Longley was advised that another message had been delivered to the State Department by the Swiss ambassador from the new state of Parsa. The letter protested surveillance over-flights in its airspace. They were considered acts of war and would be treated as such if they continued. Longley directed that the over-flights be stopped, but the satellite and offshore monitoring continued. He still didn't know the Iranian objective.

CHAPTER 35

JANUARY 27
WASHINGTON, D.C.

As the president had reported to the prime minister, satellite images showed that another ship had been detected departing Jask and heading east. This one left with great fanfare and publicity, and everything was reported by media around the world. The Iranian population, and many Muslims outside of Iran, had applauded Iran's dramatic announcement. Celebrations were widespread in the Middle East, rejoicing that the Americans and their puppet Israel were finally getting a comeuppance. President Talabani announced to the world that he was going to personally visit the new outpost and head a huge celebration on the island. He explained that there was not yet any airfield, and no Western country would permit him to travel through its borders, so he would go by ship in the same way the island had been built and armed.

Televised newscasts depicted ceremonies in both Tehran and Jask seeing him off. Before boarding, the president had a final meeting with the Ayatollah and General Mussahrah.

"I'm a sitting duck on that ship," Talabani complained. "I should fly to Cuba, or Argentina. I'm sure they'll let me land."

"No, actually, they won't," replied the general. "We've talked and argued with them . . . and others. No one wants to invoke the wrath of the Americans. We expected a response from the West by now, but it hasn't happened. Probably the indecision of a woman, as we thought. We'll put Al-Jazeera and plenty of civilians on the boat. They won't attack it and kill innocents. They're too weak to do that. You will be safe on the ship."

. . .

Following the recommendation of the vice president, the announcement from Washington came first from General Boyer and the secretary of defense. They held a press conference on the afternoon of January 27 at the Pentagon.

First, they announced that the president was at that moment on her way home to the "Western White House" in Bel Air, California, to assure her home state that Californians had no need for fear. That would hopefully slow the panicked departure that was taking place in southern California. Automobiles continued to stream north. Airlines were fully booked. Some airlines had even attempted to cancel all flights from the area and redeploy their airplanes to the north, as they often did in advance of hurricanes and floods. Prompt intervention by the FAA had stopped that. But no one could force the ground crews or cockpit crews to show up, and some were not appearing for work. The secretary of defense also reiterated the president's message from the night before that this development was not a surprise to the military or to the intelligence community. They had been watching this island for quite some time. Questions were invited.

"Sir, is there a nuclear bomb on that island?" yelled an Associated Press reporter.

General Boyer stepped forward. "We know there is a missile there, but we cannot confirm the nature of any bomb or weapon. We take Iran at its word, stated repeatedly over the last five years that its nuclear program was for civilian and peaceful purposes. Their recent pronouncement belies those earlier statements. They either lied before, or they're lying now. We are, however, prepared for any and all eventualities. If Iran wants to pick a fight with the United States, they will find, as others have in the past, that we are a worthy adversary. We would not lose such a fight."

"But what about the report that there is another nuclear bomb in Iran, aimed at Israel?" shouted another reporter.

The secretary of defense took that question. "Once again, Iran has made such a threat, but there is no evidence that it is true. We assume that Iran wants to live peaceably with its neighbors rather than be destroyed by them. I will let Israel respond with any more detail."

"Will you be going to the United Nations?"

"We see no need to do that at this time," said the secretary. "We have the matter under control."

"How does Mexico explain what it has done to us by making our enemy our neighbor?"

"Mexican officials feel they have been duped," answered the secretary. "As we speak, they are reviewing their options. They transferred this island to what they understood was a private group for development into a retirement community. They were misled."

The secretary of state had been assured by Mexico that afternoon that whatever nullification votes or resolutions were requested would be immediately forthcoming. It would be impossible to keep quiet a vote of the full chambers of the Mexican senators and deputies, over six hundred politicians, but the leaders of each chamber would sign an appropriate resolution. Mexico's president had already requested any and all necessary military action to rid Mexico of this embarrassment. That request would also be put into writing. It had been decided that they would downplay the military preparations. No one wanted to set off a trigger-happy Iranian.

CHAPTER 36

MID FEBRUARY
TEHRAN

The Ayatollah and General Mussahrah were surprised by the American response. They thought it was too muted, as if the Americans had something up their sleeve. The Iranian strategy depended on the continued secrecy of the location of the missile pointing at Israel. If the location of that missile in Saqqez became known, Iran's trump card was severely compromised. Mussahrah therefore ordered a careful review of security measures at Iran's nuclear facilities to see if there had been any leak. The review included electronically scanning outgoing emails over the last ninety days for any message containing the word *Saqqez*.

Maked's last unencoded message had identified Saqquez. His message was uncovered by Mussahrah's review. Once he received the report, Mussahrah had Ishmael's background file pulled. Nothing stood out until he saw the entries about the death of his parents. He thought he understood. The general was in Tehran. He ordered Ishmael's wife and children immediately picked up and transported to Saqqez. Then he left, heading for the same place with an entourage of three heavily armed vehicles. He didn't think it would take him long to break this traitor.

Ishmael was at his work station in Saqqez when the security detail arrived. Three uniformed men barged into his area, brandishing weapons. They ordered everyone to stay put. Once they located him, he was pulled out of his chair, dragged to a waiting car, and taken to a shed-like building. The room inside was dimly lit, with a drape across one end. As Ishmael was roughly escorted into the room, he saw General Mussahrah sitting at a desk at one end. Makad's hands were tied behind his back, and he was pushed roughly to the desk, where he stood quaking with fear.

"Ishmael Makad, I am General Mahmoud Mussahrah. Do you know of me?"

"I know who you are, sir."

"We have some very serious questions to ask you."

"Yes, General. I will try to answer." He knew what was happening. He tried to appear calm, but he was trembling inside.

"Why did you recently send a transmission to outsiders about Saqqez?"

Thinking quickly, Makad decided he had to try to cover. They didn't seem to know too much. "I do not believe I ever did, General. Maybe I mentioned its name in a transmission. But I certainly would not have said anything about our operations . . ."

Mahmoud nodded to the men, and Ishmael was struck hard in his face with a rifle butt. It smashed his chin and nose, and blood gushed down his shirt.

"Don't play games with me. We have the message. It makes no sense, unless you were trying to send a coded message. I assure you that you will die in Saqqez as you said in the message. But before you die, you will see your wife die, and then your two children." He gestured again, and the drape was pulled open to reveal three chairs in which his family members were tied and gagged. The children's eyes bulged with fear. His wife's were closed, as if she were praying. "Their deaths will not be pleasant to view."

Makad turned and saw them. His wife's eyes opened, and they were filled with hatred and the accusation of betrayal.

Spitting out blood and broken teeth, he cried, "They know nothing! They are innocent. You must not harm them!"

"I don't care what they know or whether they are innocent. You will either talk right now and tell us the truth, or I promise to Allah that I will rip their bodies apart before you. Now to whom did you send that message, and why?"

Makad knew he had reached the end of the line. He hoped he could save his family. He had settled his blood oath and done all that he could. He knew he would soon join his parents. He told everything.

Immediately after the interrogation, General Mussahrah reached the Ayatollah.

"Ali, we have a serious problem. I believe they know of Saqqez."

"How could that be?"

"We had a traitor. A spy. He disclosed the location to the Israelis. That explains the strange silence from the Americans and the Israelis. By now, we expected them to be clamoring before the United Nations and trying to negotiate with us. None of that has happened. If they know of Saqqez, they are almost certainly planning a surprise joint attack on both sites."

"That is certainly possible," mused the Ayatollah out loud. "Let me think for a moment." There was silence. Then he spoke in a conspiratorial voice. "But what if there is a third bomb?"

"You know there isn't. Let us not play games."

"Don't be so sure, my general. You do not necessarily know everything. Remember, the plans were to build three bombs. We have never talked of the third. The more important point is that they know nothing about the third bomb. At least, not yet. As we have said before, we cannot beat them with bombs. They have too many. We can only beat them with the threat of bombs. Put together an immediate message for delivery to the Americans and the Israelis, playing, as they would say, our ace in the hole. Tell them we detect a sense that they might try to destroy our two bombs. That is why we have a third, which we have not yet talked about. Tell them the third will detonate if they attack the other two. We will not tell them where it is."

"As usual, my esteemed one, you are a genius. The letters will be delivered before day's end." Mussahrah wondered whether there was any truth to this new threat. Had his cousin the Ayatollah, or the president, really placed a third bomb somewhere for this eventuality without telling him? He met with his advisors to prepare the letter. But he also started to think that he might have to implement his own contingency plan.

CHAPTER 37

LATE FEBRUARY

THE LETTER

On February 1, two envelopes were delivered by the Swiss ambassador. They quickly reached the president and her military staff at Colorado Springs, where Longley and Morad had been sent.

To the American President and the Israeli Prime Minister:

We believe you have ignored our warnings and that you are planning to attempt to destroy our bombs. For your information, your agent "Paul Revere" has met his death as he predicted. All along, we have had a third bomb which we chose not to disclose. Be assured that any military action by you will cause the detonation of this third bomb. It will cause many deaths. They will have been caused by you.

"Charles, this is a hoax," concluded Morad. "They might have found and killed our agent, but they're bluffing about the third weapon."

Longley nodded hesitantly. "I tend to agree, but it does create a dilemma. What if they're not bluffing? They're careful not to say that there's a missile, or where it is. There could be a bomb already somewhere in either one of our countries. We need an immediate teleconference of the group, with our President and your prime minister patched in. We only have days before the attack."

The telephone conference was immediately set up.

"Okay, gentlemen, since ladies go first and I'm the only lady here, I'll go first. Who can shed any information on this message?"

After a short silence, the prime minister spoke. "This is very troubling, but we think it is clearly a ruse. They have found and killed our agent, so they now know we are aware of Saqqez. Iran must now come up with another way to deter our attack, so they come up with this story about a third bomb. Our agent was very good. His information has proven accurate for over ten years. We believe his last message was telling us to bomb Saqqez and that he expected that he would die in that assault. He would not have said that if he thought there was a third bomb, and I feel sure he would have known if there was one. That is my opinion and that of my security people."

"Colonel Longley?" asked the president.

"I agree, but for a slightly different reason. If I were the Iranians, I can think of no reason why I wouldn't have disclosed the third bomb from the outset. It would only have strengthened their hand. They've come up with this because they think we might be planning to attack both locations – which, obviously, we are."

The discussion continued, but nothing more of substance was said.

President Menton finally closed the meeting. "But we don't know for sure, do we? The only certain thing is that we have a renegade nation on our hands which must be stopped. For now, I think we have to take the risk and ignore the threat of a third bomb. Continue your plans. And by the way, I like the idea of timing the attack with Talabani's arrival, rather than before his ship arrives. I am advised that the FBI uncovered a small electronic chip in one of the television cables which permitted him to take over our airwaves. That will not happen again. I'm praying that we are making the right decision. I'm sure you all are, too."

A few minutes later, Longley was advised that the president was back on the line. He wondered why she was calling him again. She had grown in his respect during the crisis. She was now ensconced in her California home in Brentwood Country Estates, a private walled community off Mandeville Canyon Road in the foothills of Bel Air. She was on the line.

"Colonel, I'm calling you one-on-one. No one else is on the line. What do you think I should do?"

"That's not really for me to say."

"I know, but I'm asking you. I need to be able to talk to someone I trust. I know I'm the president. But I'm also a person, a woman, and as you probably know, I no longer have a confidante. I'm a bit alone in this job."

"I'm alone too, ma'am, so I think I do know what you mean. I'll help if I can. I think you should follow your gut instinct and the advice you're getting. You did that when you listened to the vice president, and did him one better by returning to California. The advice is basically unanimous. Get rid of the threat. There's a risk that they're not bluffing about the third bomb, but the alternative is to let them leverage us on every issue that comes up. Next it will be a U.N. vote, or an aid package to Israel. They cannot beat us militarily. They can only threaten and play upon our fear of being hurt. We have to risk being hurt. There's no other way." Suddenly, realizing that he was talking to the president of the United States, Longley stopped. "I'm going on too long. I'm sorry."

"No, that's what I wanted to hear. I wanted to hear your heart. I think I did." She paused. "How am I doing, Colonel?"

"Much better than many expected, ma'am, including myself." Longley had always been direct. "I thought you were a good actress. I wasn't so sure how you'd be as president. I'm impressed."

"I appreciate your candor. I'm new at this. I feel better hearing that I'm not messing it up."

"No, ma'am, you're not messing it up. You're doing fine."

"Thank you, Colonel. Guess I'd better get some sleep. Hope to see you someday under different circumstances. One more question. What's this reference to Paul Revere in the Iranian letter?"

Longley realized he hadn't discussed that part of the message with her or the Security Council. "Actually," he answered, "I had almost forgotten about that. The last message from the Israeli agent made a strange statement that we still don't understand. As I recall, it said, 'As Paul Revere signaled, they are by water.' We've not been able to figure it out, other than warning us of an Iranian attack, just as Paul Revere warned the revolutionaries that the British were coming."

"How's your American history, Colonel?"

"Probably not that great."

"Do you know what Paul Revere's signal was?"

"Can't say that I do."

"One if by land, two if by sea. . ." she said slowly and distinctly. "Colonel, do we have two bombs on that island?"

"Oh my God. That's what he meant. Two missiles by water. He was saying that the ship carried two missiles, and we've assumed there was only one. We have to get someone onto the island."

"I think that would be a very good idea. And quickly. We don't have much time."

CHAPTER 38

LATE FEBRUARY
SAQQEZ

Mussahrah was not certain that the new ploy of the third bomb would succeed. As a backup, he traveled again to the launch center at Saqqez and visited the launch site. He spoke with the chief of the missile guidance and firing staff.

"How quickly can this missile be fired?" Mussahrah asked.

"From the moment of the order, we can have it off the ground in forty-five seconds," responded the chief engineer.

"And where is it aimed now?"

"As ordered, we have avoided Jerusalem. Tel Aviv is the city with the largest concentration of Jews without great numbers of nearby Arabs. That is where it will go. To Tel Aviv – their money capital."

"Can it be redirected?"

The engineer looked puzzled as he answered: "Yes, certainly, General Mussahrah. To any target within fifteen hundred miles. But the plan has always been Tel Aviv. A change would take only an hour of reprogramming. But it would require confirmation."

"What do you mean, *confirmation?*" said Mussahrah, his voice rising in anger.

"Our orders are to make no changes to the plan without a joint directive from the Ayatollah and President Talabani. Surely you know all these things, General?"

General Mussahrah calmed himself. "Certainly. I am just testing you. But what would you do with an order from me to redirect the missile to the Green Zone in Baghdad?"

"We would hope for the required confirmation, General."

"Good. Carry on. Let Allah be your guide. And please make the arrangements to redirect the missile to Baghdad. Naturally, do not implement them unless you receive the necessary confirmation. But be ready. The confirmation will be forthcoming. "

I'm going to work on that confirmation, Mussahrah thought to himself as he turned and marched out of the room. He was starting to think that the American forces in Baghdad would be better than nothing. If his ace in the hole at Saqqez was now compromised, and it certainly was, Iran would soon be attacked. If he initiated a preemptive attack, everyone would pause. He knew the Americans had nuclear weapons in Iraq. He could orchestrate it as an American nuclear weapon malfunction. After all, the world had believed his lies up till now.

As for the required confirmation, his man Kazam was on the island and could extract authorization from President Talabani once the president reached the island. Mussahrah himself could control the Ayatollah. Those sexual indiscretions might be helpful after all.

When he reached his car, he placed the call. "Get me Kazam from Guardian Island on my line," he directed his assistant. "Then leave so I can speak to him in private."

This will cause the Americans to delay their attack to another day, he thought, *and at least the Baja weapon will be saved.*

A few minutes later, he said, "Kazam, are you ready for one final, heroic assignment?"

"Of course, my General . . ."

General Mussahrah told Kazam what he needed. "It must be done quickly, as soon as he arrives on the island."

"I will attend to it."

CHAPTER 39

MARCH 1
CHEYENNE MOUNTAIN

Maria had also been brought to Cheyenne Mountain in Colorado Springs to be available for inquiries about the island. After his conversation with the president, Longley ordered the SEAL team flown in immediately. He also summoned Professor Abbey from Albuquerque. Late that day, he met with all of them to decide how to get on the island to determine if it held a second missile.

Henre Morad also attended. He could not believe that he and his intelligence people had missed the code in the message. He retrieved a dossier on General Mussahrah, whom he assumed was in charge of this project. Both against the Afghans and the Iraqis, Mussahrah had been masterful in the use of decoys. The invaders had almost been invited to attack apparent weak points in Iran's defenses. When they took the bait and attacked, the attacking forces were crushed by overwhelming forces from other hidden locations. Was the fully visible missile site on the southern tip of Guardian Island another such decoy? Was there another missile on the island in a different, hidden location?

The group began to review the maps and photographs to find a location for another missile. A second could have been brought along as a spare, in which case it had to be stored somewhere. Such a spare missile did not concern them. What they were worried about was a second oper-

ating missile armed with a nuclear warhead. There were
many possible sites, particularly on the northern half of
the island, where a simpler and more concealed second
launch pad could have been built. It could even be a mobile
launching platform such as used for the Scud missiles. It
was going to be difficult to get on the island surreptitiously
and search for other sites within three days. Because of the
president's mention the night of January 26 that American
forces had already been on the island, the Iranians had increased their shore patrols. They were also now bolstered
by new small motor boats which had been delivered with
the missile ship. The group was stymied.

Longley summed up their dilemma. "We have to put
a resource on the ground on the island. We need to know
about the second missile, and we also need some independent ground confirmation of what is there. We have
that confirmation from Henre's source in Kurdistan. He
crossed into Iran, and he reports there is a camouflaged site
at Saqqez which appears to hold a missile. It is newly constructed. If we don't put someone onto the island, and if we
attack, we could be pilloried in the world press. They'll say
we attacked prematurely, like in Iraq, and that we should
have talked and negotiated. They'll say that Iran was bluffing and that no one would put one bomb against our thousands."

Professor Abbey was in the room but had been silent.
He finally spoke: "I have an idea."

Everyone turned.

"There's only one way to get the answer in time. Someone has to go to the island who is not military. Someone who
might be accepted as a friend of the Iranians. I'm the only
one who can do that. Tomorrow President Talabani's ship is

supposed to arrive. I should go to greet him. I'm sure they know my name. After all, I'm the one who made this whole thing possible. In talking with them, I think I can flush them out as to whether there's a second bomb on the island."

"Sorry, Professor," Longley said dismissively. "This isn't for amateurs. It's a brave offer, but foolhardy. You weren't a voluntary participant. You were tricked along with everyone else. They'll shoot you on sight."

Morad held up his hand, asking for a moment. "Let's think for a moment. Remember, they don't know what we know. They don't know that we've interrogated everyone. They probably don't know exactly how Duprey recruited the professor. For all they know, he's a left-wing academic who believes some of their lies. Hispanic Studies professors are, after all, known for that leaning. Look at all the anti-war movements in your country. Many foreigners believe that mainstream Americans don't support your policies. Only Duprey knows how he recruited the professor, and he is under our control."

"I could go with him," added Maria. "I know the island, and he would need my help."

"No, Maria, this time I have to do it on my own. They know you too well. Your encounters with them haven't been good. There's no way they would ever think of you as a friend. I had an opportunity months ago to raise an alarm and maybe stop all this. I did nothing. I have to do something now."

"I'm concerned about that previous encounter at the dock with Ashkan, when Maria was in the boat with him," added Longley.

"It really wasn't all that hostile," Abbey responded. "I didn't argue or give him a hard time. I did as he directed."

He added wryly, "I even destroyed the worthless film without an argument."

"Professor, it's not too difficult to get you there," added the SEAL commander, Major Keiser. "Under your scenario, I assume you just pull up to the dock. But we're going to destroy the place. How do we get you out – alive?"

"Hopefully you'll work on that," Abbey responded. "I got off the island once. I'll take my chances a second time."

Longley had remained quiet since his initial dismissal of the idea. He was thinking. "It might be the only way," he murmured, almost to himself. "I've never sent a civilian into combat. Maybe there's a first for everything. Let's talk about it. If you're serious . . . ?"

"I'm serious, sir."

The discussion continued. It did appear to be the only way. Abbey thought he could play the role of a welcoming host for Iran's President Talabani. Iran wanted acceptance and legitimacy, and the Iranians would probably go to some lengths to grasp an apparent straw of welcome.

"I can play the role of an American wanting peaceful coexistence. I also happen to be the one who found the site and set it up for them. I'm sure they'll try to contact Duprey, make sure he's available to confirm my story. They'll be suspicious, but I don't think they'll shoot me on sight. If I can get past their initial resistance, I think they'll try to use me as a publicity tool."

"You know," said Longley, "this will destroy your reputation and make you a pariah. Do you understand that?"

"I'll take that risk, Colonel."

Morad looked at Longley. "We need to turn the professor into a traitor. Can you do that?"

Longley picked up the phone and asked to be put through to the Director of the Central Intelligence Agency. Since his status was now a direct presidential advisor authorized to act with full presidential authority, the connection did not take long. As he waited, holding the phone to his ear, he explained to the group, "We'll do better than just make Duprey available. As Henre said, we're going to alter Professor Abbey's stripes. We'll turn him into a rabid, anti-government, screaming liberal. And we're going to do it overnight.

"Hello, Director Johnson. Thank you for taking my call. This involves Operation Thunderclap . . . Yes, I am speaking for the president. We need an operation to be conducted immediately to label Professor William Abbey as an extreme, left-wing liberal who appears to hate and distrust our government . . . It has to be in place by noontime tomorrow, Pacific Time." They agreed to alter the university website, write some newspaper articles and letters to the editor in his name, and fabricate a criminal record from protest arrests, all by the following morning.

Looking at Abbey, Longley said, "You're going to morph overnight into such a despicable son-of-a-bitch that the Iranians might even like you. I'll have a short synopsis for you to read first thing in the morning, summarizing the high points of your past. You might now fit right into that Chicano Studies field. You were much too mainstream.

"We need to know the status of any second missile," he continued. "Is it a spare, or is it sitting armed somewhere on the island?"

"I'll find out," Abbey assured them. "They're so damn proud of what they've accomplished, they'll brag a bit. I'm sure I can get the information."

"Professor, we need you to communicate it to us. I don't think there will be a phone available," added the always-practical SEAL commander.

Abbey sat thinking. He nodded his head back and forth, as if considering and rejecting options. Finally, he nodded.

"Well, will you be watching me?"

"We'll be watching," said the colonel. "You can be assured of that."

"I'll try to welcome President Talabani at the dock when he arrives. At that time, I'll show what I know. If, when I greet him, I bow in respect but do not extend my arms, that will mean I don't have the answer. If I shake his hand with only my right hand, that will mean there is only one armed missile. But if I grasp his hand with both of my hands, there are two. Will you be able to see all of that?"

"Professor, we'll see if you've cleaned your fingernails."

Maria spoke up with concern in her voice. "How will we save you?"

"I'm not sure. Any ideas yet, Major?"

"Yes, I have an idea. But I have to protect you from knowing too much. No matter how brave you turn out to be, you will be no match for their chemicals, or their other methods, if they interrogate you. So I'm not going to tell you exactly what we're planning. Do you understand?"

"Yes, but . . ."

The major cut him off. "Just listen to me. At four o'clock, morning after next, you should be prepared to flee. There is a cave you know of, about five miles up the beach, on the west side of the island. At four in the morning, head for that cave. If you reach it, I think you'll be safe. I won't tell you anything more."

"I'll reach the cave, Major. I'll reach it."

CHAPTER 40

MARCH 2

ABBEY'S MISSION

Abbey, Maria, and the SEAL team were immediately flown to the airstrip at Bahia de los Angeles. Soon after dawn the next morning, Abbey pulled away from the village docks in a twenty-four-foot center-console Boston Whaler. It had been decided that it would be a mistake for him to use Maria's boat. He was dressed as a professor, in Chinos, an open shirt, a blue blazer, and Docksiders with no socks. He wore his glasses, which Karen had always told him made him look more professorial. He headed southeast toward the new docks at Guardian Island. Maria was dockside and waved as he pulled away, holding back her tears until he was out of sight. She didn't think he would return.

As he approached the new docks, a small power boat sped toward him. Two heavily armed men sat in the approaching boat. He waved and yelled. "Hello. I'm here to welcome your President Talabani when he arrives. I'm Professor William Abbey. I found this island for you. I come in peace to try to ensure peace. I am your friend!"

They spoke briefly on their radio phone and then responded. "Who do you say you are?"

"Professor William Abbey. I worked with John Duprey from Denver."

After a few more moments talking on the phone, they waved with their arms. "Follow us," one directed.

Abbey pulled his boat gingerly into the slip next to the lead boat, as he was directed. Two armed men stood on the dock. They gestured to him to get out. On the dock, they frisked him thoroughly. The only thing of interest they found was his container of pills, which they took. They then gestured for him to walk toward shore. No one had spoken a word.

Standing on the shore was General Ashkan, whom Abbey recognized from the previous encounter at these same docks and also as the man he had seen inspecting Maria's boat the next morning. Standing next to Ashkan was a man with a pinned sleeve where his left forearm should be. They did not look like welcoming greeters.

As Abbey reached the shore, the general looked him over slowly.

"So you are William Abbey, you claim?"

"Yes, I am. I would like to offer my assistance to avoid violence and bloodshed. I was involved in helping to locate this island for you. I don't want my efforts to lead to war between our two nations. Although I am not an American official, I am willing to be an intermediary between you and those officials."

Kazam leaned over and said softly to the general, "Yes, he is Abbey."

General Ashkan continued, "So, yes, you are William Abbey. I know your name, Professor. I think I know your face also . . ."

"Yes, definitely. You have a good memory. Some weeks ago a lady on the mainland brought me here in her boat. I think I spoke briefly to you when you sent us away. I was hoping to see the fruits of my labor. But it was not to be, so I went home."

"Yes, I remember. I think she came back again that same night. She claimed to be alone then."

"I know nothing about that, sir. I come today in peace and hope to help keep peace between our countries."

"Let us think about that for a while, and also make some inquiries about you." Ashkan turned to the man at his side. "My assistant here is Abdul Kazam. He is a great Iranian patriot. He will be your guide and your guard. You will understand that we must maintain security. Abdul will show you to a tent in which you may relax while we think. Please do not leave the tent."

Abbey bowed slightly and turned to follow Kazam. He thought that he had passed the first test. He was still alive. As he walked after the man, he directed a few questions to him, but his questions were met with silence. Talabani's ship was due to arrive soon, and Abbey was supposed to make it to the cave before morning. He had to quickly think of some way to communicate with his guard.

He turned, while still in earshot of the general, and shouted, "Sir, one request!" He caught Ashkan's attention. "President Talabani's message offered that an American could view your missile. I think I am the only American here. Could I see it, so I can confirm to everyone that it is here, as you say?"

The general was visibly irritated by the request, but he remembered that the president's message had made such an offer. Maybe it would be helpful to have an American who could say he had seen the weapon.

"Take him to the site," he ordered Kazam. "Secure his hands, and watch him closely. We don't want him to injure himself. Then to his tent."

Abbey stood still as a guard tied his hands in front of him. He was then led to a small all-terrain vehicle parked nearby and eased into the passenger seat. He watched Kazam get in and start the machine, operating it with one hand as smoothly as if he had two. They headed north along a dirt trail. After about a half mile, a concrete walled enclosure loomed in front of them.

The wall looked enormous. Towering eight feet high stood a grey concrete façade which ran on as if forever. A cleared strip about ten feet wide ran around the wall. Abbey was reminded of the Maya temples, which rose starkly and suddenly from the forest floor. At one corner of the enclosure was a large double door, and a smaller one beside it. Kazam stopped in front of the smaller door, got out, and spoke to one of the men guarding the enclosure. The man made a brief radio phone call and then swung the smaller door open. Abbey walked hesitantly to the opening.

The football-field-sized area before him held a large missile elevated at about a thirty-degree angle, pointing north. It looked huge. Many electrical cables ran across the ground, and on the tip of the missile was a large, cylindrical nose cone. The missile and cone were black. There were no markings on either. Abbey walked in as far as they permitted him and scanned the area. It took his breath away to be so close to the bomb . . . a bomb he had been reading about since childhood. He felt chilled even though enveloped in warm, moist air.

But he had a job to do. Looking closely at the base of the east wall, he was sure he saw another missile shape covered by the tarp which had once covered the whole site. Kazam strode up and said in perfect English, "So now you have your proof, American. Let no one think we lie about our missile."

"Not only your missile, but your *two* missiles," said Abbey somberly while nodding towards the shape at the base of the wall. "Do you really need two?"

"One is all we will need to right the injustices of the past. It is fully tested and operational. No need now for the spare."

Professor Abbey had his answer. Now he had to communicate it.

He was driven back to a small tent near the dock and put inside with his hands still bound. He asked Kazam to remove the bindings so he could sit without pain while he waited. The Iranian simply smiled, saying, "Stand, if you wish. The restraints will stay. And I think I will also take your glasses. You have seen enough." He removed Abbey's glasses with his one hand and stuffed them into his pocket.

After a few hours, Abbey heard much commotion outside his tent near the docks. Many people spoke in a language he had never heard before. Eventually, the deep horn of a large ship announced its approach. He assumed President Talabani was about to arrive.

All of his activities had been viewed by satellite transmission at Cheyenne Mountain. They even knew the location of his tent. Abbey had been seen visiting the missile site, and it was hoped he had learned the answer to the question about the number of bombs. All they could do now was sit and watch as the clock ticked toward the following morning.

Suddenly the tent flaps were pulled open. Kazam entered and grasped Abbey's left arm to lead him outside.

"We have found there is some truth to your story, Professor Abbey. Some. But I remain unsure. I know more about you than you realize. You might remember a lonely night in a cave a year ago. I broke that ladder, snapped it right off at the roof line, and then spent quite a bit of time with your computer. I did not find this radical streak. If you are up to something, I will cut off this left arm of yours to make us an even match," he growled as he squeezed Abbey's arm in his iron grip.

Abbey was shaking with fear, but he stayed quiet.

"Then I will make you wish you were dead. And you will be. First, however, you are to welcome our president at dockside. Just as you suggested. I will be behind you at all times." He led him towards the docks, where the ship Birania was tied up.

"My glasses?"

"You will not have to see anything very well. I will keep your glasses."

As they approached the dock, Abbey saw a ramp leading down from the ship and television cameras set up on the docks at the bottom of the ramp. His hands were still bound behind him. He knew he couldn't send the signal with his hands tied.

"I can't welcome your president tied up like a prisoner," he whispered loudly to Kazam at his side. "On TV, before the entire world, the welcoming committee is bound? Why don't you gag me, too? Then you'll send a great message."

Kazam paused. After a moment of thought, he released his grasp and pulled a knife from his belt, quickly slicing the lines which tied Abbey's wrists. "Remember, I am right behind you," he hissed.

A huge production was made of the Iranian president's arrival. With the cameras rolling, he descended the ramp and greeted General Ashkan and many of the force who had been on the island for the last months. Ashkan then led the president to where Abbey was standing, announcing to the cameras that there was a welcomer from the United States, an American professor who had provided great assistance in establishing this new nation and who had now offered his assistance in negotiating with the American authorities.

Abbey stuck his left hand in his pocket, stood as rigid as possible, and extended his right hand to President Talabani. There was an awkward scene as Talabani attempted to give the traditional Arab welcoming embrace, and Abbey stood stiff with his right hand extended. The moment passed quickly. The signal was, however, received and understood at Cheyenne Mountain. They didn't know how he had done it, but Abbey had apparently determined that there was only one armed missile on the island. Preparations continued for the attack the following morning. After the greeting, President Talabani gestured to Abbey and asked him to speak to the television audience.

Abbey knew that he had to continue to play his role. He spoke into the assembled microphones: "I only wish my government had a representative here more powerful than me," he said. "I hope that I can assist in some small way to right the injustices of the past. Americans want peace. Iran and America should be friends, not foes."

In Washington, that interview was seen by many, including Madeline Cartright. She remembered the name William Abbey from last year. She had done her job. Had others done theirs?

Across the continent, in Eureka, California, Abbey's parents looked on in shame and dismay. He was speaking as a traitor. What had happened? His mother walked silently to his old bedroom, saying nothing. She sat on his bed and looked around the room, crying. This was her boy.

The commentators labeled Abbey a traitor. Quick electronic research showed him to be a far-left anarchist with little love for his country. To the conservative talk show hosts, he was today's Benedict Arnold, for whom a firing squad would be too lenient. The more reasoned television media scrambled to interview his university colleagues, who expressed shock. He was labeled an American enigma, all within hours of his dockside interview. The CIA had done its job well.

As for Talabani, he had a speech ready to give at dockside, which he knew was being transmitted around the world by the crew from Al-Jazeera which had accompanied him.

"Friends of the world, I am Tariq Talabani, President of the Islamic Republic of Iran. I am speaking from Iran's new outpost in the West, our new Guardian Island, which we now call Parsa, in honor of the once grand and majestic Persian Empire. This island will help us guard all people, including all Arab and Persian true believers, from the oppression we have received from the West. I today announce a way to end the hostilities which have been foisted upon us by America and which have forced us to defend ourselves from this island. Just as Persia's great leader Cyrus issued a call to peace to the Babylonians centuries ago, I today issue a modern-day call to peace to the Americans. All we require is peace and parity to permit us to deactivate and remove our weapons. For peace, we require a United

Nations vote, to be supported by the United States and Israel, that our great country of Iran will never be attacked by them and that all economic sanctions will immediately be vacated. For parity, we require that the United States provide the Palestinians with the same amount of financial support that they give the Jews, once again to be enforced by a United Nations vote.

"So, with peace and parity, we will disassemble and remove our weapons. That is all we ask. We await an answer."

Talabani left to inspect the missile site. No pictures of the site would be permitted. He said he wanted to enter the enclosure alone, to pray for continued guidance from Allah.

After his speech, the Americans finally knew what Iran wanted.

• • •

The president and her cabinet in Bel Air, and the military gathered at Colorado Springs, listened attentively to the televised speech. They immediately arranged a televised conference call between the two groups.

"As I suspected," opened Colonel Longley, "it's blackmail. They hope to gain by threats and blackmail what they cannot obtain by force."

"What about a second bomb, Colonel?" asked the president.

"There's no second bomb, according to the signal we've received from Abbey," he answered. "Might be a second, spare missile. But his handshake signal says only one bomb."

"Before we use force," interjected the secretary of state, "President Talabani has left the door open for negotiation. Shouldn't we at least try to talk with them?"

The airwaves were silent as everyone wondered who would rejoin. Then President Menton spoke. "No, Patricia, we will not negotiate," said the president, with sadness in her voice. "Iran has lied to us for years, and now they're trying to give us an ultimatum through nuclear blackmail. It wouldn't stop with these demands. We will stop it now. General Boyer, Colonel Longley, be ready to attack as planned, in the morning."

CHAPTER 41

FEBRUARY/MARCH
THE MILITARY PLANNING

A coordinated, simultaneous attack by Israeli jet bombers and American submarine-launched cruise missiles had
been agreed upon by the military and approved by the
president. It was decided to delay the attack until Talabani
was on the island and had actually visited the missile site.
Not only would that eliminate the troublemaker who had
shown the arrogance of taking over America's airwaves, but
his death might permit the growing popular insurrection
in Iran to expand. More and more, Iranians were becoming
tired of their religious and military leaders making them
the pariahs of the world.

Colonel Longley and his staff thought Talabani would
certainly visit the launch site soon after his arrival. After
that, the attack would take place, thereby assuring his death
along with the destruction of the missile site. The military
planners did not want another Bin Laden surviving to martyr himself. In case he entered the site at night, Longley
ordered a personal infrared heat profile of Talabani to be
recorded so he could be detected and identified even in
the dark by the hovering satellite. He also ordered a search
for the Iranian's DNA, so that a body could be positively
identified. The plans were set before Talabani's dockside
speech. Nothing in the speech caused them to change.

The attack would also bomb the three sites in Iran
which were involved in the present threat. Everyone knew

that Natanz and Jask were involved in the nuclear program. By now, Longley had received satellite photographs of Saqqez, which revealed a suspected launch site with a camouflage cover very similar to what they had seen on Guardian Island. This confirmed the message from the informant Ishmael. The colonel was also advised that the Israeli Kurdish agent was in place, ready to help guide the Israeli bombers, and that a signal had been received from him confirming a missile in Saqqez.

The Israeli planes necessary to bomb the two sites in northern Iran had caused a planning problem. The only routes to northern Iran from Israel crossed over Turkey, Jordan, or Lebanon. None of those countries would approve such an overflight, and secrecy would be lost if permission was requested or if the overflights went forward without permission. Because of the time difference between Iran and the Baja, and the American insistence that Guardian Island be hit at night, the attacks in Iran would be in daylight. Even a few minutes' advance warning could not be risked.

The Israeli planners came up with a way around the dilemma. Both Israeli and American Iraqi forces flew the F-16 fighter/bomber. A joint training exercise was staged, in which Israeli F-16s flew through Jordan airspace into Iraq. They landed at the Kirkuk airfield in northern Iraq for a ground maintenance exercise involving crews from the United States and Israel working on the planes from the other country. The Israelis were supposed to fly into Iraq in the morning and return to Israel the same day after dark. The flights were disclosed to Jordan. The planes returning to Israel, however, were the American F-16s. The Israeli bombers, with crews, maintenance personnel, and armaments, stayed on the ground in Iraq. From Kirkuk, it was only a short flight to Saqqez, and then only another two hundred miles to Natanz. The attack would occur before anyone would know of the plane switch. No flight over hostile territory would be necessary. Afterwards, although Jordan might not be happy, the attack would have been by Israeli bombers flying from Iraqi soil. Jordan could say that it was not involved.

As for Jask, another nuclear submarine was in the Indian Ocean off the Iranian coast, the same distance from shore as the two submarines now in the Gulf of California were from Guardian Island. All were nuclear-propelled Fast Attack submarines, Los Angeles class, armed with the new Fasthawk cruise missiles. All three submarines would launch their missiles simultaneously. They were all well within the one-thousand-mile range of the missiles. Most of the missiles carried a one-thousand-pound conventional warhead. Two of each of the missiles at Guardian and bombs at Saqqez carried electronic disturbance devices which would disable all nearby electronic equipment.

Everything was in place, waiting for the go directive which was to issue after Talabani's visit to the launch site. The attack was tentatively timed for 4:30 a.m. Pacific Time, March 3. For the attack to launch required a signal at least thirty minutes before launch. The signal was to originate from Colonel Longley in Colorado Springs after he received final authorization from the president.

CHAPTER 42

MARCH 3, 4:00 A.M.
ABBEY'S ESCAPE

Abbey was escorted back to his tent after his visit to the missile site. He was given some food and water. Luckily, his hands were not retied. Kazam stayed in the tent briefly to tell him that the professor would remain for the night and that they would meet in the morning to decide his future role. The Iranians expected to receive more information from Abbey. Maybe he could be useful. But he was not to leave the tent.

"But I'll have to go to the bathroom. And I had some pills that your men took from me." He didn't want to risk a seizure on this important night.

The Iranian responded gruffly, showing no compassion. "The latrine is the tent next door. I would not expect it to take you long to pee. And without your glasses, you won't want to go further than to pee. I don't want you to get lost. As for the pills, you look healthy enough. You can do without them." He turned and stalked out, pushing the flap open quickly with his right arm. Kazam was headed to his new assignment with President Talabani. He expected to have the information General Mussahrah wanted very soon.

Abbey had looked carefully at the surrounding area before being put back in the tent. He had seen and smelled the latrine. It had door flaps at each end. That was going to have to be his escape route. Beyond the latrine, he saw some other structures and a long, sandy beach extending to the north. He was in good physical shape. Five miles was not a long distance. Even running on the sand, he should be able to make it in about half an hour. He hoped he would have that long.

• • •

Abbey was too nervous to sleep. He had to be ready to flee at 4:00 a.m., and he couldn't risk the noise of his watch alarm or a seizure occurring while he slept. At 11:00, he went to the bathroom and saw no guard. Returning to his tent after a few moments, he heard some voices and laughter from some of the other larger tents. Maybe they were celebrating.

When his watch showed 4:00, he propped a small rug under the blanket on his cot, as he had seen in the movies, and left quietly. He entered the latrine tent. It was dimly lit. He ran quickly to the other end and slipped through the flaps. He moved rapidly, but quietly, till he passed the last structure. Then he started running along the water line, where the sand was firm. All of a sudden, he heard a soft click on his right at the top of the beach.

Looking back over his shoulder, he saw a dim, blinking red light. Probably an infrared beam across the beach, which he had tripped. There was nothing to do but run faster. The Iranians would probably first think someone was trying to enter the complex, not depart. He hoped they would not immediately check his tent.

He heard sounds of an alarm spreading behind him: loud voices, engines starting, and a glow which reached him on the beach as lights were turned on.

• • •

At that moment, Kazam was in the president's state-room on the ship. He had tied Talabani's hands and injected him with a strong dose of sodium pentothal.

"Mr. President, the Ayatollah and General Mussahrah require that you issue a directive to re-target the Israeli missile to Baghdad."

"Kazam, you are crazy and misguided. Cut these lines now and leave immediately, or I will summon my aides!"

"Your aides are not available, Mr. President. Let's say they are indisposed. If you raise your voice again, I will gag you. Your death will not be a problem. Your deputy president is in Tehran. You authorized him to act for you should you become unable to act in your absence. He will do so if you die. And, if Allah wishes, you will die. Now, I need the directive to go via this cell phone. The people in Saqqez are on the line. The missile is to be redirected and launched immediately."

As he held the phone to the president's head, alarms began to blare on shore. Kazam thought for a second. He disconnected the phone and grabbed a role of duct tape off the floor, bit the end with his teeth, and quickly wrapped it around the president's head to gag him. Then he ran out of the cabin for shore.

• • •

Abbey ran as fast as he could, almost sprinting. He gasped for air as he took long strides. He had left his shoes behind, and his bare feet sank partially into the sand on every down step, with his toes scraping and lifting sand as they rose for another stride. Eventually the glow of lights was behind him, and he was running in the dark. No moon this night.

He was starting to think he might make it all the way to the cave without being detected. Then he heard the sound behind him, the harsh roar of a vehicle driving behind him on the beach and getting closer. Probably the same all-terrain vehicle he had been in the afternoon before. He ran for his life, but soon a headlight started bobbing on him as the vehicle narrowed the distance. He kept going, but he still couldn't see the rocks or the beach he had to reach. Finally, the headlight was next to him. He glanced over in a panic and saw Kazam driving and steering with his one arm and leering menacingly at him. The face was contorted with hatred, teeth bared.

Rather than shout any warning or command, Kazam abruptly turned the vehicle toward Abbey and slammed into him. The professor went sprawling onto the sand at the edge of the water. He couldn't get up. His right leg felt like it was broken, and he was bleeding from his chest and head. Blood ran into his eyes, making it difficult to see.

Kazam got off the machine and walked slowly toward him, holding the knife from that afternoon. "Now we will find out what you are up to, Mr. Abbey. But first, I think I will have that arm I spoke of before. Then we will talk." He stamped his left foot onto Abbey's neck and reached down with the knife in his right hand.

Two shots rang out. Kazam's head exploded in a bloody spray in front of Abbey's face. The body fell on top of him, with the knife still grasped in Kazam's right hand. Abbey looked up the beach. Maria was standing twenty feet away, holding her pistol.

"I thought you might need help. I was offshore in my boat, watching, when I saw the headlight chasing you. The others are in the cave. They don't know I came. Now let's get you to the cave. It's not far. You almost made it on your own." She helped him hobble toward the small vehicle which stood a few yards away with its engine still running. She helped him onto the passenger seat and drove the vehicle north.

Just as they reached the cave, all hell broke loose to their south. The sky was brightly lit with multiple explosions, larger and brighter than any Fourth of July display Abbey had ever seen. The explosions continued for five minutes. After a short pause, they started again.

As Abbey lay in the cave area with his leg throbbing, the events of the last year ran through his mind in a flash. First, being stranded in that Mesa Verde cave by Kazam. Then receiving the assignment and traveling to Mexico, and twice escaping. His liaison with Maria, and, finally, the cataclysmic events of the last few weeks. It was all like a dream. *A bad one*, he thought as he continued to hear explosions to the south. *But maybe one with a good ending.*

CHAPTER 43

MARCH 3, 4:30 A.M.
THE ATTACKS

Colonel Longley had returned to NORAD headquarters at Cheyenne Mountain to monitor the attacks. He was in a large, concrete and steel-clad room hundreds of feet inside the mountain, an adjunct room to the main operations center, available for special operations. As soon as President Menton gave the order, the countdown for the 4:30 a.m. attacks began. His monitors blared live reports of the action.

"Missiles away, Seawolf," came over the speakers, almost simultaneously with, "Missiles away, Monitor." Longley had positioned each submarine the same seven hundred miles from its target. *No room for error,* he thought grimly. *Same distance from target, same time on target.*

He was impressed by the Israelis. Interfacing with their communications, he heard the planes gather over Kurdistan, playing the role of Americans perfectly.

"Permission to fly over the oil field, sir?"

"Negative. Just test the plane."

At the appointed time, six minutes after cruise missile launch, the coded attack order issued: "Time to land, gentlemen. Immediately."

The attacks went like clockwork. Two squadrons of Israeli F-16s immediately streaked east to their targets. A second nuclear submarine had joined the first at the southern end of the gulf, seven hundred miles south of the island.

A third was submerged the same distance from Jask in the Arabian Sea to take care of that target. Once Longley initiated the go order, each force had a prearranged timetable to make the attacks simultaneous. The only preset schedule was that the attacks were not to begin before 4:30 a.m. Thursday, February 5, Pacific Time. That was when they occurred.

One Israeli squadron bombed the missile pad in Saqqez, while the other destroyed the enrichment facilities at Natanz. The Israelis had proposed a third squadron to bomb Tehran, but they had been overruled by the Americans. The warehouse and dock facilities at Jask were quickly destroyed by Fasthawk cruise missiles. Similar cruise missiles descended on Guardian Island just as the Israelis were dropping their bombs in northern Iran. Large, two-thousand-pound bunker buster bombs were not necessary, because they were not dealing with a hardened facility. It was also hoped that the blasts would not shatter the nuclear warheads.

Eight cruise missiles hit the launch pad, as four others hit each of the two ships at the dock. Another eight targeted the security positions and apparent barracks. Then the second barrage hit again. All were fired in a ballistic flight mode which maximized their range and dropped them onto the target vertically. The first wave was set for contact burst to explode upon impact. The second wave exploded thirty feet above the ground. Traveling at speeds over three thousand miles per hour, the missiles arrived with no warning.

Within five minutes of the cruise missiles exploding, Longley ordered a company of radioactive-suited marines to the island to finish the work and attempt to recover the warhead. They discovered that the bomb had been shattered, but the disbursed radioactivity was less than feared. The few remaining Iranians were shot if they resisted, and captured if they did not. President Talabani's charred body was found in what remained of his stateroom. It appeared, however, that his hands had been bound before he died, and remnants of duct tape circled his head. An autopsy later revealed an unusual array of chemicals in his blood. No one could understand what had happened to him before he died.

Epilogue

By nightfall, Maria and Abbey were in a military hospital at Edwards Air Force Base. Abbey's leg had been reassembled, and his other wounds cleaned and dressed. He was drowsy, but they both wanted to know what had happened. Maria turned on the television.

The news anchor was saying, "In coordinated attacks which encircled the globe, the United States and Israel this morning eliminated the nuclear threat that Iran recently announced. Apparently the attacks were assisted by the unknown Albuquerque professor who was yesterday labeled a traitor. Today, Professor William Abbey is being called an American hero . . ."

No third bomb ever appeared.

The only American casualty was President Overton of the University of New Mexico, who was found dead in his garage. He had killed himself, wondering if he could have prevented all of this by being more truthful in that first phone call from Madeline Cartright. He couldn't live with the shame of the new campus building, forever commemorating his indiscretion.

In Mexico City, attorneys Alvarez and Cox were shunned. Their law firm closed its doors.

As for Duprey, although it was concluded that he had been duped along with the others, his mail campaign to the Walker heirs became his downfall. He was indicted for mail fraud, convicted, and sentenced to ten years in federal prison.

After a week camping in the desert, including a trip to the Canyons at Joshua Tree to re-take the cave photos,

Maria and Professor Abbey returned to Albuquerque. They found Abbey's desk piled high with requests from agents looking for book and movie deals. His first task, however, was to take Maria home. They drove south with two new possessions: a new, clean passport, which Colonel Longley had personally delivered to his office, and a new puppy for Maria. "A birthday gift," he told her, "a little late."

His final dream from the desert echoed in his mind:

Mommy, did I do good?

Yes, my dear, just as you should.

And now may I leave my room?

You're out, my dear. You're out of your room.